Readers love the Ready or Knot series by K.A. MITCHELL

Put a Ring on It

"This is a book you will not be able to put down until the last page, so be prepared! The writing is excellent, the story intriguing and the characters very real, very human…"

—Three Books Over the Rainbow

"I absolutely loved this book."

—Gay Book Reviews

Risk Everything on It

"This is definitely a well written story, one with totally fleshed characterization. K.A. Mitchell's writing is always first rate, and I will always recommend her books, including this one."

—The Blogger Girls

"I truly enjoyed Jax's journey of self-discovery and love. It was a slow and steady progression that was never boring."

—Prism Book Alliance

Take a Chance on It

"Romance… yes, emotion… by the bucket load, an engaging story, and such deep love, make this a book I know I will go back to again and again."

—*Divine Magazine*

By K.A. MITCHELL

BAD IN BALTIMORE
Bad Company
Bad Boyfriend

READY OR KNOT
Put a Ring on It
Risk Everything on It
Take a Chance on It

Published by DREAMSPINNER PRESS
www.dreamspinnerpress.com

BAD
BOYFRIEND

K.A.
MITCHELL

REAMSPINNER PRESS

Published by

DREAMSPINNER PRESS

5032 Capital Circle SW, Suite 2, PMB# 279, Tallahassee, FL 32305-7886 USA
www.dreamspinnerpress.com

Bad Boyfriend
© 2018 K.A. Mitchell.

Cover Art
© 2018 Kanaxa.
Cover content is for illustrative purposes only and any person depicted on the cover is a model.

Trade Paperback ISBN: 978-1-64080-417-3
Mass Market Paperback ISBN: 978-1-64108-063-7
Digital ISBN: 978-1-64080-416-6
Library of Congress Control Number: 2017915315
Trade Paperback published February 2018
v. 2.0
First Edition published by Samhain Publishers Inc., December 2011.

Printed in the United States of America
∞
This paper meets the requirements of
ANSI/NISO Z39.48-1992 (Permanence of Paper).

For all the Elis out there.
Thank you to the Dreamspinner team
for giving the Baltimore boys a new home.

Chapter One

WHEN QUINN straightened from brushing his teeth, the face in the mirror scared the shit out of him.

Christ, I'm my grandfather.

It had been cold in the kitchen while he sat at the table, surfed the internet, and pretended not to listen for Peter's car in the driveway—or to check for any breaking news involving fires—so he'd thrown on a sweater Peter's mom had given him for Christmas. With the off-brand matching luggage set under his eyes, the gray at his temples, and the old-man brown wool, he looked like his grandfather. After his heart attack.

No wonder he and Peter hadn't had sex in…

Hell, Peter, it's been three and a half months.

I didn't know you were keeping track. I've worked eight days straight and I'm thirty-six fucking years old. Do you mind if I pass out now?

Yeah, I remember how fucking old you are. Especially since your birthday was the last time I got laid. So watch porn. You're always on the damned computer anyway.

…two more weeks since that conversation added up to four months. Quinn was starting to wonder if he'd forget how to do it. Maybe he couldn't blame Peter for dropping off to sleep when he came home and found dead grandpa in their bed. Ten years as a fireman's partner could leave anyone with gray hair and worry lines.

He'd thought about an affair—about Peter having an affair—but the checks Peter was bringing home meant he was telling the truth about working all the overtime. And Peter was in such a panic that anyone would find out he was gay that he'd be afraid to go near another man.

Peter's truck growled into the driveway, and Quinn dropped his toothbrush in the holder. He was too short on time for a dye job, but at least he could ditch the grandpa sweater.

He traded his sweats and saggy boxers for a close-fitting pair of black briefs and shivered his way under the covers.

He thought about trying to pose, but Peter had always been able to see through Quinn, so he propped himself up against the pillows and hoped it didn't look like he was in a coffin. Hubert's tags chimed in warning, giving Quinn time for the futile hope that the big St. Bernard mix wouldn't shake his shaggy head and send drool around the room.

Hubert yawned, and then Quinn was wiping the spray from his cheek as Hubert shook off sleep and climbed out of his bed, stalking stiff-legged out to meet Peter in the hall.

Peter's keys hit the kitchen table, and Hubert's tags jangled as Peter rubbed his head and neck. "How's my old man?"

Hubert whined and, after a satisfied sounding yawn, made his slow way back to bed.

Peter slammed around in the kitchen for a few more minutes, leaving Quinn to wonder if this was a beer- or orange-juice-before-bed kind of night. Beer meant on the couch for TV, ignoring the bedroom, orange juice meant he might come to bed in a few minutes. Quinn heard him in the hall.

"Hey. You're still up."

Something was different about the man Quinn had lived with for ten years, like he'd shrugged off something that had been hanging on him for weeks, months, maybe this whole past year. It was in the broad shoulders, the steady hazel eyes, the way he stood straight in the door of the bedroom and offered Quinn the first smile he'd seen in who knew how long.

"You're home early."

"Lupi's back from his suspension. We can finally stop covering for his ass."

"Shit. I was counting on those big paychecks so I could run off to Vegas."

"Yeah. Right. Like I can see you dropping something bigger than a nickel in a slot machine." Peter pulled off his shirt, reaching over his head with arms crossed, dragging the material up from behind. Something about the familiarity of that quirk eased the ache

Quinn had been wearing under his scalp for so long he didn't notice it until it was gone.

Peter was back. And they were going to be okay. The weirdness was gone, just one of those bumps in the long, long road.

"Hey, I can spend someone else's money, no problem. And it's not like you'd even notice I was gone." Quinn said it lightly, but Peter looked up from where he was folding his pants across a chair, lips twisted in a grimace.

"Sorry," Quinn added quickly.

Peter stared at him until Quinn wondered if they were back to the land of weird. Then Peter's face relaxed, like he'd made up his mind not to get all pissed off again. "Not tonight, okay?"

Quinn's throat went dry. "Got something else in mind?"

For a big guy, Peter could move fast and quietly—maybe he snuck up on fires. He had a hand on Quinn's ankle, yanking him toward the edge of the bed. "Yeah. Get your slut panties off so I can suck your cock."

Peter knelt at the edge of the bed and ran his hands up the inside of Quinn's legs, the touch revving Quinn's engine faster than he thought his thirty-four-year-old tachometer could handle without redlining.

Shit. Why had he put on such tight briefs? "A little help?"

Peter ran his thumbs along Quinn's groin. "So not helping."

Finally Peter hooked fingers under the waistband, and Quinn lifted his hips. Peter yanked.

Ow. "Fuck."

Peter kissed it better. Kissed everything better and swallowed Quinn's dick like he was starving for it, because God knew Quinn was. Their fingers locked together on Quinn's hips as Peter sucked and bobbed.

It had been so long. And it was so fucking good. Quinn mentioned that last bit out loud, in case the throb of his hard cock in Peter's mouth wasn't enough to tell him how fucking good it was.

Peter freed one of his hands and grabbed the base of the shaft, giving the head perfect, wet, flicking-tongue, tight-lipped attention. "Don't come." Peter stroked his hand over the length as he licked and sucked on Quinn's balls, pulling one into his mouth for the stretch and tug guaranteed to make him want to do exactly what Peter had told him not to do.

"Uhn?" Quinn asked. If he'd known Peter would be launching the blitzkrieg of blowjobs tonight, Quinn might have taken the edge off so he could last longer than sixty seconds.

"Want you to fuck me," Peter said with his chin bouncing into Quinn's sac, scrape and pressure, and Quinn smacked Peter's stroking hand away before it was all over.

"Now who's the slut?" Quinn asked, scuttling back to reach for the lube on the nightstand.

"Shut up." But Peter smiled as he stretched out on his back.

Quinn dragged Peter's ass to the edge of the bed, and Peter grabbed at the lube, pumping some over his fingers and stroking down under his balls to his hole. Quinn shifted from trying to read Peter's eyes to watching him slide two fingers into his ass.

"Hey, hon, what's wrong? You're not even hard."

"Went a little fast." Peter's words whistled through a clenched jaw. "Why don't you do something about it?"

"Okay." Quinn knelt next to the bed and licked up the length of Peter's dick before mouthing the head. The flesh pulsed and thickened against Quinn's tongue, and he groaned as Peter hardened enough to stretch Quinn's jaw, press into his throat.

Sliding a thumb down the thick ridge under Peter's balls, Quinn tested the stretch of muscle.

"Stop. I'll come."

"You can come like this. I don't care."

"I do. Want you in me." Peter's last word was muffled by a hoarse groan as Quinn popped his thumb past the tight rim and back out.

"So tight." It had been a long time, and Quinn didn't want Peter taking one for the team because he owed Quinn something.

"Just fuck me." Peter pulled Quinn's hair hard, dragging him off, but not before he gave the salty crown a last noisy kiss.

"You got it."

Quinn stepped back off the bed and lifted Peter's hips, hauling him forward enough to get just the head pressed to the slick hole. God, he'd missed it. The flutter of muscles, the wet textured heat against his cockhead, like a mouth sucking him in. Quinn's hips and ass and thighs clenched, fighting the sweaty, hungry need to drive in, force the muscle wide and open. As he held himself still, he watched Peter shift around, mouth thin, eyes squeezed shut.

Peter's face relaxed, and he wiggled down farther onto Quinn's cock, and Quinn slammed home, sheathing his dick in hot flesh. His abs ached from the strain of holding back, and he worked himself in and out, deeper every time, and Peter arched to meet the thrusts, head thrown back, fingers grabbing hard enough to bruise wherever he could reach.

Four months of distance disappeared as they moved together, with Peter's ass pumping and pulling on Quinn's dick, mouth open to whisper his name. No space between them now. Quinn drove him forward so he was on the bed too, hands on Peter's hips to drag him down on his cock with every thrust.

The muscles on Peter's chest and belly shuddered as Quinn angled them to get his dick rubbing inside on the right spot, and Peter's eyes snapped open, hand shooting down to grab his own dick.

"You first." Peter's voice was always deep. Now it was all rough and wet. His sex voice. "Want to feel you come in me."

"How bad?" Quinn slowed his strokes to a rub where he knew it would make Peter crazy.

Peter bit his lip. They both loved it when he begged, Quinn for seeing his big strong lover desperate for it, Peter for being driven out of his mind. Why had they gone so long without doing this?

"Just come, you son of a bitch."

Quinn swiveled his hips and held Peter's as still as he could to keep him from starting his own thrusts to drag the orgasm out of Quinn.

"Fuck you, Quinn." Peter's breath raced out of him, then his fist pounded the mattress. "Please, please. Come on. Fucking fill me with it."

Peter's plea hit Quinn low and deep like it always did, and he started thrusting, quick and hard like his balls were screaming for him to do. Peter bit his lip, and that was all Quinn saw before his eyes squeezed shut, body locked in the sweet explosion that emptied his dick in Peter's ass.

When Quinn opened his eyes, Peter's hand was a blur on his cock. "Want me to suck you off?"

Peter shook his head. "I'm good."

Quinn stroked his hands over Peter's chest, a forceful rub on his pecs, then flicked his nipples with his thumbs. Peter shuddered and gasped and came, warm spurts landing on Quinn's wrists and belly.

As soon as Peter let go of his cock, he dragged Quinn down against him, mashing their sticky, comey parts together. A towel would be good. Quinn was going to get one as soon as he was sure his legs would handle the long trip to the bathroom.

Quinn started to move, and Peter grabbed him tighter. "No. Wish you were still in me."

Quinn couldn't remember Peter ever saying that before. He shifted a little, and Peter rolled onto his side. Peter reached back for him, and Quinn's dick had just enough blood left it in to ease into Peter's slick, open hole. Peter made a grunt like it hurt, but he held Quinn's thigh.

"It's okay," Quinn said, but he didn't know what he was offering reassurance for, only that Peter needed it. Stretching out an arm, he managed to free a sheet and blanket to get a cover over them and fell asleep with Peter snug in his arms.

Quinn was on his second cup of coffee, Hubert keeping his feet warm under the kitchen table, when Peter came in with a cardboard box in his hands, wearing sweats and a purposeful expression.

"Jesus." Peter jumped. "I thought you'd be at work."

"It's winter break. We have the week off."

"Right. I forgot." Peter slid the box onto the counter.

Quinn gestured at the box with his coffee cup. "Early spring cleaning?"

"Not really. Shit. I can't believe I forgot about winter break."

"It's okay. I figured you'd be working. I didn't have plans." The last time they'd had vacation time together had been... three years ago.

"Quinn." Peter sat down, clutching at the table like it was the only thing keeping him upright.

The coffee was barely warm, but the sip Quinn had just taken burned all the way down his throat. Tension strung rusty wire through his neck, under his scalp, warning prickles erupting on the skin. "What?"

Peter's face went motionless, calm. Did he use that face when he was keeping people from running back into a burning building after someone they loved? Quinn had a sudden premonition he was about to know what that desperation felt like.

"I've been dealing with some stuff."

"I noticed." A preliminary skirmish, no casualties.

"I've been with other people. Not a lot. Just sometimes."

"Okay." Quinn managed to keep that word even, despite the flare of panic. *Christ, how many? Were you safe? When the hell did you manage that in your double shifts?*

"Do you remember the Christmas party? When I asked you to come get me?"

Cops and firemen and paramedics drinking. Together. God help the innocent bystanders. "Yeah, some guy met me in the bar and told me they were going to get you home later."

"Yeah. That was one of those times. And…."

So it *was* possible for one breath to last a lifetime.

Peter couldn't look at him. "She's pregnant," he finished.

Quinn knew there weren't too many different ways to interpret that, but he heard himself stupidly ask, "What do you mean?"

"I mean, I had sex with a woman eight weeks ago, and she's pregnant. And before you ask, yes it's mine and no I wasn't too drunk to know what I was doing. She's going to keep it and—that's what I want. We're going to get married."

Married. Quinn heard himself repeat the word, but it sounded far away.

"This—" Peter made a vague gesture that was supposed to cover ten years of sharing an apartment, a home, a dog, a life together. "It's never been all I wanted."

"We could—" But Quinn stopped himself before he finished it. *We could do it together?* The three of them? Did he even want to suggest it?

Peter shook his head. "I'm going to marry her. She's—It wasn't something she was expecting either, but I need to do this."

"And the fact that you also need a dick up your ass or down your throat when you want to really get off? Is that something she can expect?"

"I don't—I'm not gay, Quinn."

"You've been faking it pretty good for ten years. And it's not as if I made a pass at *you* at your brother's birthday party all those years ago."

"You're the only guy I've ever fucked. And I was married before."

"Yeah, to Stacy, I remember. All two months of your marriage. After you jerked me off at your brother's party."

"You knew what you were getting into."

"And I'm to blame for not saying to hell with your closeted ass?"

"No one's to blame." Peter looked down.

"Yes, someone is. You."

Peter pushed away from the table. "I never made you any promises."

"Living together for ten years is a fucking promise, Peter."

"You were on active duty for four of it." Face implacable, Peter leaned back against the counter with his arms across his chest.

Quinn itched to get that look off his lover's face. "I'm confused. That wasn't you begging me to come in your ass last night?"

Peter's gaze was steady, like Quinn was the irrational one in this conversation. Not irrational, clueless. Months of Peter pushing him away, spending all his time at work, coming home last night acting like he'd finally figured something out. Leave out the sex and it almost made sense.

When Quinn didn't get an answer, he said, "Then what was last night about?"

"I wanted to give you a nice goodbye." Peter turned away and opened a cabinet. "I'm only taking the stuff my mom gave me."

Gave us, Quinn wanted to point out, but he stared at the box on the counter as another horrible realization pierced his brain. "So when I came home from work, you were going to be packed and gone?" Did his voice break? Did he care?

"Yeah, but I was going to talk to you."

"Why bother? I'm sure a note would have covered it."

"Don't get—"

Quinn shoved the table away and stalked over to box Peter against the counter. "Dear Quinn, The last ten years were a mistake. I'm straight. Except when we fuck. Later, Peter."

Peter shoved Quinn away.

"You don't have to marry her to be the kid's dad." Quinn wanted to pin the son of a bitch against the counter again, but he was afraid that would lead to one of them taking a swing.

"Yes, I do. He deserves better than that."

"Than what? A father who's so ashamed of himself he wraps himself in a lie?"

"It's not a lie." Peter's face flushed. "My dick got hard. I came. You're the one who's having trouble with the facts."

"And what facts are you going to share with her? Are you going to tell her who's been getting your dick hard for the past ten years?"

"No. She doesn't have anything to do with that. I'm not asking her what she's been doing either."

"Maybe I owe her a warning. I hate to think of her waking up to this same shit ten years from now with a kid to think about too. Don't worry. I'll be sure to explain how not gay our relationship was."

There it was. An honest emotion on Peter's face. But it wasn't love or sorrow. It was fear. "Don't. Please, Quinn, don't. I know—I know I'm hurting you, but don't do that to me. You can't tell anyone."

"You know how I love it when you beg." The words felt like he was swallowing dirt, clumps falling cold and dry into his stomach.

"Quinn."

"I'm not going to say anything. Ten years is a hard habit to break."

"Thank you." Peter went back to taking dishes out of the cabinet.

"But I gotta say, if you're trying to pass, you might want to try harder. I don't think many straight guys pack their stoneware before they walk out."

"I moved some clothes last week." Last week.

"Where?"

"I know we've got another month on the lease, but I found a place that will take dogs."

Quinn couldn't make his mouth form a word. His body snapped to attention, braced for whatever abuse was coming his way as the commandant looked for some kind of weakness in his eyes. He must have made some kind of sound, because Peter turned around.

"He's my dog."

Quinn knew that. And he could remember dress whites covered in dog hair, chewed shoes, and endless drool. But he was the one who fed him and took him to the vet when Peter was working.

Quinn started for Peter. Maybe to punch him, maybe to kiss him, one argument no better than the other, but after the first step, the floor turned to quicksand. What had ever happened in his life to make Quinn think this was safe, that this would last? He fucking knew better than that.

His hands closed on the box instead of Peter. The box made a satisfying crunch as it hit the wall, and Quinn stepped over the pieces as he left.

Chapter Two

"THE BABY'S godfather? Seriously? He is so fucked-up." Jamie Donnigan offered his Corona bottle for a toast.

Quinn lightly touched the neck of the bottle in his hand to Jamie's. What were they toasting? Peter's son's birth, or the fact that Quinn's ex-lover was his own special classification in denial?

"Weren't you, like, his best man or something for the wedding?" Jamie's version of commiseration felt a lot like pouring salt into wounds Quinn thought had healed.

"No. His brother was."

"But you were in the wedding."

"Yeah." Quinn wanted to turn and put his elbows on the bar, but on a Friday night at the Arena there was barely enough room to breathe, let alone grab that much prime real estate. Instead, he scanned the writhing bodies on the dance floor. Skin shining with sweat, hips and arms an invitation and a celebration of sex. Had he ever felt that kind of freedom? The years he would have spent dancing and fucking had been spent hiding out, first in the Navy and then with Peter. A few trips out in the last eight months hadn't given him much of a taste for the kind of instant sex being advertised by the cute club rat who'd flipped long hair out of his eyes to wink at Quinn on his way to the dance floor.

"Okay. Scratch that. You are the fucked-up one, my friend."

Inwardly, Quinn agreed with Jamie's eye-rolling and his words, but he didn't nod.

"And she still doesn't know?"

She. Chrissy. Peter's wife. Quinn had really wanted to hate her, but she'd been nothing but warm and friendly to everyone. "That's what they tell me."

"I don't know if showing up tomorrow with that stupid ponytail will make it more or less obvious." Jamie flicked the tiny curl gathered at the nape of Quinn's neck. "They didn't have scissors at that commune you went to over the summer?"

"It was a summer camp for kids with cancer. And I'm going to get it cut."

"Dye it too. You look fifty."

"Fuck you."

Jamie laughed. "In your wettest dreams, Navy."

So there was a lot more gray now than just at his temples. Hell, he swore it had gotten worse in the six weeks since he'd come home.

"I think she knows—about me, anyway. Not that anyone is allowed to say the word *gay* in Peter's presence. She wanted advice about her wedding dress, for Christ's sake." That had been the moment when Quinn knew he had to get out of town.

"That is wrong on so many levels."

"Thank you, Dr. Phil. Are you charging for this? I thought we were having a drink."

"You brought it up. What did you say?"

"That whatever she decided would be exactly what Peter wanted."

Jamie wasted some perfectly good pale ale when he spluttered, spraying the side of Quinn's face. "I take it back. You don't need a beer and a piece of ass. You need a fucking therapist. And I think you are beyond Dr. Phil's help at this point. Exactly when did you flush away your last bit of self-respect—that is, whatever the Navy left you with?"

The foot Quinn placed firmly on Jamie's instep was more about the Navy crack than the personal insults. "I'm not still in love with him, if that's what you're saying."

"So prove it. Put an end to this insanity with a big *fuck you*."

"Like how?"

"Show up tomorrow with a drag queen on your arm and ask Peter if he thinks she makes your dick look bigger."

"I can't do that."

"Why not?"

"His family. They've always been good to me. I couldn't—" He hadn't worried about losing touch with Peter's brother, Dennis. They went back too far for that, had been through too much in the Academy together, but he'd thought losing Peter meant losing the rest of the

Laurents too—cracking on pop culture with Peter's sister, Alyssa, war games with Peter's dad, and worst of all, losing Peter's mom. Claire had welcomed him, mothered him, from the first time Dennis had brought him home on their break from the Academy. Two weeks after Peter moved out, Claire had called to tell him her son's business was his own, but as far as she was concerned, Quinn was still a member of her family. He couldn't humiliate them in church like that.

But the idea of showing up with a date, a very obviously gay date, someone who Peter would have to notice, got entrenched in Quinn's brain.

"Tell me you'd try something like that in front of Clan Donnigan."

"Okay, so not a drag queen," Jamie agreed. "But something…." He turned to scan the club. "Yeah, something like him." He jerked his chin at the dance floor.

Under one of the brighter spots, a short slender guy—the twink who'd given Quinn that flirty flip of his black hair—was dancing, or publicly fucking the guy he was with. A hula dancer couldn't have moved her hips like that. His shirt was black, open in the front to show off a mesh tank top that didn't do much to cover his smooth white chest. Quinn leaned into Jamie but couldn't see what assets the guy had below his waist. Given the number of guys stealing looks at him, he must have had something impressive under his black jeans.

The guy worked his dance partner like a stripper pole, swinging around him and giving Quinn a good look at his face. At the moment the pretty boy's head was thrown back, eyes shut, mouth wet and open like he'd been panting his lover's name. A shock went right to Quinn's dick, a flash of heat and blood, like those lips were inches from his cock instead of twenty feet away. Then the twink opened his eyes and stared at him, tongue tracing his lips before he went back to humping his dance partner.

"Not my type." Quinn took a long pull of his beer.

"Oh, babe, that mouth is everyone's type. But that's kind of the point, Quinn." Jamie waved his empty at the shirtless bartender. "Don't make me dare you."

Quinn shrugged. "I'm thirty-five years old. I think I can handle it."

"Really? Because I don't think you can. I think you're just a pansy crying into your beer over the one that got away. You don't have the fucking balls to face him and make him deal with the shit he pulled."

"Shut. The fuck. Up."

"Knew you wouldn't do it. You think he's going to come back, don't you? That after a year he's going to come crying back because he can't live without you and your dick?"

"How about I punch yours?"

"Snappy comeback. That all you got, Navy boy? This Marine is ready for you anytime, anywhere."

Almost before Jamie finished his taunt, Quinn slid a hand into the gap in the back of Jamie's jeans and gave him a hell of a wedgie. "If you want to act like you're twelve—" Quinn grinned and ducked the knee Jamie aimed in retaliation. "But you're right. I do need a date for tomorrow."

ELI EXCHANGED a sweaty, wet kiss with his dance partner and reclaimed his mojito from Nate's custody. "Thanks, Silver." He returned the tall blond's wave as he bounced off through the crowd.

"Silver?" Kellan asked.

"Yeah. Stupid, I know. His real name is Greg, but he won't answer to it. But we look really good together when we dance." Eli looked in his glass and glared at Nate. "I'd swear this was full when I gave it to you."

"Evaporation." Nate leaned in and sucked a little more out of the mixer straw.

"You guys go out?" Kellan asked.

"Me and Silver? No way. Totally not my type." Anyone who would rename himself Silver was way too complicated for fucking, let alone a relationship.

Since Kellan and Nate had hooked up on a permanent basis, they were doing that annoying couple thing where they thought everyone should be happily married. It wouldn't bug Eli so much because he could see the benefits in (a) being able to simply roll over on top of someone for regular sex and (b) not having to live with roommates who took up so much space and time in the bathroom and (c) rolling over on top of someone for regular sex—if either Nate or Kellan could buy a clue about what kind of guy Eli liked. Which basically boiled down to *toppy and uncomplicated. Big and stupid* would work fine for Mr. Right. Or even better, Mr. Right Now.

"And what is your type?" Kellan asked.

"You, baby." Eli jumped on him.

Kellan caught him, letting Eli slide down his tall frame with careful hands on his hips.

"You walked right into that one, Kell," Nate said.

"He totally did." Eli stretched up on tiptoe to get his arms around Kellan's neck.

"Someone's watching you," Kellan leaned down to murmur in Eli's ear.

"Let Nate watch. He'll only want to fuck you harder if you get him jealous."

"No." Kellan held Eli's hips away, but the size of his hands meant his fingers still brushed Eli's ass.

"No, you don't want him to fuck you harder or no, Eli, get your dick off me?"

"Yes I do, yes please, and no, not Nate. A guy at the bar's been watching you."

"The redhead?" Eli shook his head as he took a step back. "Redheads clash with my complexion."

"Not him." Kellan's wide mouth stretched in a grin. "Him." He pointed with his chin to a spot over Eli's shoulder.

Eli spun around to come face-to-chest with hard muscles under a thin cotton henley, unbuttoned to show some dark curls underneath, at a perfect height for Eli's lips. From there he could lick his way up the neck to a stubbled jaw. The face above was tanned and lined, lips unsmiling, eyes dark—maybe blue, though it was hard to tell in the club lighting. The dark hair was shot through with silver. Just the sight of him had Eli's dick hard. He met the guy's eyes again. Him. From the bar. Eli wanted to pump his fist in triumph. That drive-by wink had worked.

As the man's lips parted to speak, Eli decided he didn't want to ruin a sex dream come to life with anything as risky as conversation. He wrapped an arm around the man's waist. "I'd love to. Thanks for asking."

Tugging Mr. Instant Wood to the dance floor was like trying to move a boulder.

"Hey, man. Kellan." In addition to the introduction, Kellan offered a hand. His sexy but obnoxious height—and his even more irritating determination to point it out—meant his offered hand shot over Eli's shoulder.

"Quinn."

Quinn. Eli tasted the name on his tongue. That fit.

Quinn hadn't returned the offer of a handshake, which was nice, since the action would have taken place in the vicinity of Eli's ear. He tucked Kellan's still-waiting hand back behind him. While he didn't usually have an issue with being under five eight and one hundred thirty-four pounds, having two guys shake hands over his shoulder would have made him feel closer to age five, and that wasn't sexy. "I'm Eli. Kellan's taken. But it's your lucky day, because I am totally free. Let's dance."

The reluctant smile on Quinn's face made Eli think he'd said something funny at a funeral, but at least Quinn moved when Eli tugged him to a spot where the blue lights in the ceiling showed off his hair and skin. It never hurt to work all the angles.

At first, Quinn kept his distance as much as anyone could in the Friday-night crowd, but then his hands landed on Eli's hips, one leg sliding forward to let Eli ride a hard thigh. He put his hands on Quinn's shoulders, stroking the muscles under the soft cotton. All Quinn needed was a neat salt-and-pepper beard to be Eli's perfect fantasy come to life.

Quinn's expression changed from pained amusement to a genuine smile, but the kind that made Eli think he was the butt of the joke. Eli could fix that. He slid his hand down the muscle-ridged torso and landed on what he'd already felt rub on his belly. The fat length of Quinn's dick stretched up to just under the waistband of his jeans. Eli stroked and let the inside of his wrist find the damp head pushing up past the denim.

"Ooo, Daddy," Eli purred. "Is this all for me?"

Quinn didn't stop smiling, but he looked like now they were both in on the joke. "Only if you're a good boy."

"Oh, I'm always good."

"Yeah?" Quinn grabbed Eli's wrist in a bruising grip. "Because I hear you're nothing but a cock tease."

"Huh?" Eli tried to pull his wrist back.

"I did a little recon." The smile vanished. "You strut around like the biggest slut, shaking this ass at everything that moves." Quinn's other hand cupped Eli's ass, grip wide enough to lift him. "But you don't ever follow through. Couldn't find anybody who'd actually know if you're as good as you say." Quinn let go of Eli's wrist.

Eli swallowed. For some reason, he wouldn't be able to simply shrug it off if this guy walked away now. "Maybe everyone you asked wasn't worth my time." He put his wrist to his mouth, found the trace of Quinn's sweat and cock there, and licked it.

Quinn wrapped his arm around Eli's waist, leg sliding under Eli's balls. "And?" Quinn stared down at him.

Oh yeah, those eyes were blue. Dark and hard enough to make Eli's pulse jump. "I think you are."

"I'm going to need more than 'I think.'" Quinn cupped Eli's face, fingers sliding under his hair.

A thick thumb pushed between Eli's lips, and he ran his tongue over it, around it, stroked it before sucking the taste of Quinn's skin deep into his mouth.

Quinn's voice was gravel-rough against Eli's cheek. "You'd better be ready to back that up, boy."

"Here?" Eli shoved his hips forward. God, had the man seen a PowerPoint on Eli Wright's kinks?

"I wouldn't want you to get your pretty clothes all dirty. Come home with me."

"Hmm." Eli spun away, but he headed for the coat check. "Depends."

"On?" Quinn pulled him back.

"How many drinks have you had?"

"A beer and a half."

"Okay, but you have to pass a sobriety test."

"You'll go home with a stranger, but not if he's drunk?" Quinn had that pained smile again, like he wasn't sure if he was supposed to take Eli seriously.

Eli turned back toward the exit. "I'm going to be disappointed if you make me walk."

"No, I'll give you a ride."

When Quinn picked up a worn-soft leather jacket from the coat check, Eli almost came in his pants. A ride. And leather. A bike. A leather Daddy on a bike.

But once they were out of the bar and down the block, Quinn stopped at a boring dark blue Buick LaCrosse and clicked the locks. "What?" he said when Eli didn't move.

"You don't have a bike?"

Quinn's face was blank, but the corner of his mouth twitched the tiniest bit. "I have a mountain bike in my garage. Will that do, or is this where you flounce off and leave me with blue balls?"

Eli would have been pissed enough to flounce at the suggestion that he had ever flounced if his ass wasn't in the process of being shoved back onto the LaCrosse's fender and his hand being yanked onto Quinn's dick.

"No," Eli managed as his fingers curved around the shape under the denim. But a bike would have been hot.

"Such a fucking tease. What's the next test?"

God, that cock. The growl. The eyes. Test? Right. "Close your eyes." Quinn obeyed.

"No, I mean, step back. Don't lean on me and close your eyes." Eli was completely serious about never riding with drunks, in cars or on bikes. He wasn't too keen on getting fucked by them either. Quinn's balance was fine. "Put your hands out to the side and then touch your nose."

Quinn did. "Are you taking a video of me?"

The only video Eli wanted of this night would be more for Xtube than YouTube. "Maybe. Now say the alphabet backward." Eli pushed himself off the fender.

"With my eyes closed?" Quinn's voice was amused, but he didn't wait for an answer. "Omega, psi, chi, phi, upsilon—"

"What?"

Quinn's lip quirk had become a half smile. "You never said which alphabet. That's Greek."

"I know that." Sort of. *Omega* he recognized, but he thought it was some kind of vitamin. "Smartass."

Quinn laid a stinging slap on Eli's ass and walked to the driver's door.

"I said smart, not smack."

"I know." Quinn's teeth flashed in a big smile. "But I'll bet it smarts."

"That is the worst pun I've ever heard."

Quinn shook his head. "Good night, Eli." He opened the driver's side door.

"Wait. What?"

Eli didn't know how Quinn had guessed he was afraid to get in the car. But he wasn't afraid of Quinn. The way things were going said this would be one hell of a night. That was the scary part. Because while Eli could stand to have something unforgettably hot on the books for future jerk-off fantasies, the idea that this could be the high point, that he'd have hit his sexual peak at twenty-two and never have a night this good again, made him hesitate. He didn't want to spend the rest of his life measuring everything else against a one-night stand.

"If you're coming with me, get in the car," Quinn said and disappeared behind the door. But if Eli didn't get in the car, he might never get another chance with a guy this hot.

He yanked at the door handle and jumped in.

"About time," Quinn said and pulled away from the curb.

"Wait."

Quinn stomped on the brake and looked over. "My seat belt." Eli tugged it around him. "Okay."

Quinn turned and looked out the driver's window like he was checking for traffic, but Eli could see his shoulders shake. He was laughing at him.

"Why is that funny?"

"Is everything always life or death?"

"Yes. I mean, just because it isn't at the moment, it could be. Don't you ever watch disaster movies? Zombie apocalypses?"

"That actually makes some sense. Are you sure I'm not drunk?"

Eli could stand being laughed at if it meant the sex was going to be as good as he knew it would be. Just see if Quinn could laugh when Eli deep-throated him. "Where do you live?"

"Mount Washington."

Eli wasn't sure he had cab fare on him to go that far into the suburbs.

"Don't worry. I'll bring you back," Quinn said. "But it is a long ride. I don't want you to get bored and change your mind. Unzip."

"What?" But his hand was already on his zipper.

"Open your pants and take out your cock." Quinn accelerated up the ramp to the expressway north. Eli's dick didn't need much coaxing to want free of his tight black jeans.

"Move your hand. Let me see what you've got."

Quinn's approving groan echoed in the car and along Eli's bones. "Sweet-looking cock. Looks wet. Are you that hard for me?"

"Yes." God, Eli could get off on nothing more than that voice telling him what to do.

"Let me taste it."

Eli's hips jerked as he rubbed his thumb across the head and offered it to Quinn. Even though Eli expected it, the wet heat of Quinn's mouth made Eli jump like it was on his dick instead of his finger.

Quinn checked his mirrors and then whispered, "Give me the rest of your fingers."

Eli fed them to him, knew when Quinn soaked them with warm spit from the stroke of his tongue what he would say next.

"Now jack yourself. Don't come, but I want to hear you panting."

Cars streaked by them, white and red lines of light, and Eli closed his eyes as his hand closed around his dick. It wasn't wet enough, and it was his left hand, but doing this because Quinn told him to had him groaning in just a few strokes.

"Faster."

Eli gave in to it, the coil of heat in his belly snaking through his balls.

"You look so good like that. Anybody in a truck going by is going to see it too. See you jerking yourself off, mouth open and begging for a cock in it. Maybe someone will follow us. Maybe I'll let him fuck your mouth while I fuck your ass."

Eli bit his lip, abs starting to strain because fuck, he was close already. "You get off on people watching, Daddy?"

He didn't. At least he never did before. But now, with Quinn in this dark, quiet car, nothing but the hum and rush of wind, Eli wished he dared to open his eyes and see if anyone was watching while driving next to them, staring at his dick as he stroked it. His breath caught in his throat, and he gasped.

"Don't come."

The command snapped through him, leaving him hanging on the edge. "Put your hands on your thighs and look at me."

The air in the car was so heavy Eli could barely breathe. He rubbed his hands on his jeans, trying to soothe the ache sinking down from his balls. He opened his eyes.

Quinn's gaze flicked over him and then back to the road. "Christ, you're fucking hot. Let me taste you again."

If Eli touched his cock, he was going to come. If Quinn sucked on his fingers again, Eli was going to come.

"I thought you were good. Come on."

Eli clenched his jaw, his ass, his thighs, his abs and ran a finger over the slit, a hiss breaking through his lips.

Quinn didn't wait for him but lunged onto his finger, sucking it deep. "That's it. Put your hand on your dick again."

"I'll come." And he almost never came without something in his ass, but this was fucking torture.

Quinn didn't say anything, and Eli tried a light stroke. The ache, the need, came roaring back, shaking loose inside.

"Don't," Quinn growled.

"Please. I'll get hard again. God, please."

"No." Quinn's voice shook, and he slammed to a stop at the bottom of a ramp. Eli opened his mouth, and Quinn leaned over and kissed him.

"Put it away now. We're almost there."

Eli let his teeth scrape Quinn's jaw. "Please, Daddy."

"Shit." Quinn's breath whistled sharply, and he jerked back. "No." There wasn't anything but heat in his smile now. "Be a good boy."

Chapter Three

WHEN QUINN had approached the little group at the edge of the Arena's dance floor, he only had Jamie's plan in mind. Get the very obvious gay guy with the goth hair and the eyeliner to come with him to the baby's christening so they could all stop dancing around the word *gay*. If Chrissy hadn't figured out by now that Peter and Quinn hadn't just been roommates for ten years, Quinn showing up with Eli wouldn't tell her any different, but at least the rest of the family could stop walking around on eggshells.

All Quinn had meant to do was find out if Eli was free tomorrow and arrange to pick him up if he wanted to go along with the plan. Not in any permutation of said plan was having the twink look up at Quinn like he was the answer to all Eli's prayers. That kind of admiration had gone to both Quinn's heads. Still, Quinn hadn't meant to do anything but use the attraction to convince Eli to come with him tomorrow, but then Eli had rubbed Quinn hard and grinned up at him with those light eyes ringed with black and called him *Daddy*.

That was a game Quinn would have never pictured himself playing until a rush of arousal hit him like a punch to the gut, and he had to stop himself from dragging that smiling mouth down onto his cock in the middle of the dance floor.

But what was hot and fun in the club and flying up the expressway in the dark looked different in the warm light of his front hallway. He shut the door behind them. In the club, Eli had fit. Here… he had on black nail polish and a long silver chain hanging to right between the nipples showing through the mesh of his shirt.

Eli stopped under the hall light, and that only made it worse. Quinn wouldn't go so far as saying Eli looked as young as the ninth graders Quinn taught world history to, but he didn't look too many years older. Christ.

Eli's lip curled and then he stepped into Quinn, pushing him against the door. One scrape of teeth against his jaw and Eli dropped to his knees with the kind of graceful motion that said he'd done it way too many times to have earned a label of cock tease.

Now would be a good time to ask how old he was, but Eli already had Quinn's belt unlatched and his fly down. When Eli rubbed his face into the cotton stretched tight over Quinn's dick, Quinn forgot everything but that there was someone hungry for his cock.

"Can I get a taste?" Eli looked up.

"Yeah." Quinn's hand brushed Eli's hair out of his eyes, though Quinn would have sworn he only meant to urge Eli closer. The hair was softer than he'd thought it would be, not gelled hard. In this light Quinn could see it wasn't a true dyed black, but a brown as rich as fresh coffee.

Pulling Quinn's dick free of the fly, Eli used his lips in quick sucking touches around the head. Quinn forgot all about the hair in his hand, leaning back, bracing himself against the need spiraling through him, against the next whispered *Daddy* to push him to the edge of control.

Quinn let his head *thunk* against the door as Eli's tongue curled around the rim in a slick caress before he pulled off.

"Can I have some more, Daddy?"

Quinn rubbed his thumb across Eli's lips. Something in Eli's voice, in the light eyes that stared up at him, said he sensed Quinn's hesitation. Maybe Eli was falling back on their game as a way of pretending diffidence in case Quinn was about to throw him out.

Quinn wanted to tell him to relax, that it wasn't so much Eli as Quinn's tendency to think too damned much that had put a chill on the heat they'd created in the car.

Tightening his grip on the long hair, he tapped his cock against Eli's cheek. "Don't get greedy, boy."

Eli grinned, and they were back on script. He waited, lips soft and open, while Quinn rubbed his dick across Eli's face. When Eli tried to catch a taste with his tongue, Quinn shoved forward, then hung on a sweet edge as the pressure of Eli's throat tried to work him in deeper. With a hard yank of hair, he tipped Eli's head back and away.

"Bedroom?" Eli whispered.

That would be good. Except there was a question Quinn kept forgetting to ask with that mouth so close to his dick.

"Eli...."

Eli sat back on his heels, lips twisting in a wry smile. "Twenty-two. I'll be twenty-three next month." He reached back into his pocket.

The condom he slapped into Quinn's hand wasn't a surprise, but the wallet was. "I get carded at R movies." Eli flashed a real smile and then his face stilled. "I don't go bare. Ever. That goes for coming in my mouth too."

Quinn couldn't help himself; he had to check the ID. Eli's license—hair swept away from his face and a wide-eyed stare at the camera that made him look twelve—said he'd be twenty-three on November 18, next month, like he'd said. "Okay." The matter-of-fact way Eli had covered his age and safety issues with a patience born of repetition made him seem twice his age. The guys Quinn had been with since Peter had either covered the issue quickly with a "Got one?" or tried to tell him they wouldn't need it.

Eli tucked his wallet away and reached for his front pocket. "I've got lube—"

"I have that."

Eli's quicksilver mood shifted again, lower lip sliding out in a surprisingly sexy pout. "Can I show you how good I am now, Daddy?"

Quinn pitched his voice as deep as he could. "Get your ass upstairs and we'll see."

Eli clearly had no trouble finding Quinn's bedroom, since he was leaning back on the bed, legs spread wide, wearing nothing but his mesh shirt, jewelry, and a pair of tight black boxers by the time Quinn came through the door. The bedside lamp warmed Eli's pale skin.

"Lie back." Quinn shucked his jeans, briefs, and shirt before stepping to the side of the bed. "And get over here."

Eli slid, spine and hips rippling like he was dancing as he moved his head where Quinn wanted it, hanging over the edge of the mattress. He stretched his neck to put his tongue on Quinn's balls, a growl in his throat as Quinn rocked close enough to let him get his lips on the sac.

"Suck," Quinn gasped, but he was pretty sure Eli didn't need the instruction. With his hand, Eli managed to feed both balls inside stretched-wide lips and gave a sweet, spit-sloppy tug.

Eli reached back and held on to Quinn's thighs, the pull on the sensitive skin sending pulse after pulse of blood to make his cock lift toward his stomach.

"Good boy. Knew you could use your mouth for something besides pouting."

Eli let go and took a deep breath, using the point of his jaw to outline the shapes under the wet skin, burying his nose at the base of Quinn's dick.

The way Eli made no secret of how much he wanted Quinn, loved the sweat and smell and taste of another man, dredged up an unwilling comparison to the man who'd acted like he'd been humoring Quinn's needs for too long. Anger with himself for letting Peter still get to him, especially here and now, forced a rougher demand than Quinn intended. "Gonna take it all, boy? Are you a good little cocksucker?"

"Please. Give it to me." Eli licked around the base, lips tugging on hair, sucking the skin.

Quinn rolled his balls across Eli's chin again, and Eli licked the skin behind, tongue flicking up, a teasing shock as he brushed Quinn's hole.

He stepped back. "Did I say you could have my ass?"

Eli gave him an upside-down smile and then faked an apologetic pout. "Sorry, Daddy."

Quinn wanted to erase that cocky grin. Erase every other guy who'd played Eli's game and let him win. Wipe away both their histories in a flood of come until Quinn and Eli were the only people in this bed. Until Eli couldn't say "Daddy" without seeing Quinn there instead of one of any of those other tricks.

"Stop talking and do it." Quinn laid the tip of his dick against Eli's lips.

"Want a condom?" Eli twisted his neck to try to see Quinn's face as he asked.

"Don't worry. Daddy's not coming until he's deep in your ass."

Eli moaned and opened his mouth. Smooth lips, hot tongue, hard slick bone at the top, then the soft twitching pressure of Eli's throat closing around him.

"Let me in, honey. I won't choke you."

Eli straightened his neck, and Quinn moved deeper. The flutter of muscle as Eli worked to swallow him down made Quinn have to grab hard on to his own ass to keep control. Eli swallowed again, and his lips brushed the hair at the base of Quinn's dick. They both groaned, the vibrations against Quinn's skin peeling another layer off the thin hold he had on the need to fuck into that yielding flesh, batter Eli's throat, and drown him in cock.

Quinn slid back to give him a chance to breathe, and Eli grabbed for him. Quinn pushed the hands off his thighs. "Daddy's driving."

Eli's chuckle teased the head of Quinn's dick, and he thrust forward to stop it. Eli took him in, swallowed, and let Quinn fuck his mouth. Pleasure curled tight and hot in his belly from the sensations, from the knowledge that he finally had all of Eli's focus at the moment. Quinn shuddered, felt the echo in the man underneath him, and opened his eyes to find Eli's briefs down, hand busy on his cock.

He pulled out and slapped Eli's forearm. "That's mine, boy."

Eli twisted his head until he could see Quinn's face, scanning it as if he doubted Quinn was serious.

Quinn might have been surprised by the new kink in his sexual repertoire, but that didn't mean he wasn't going to give it everything he had. He pitched his voice as deep as it would go. "You don't come until Daddy says so."

Eli groaned and lunged back for Quinn's cock.

Quinn moved around the bed, scooping lube and a condom from the drawer in the nightstand and tossing them on the bed. Eli kicked his briefs the rest of the way off, but before he could pull off his shirt, Quinn reached out and pinched a nipple peeking through the mesh.

Eli jumped and then moaned.

"That's why you wear that, right? You want people to think about this." Quinn leaned in and sucked hard, tongue flicking over the tight bud.

Eli's fingers threaded through Quinn's hair, breath making quick pants in his ear that turned into a whine when Quinn used his teeth.

Quinn pulled off when he heard the whine shift from pleasure to pain.

"Shit." Eli panted and looked up at him, something less self-assured, less practiced in his eyes.

"Roll over."

In a flash Eli was on his knees with his ass in the air.

Quinn bent over him, shoved the shirt up over Eli's head, and kissed along the bony spine to give him another press of teeth in the thicker flesh of his shoulder.

"Oh yeah." Quinn slid his hand over the sharp bones of Eli's hip, wrapped a fist around the hot skin of his cock, and held on tight enough to feel the vein pulse with blood. "Those two little words get you hard and dripping like nothing else."

Eli groaned, head thrown high, hair soft against Quinn's cheek.

Quinn straightened and pressed his other palm against Eli's ass. "You grind this ass against all the guys, wanting someone to throw you on your knees and fuck you blind."

"Yes. Please. Fuck me."

"You like to get done, boy. And you think because you can suck cock and take it up your ass you can make guys crawl for you."

Eli shook, trying to get pressure somewhere, but Quinn's hands weren't moving, and nothing Eli did earned him any friction. "Come on." The words were wrapped in a soft whine.

"And that makes you want a Daddy to tell you how to take it?" Quinn took his hands away and shoved his cock against Eli's balls.

"Yes. God, Daddy, please."

Quinn shifted again so his dick slid up along the crack of Eli's ass, letting his chest settle along Eli's back, and put his mouth right next to Eli's ear to growl, "Not good enough, boy. You want to get off tonight, you're going to have to work for it."

"Fuck." The word seemed to jump out of Eli, followed by a low laugh. "You're killing me." His voice was still full of hunger, but Quinn thought he was hearing the real Eli.

Quinn slicked two fingers and rubbed them over Eli's hole, slowly increasing the pressure until Eli rocked toward him.

"That the kind of work you mean?" The self-assured grin was back in Eli's voice.

"Not even close." Quinn gave in to the desire to chase the smugness away with a hard slam in.

"Oh shit." Eli's breath rushed out in a gasp as his muscles clamped around Quinn's fingers. Quinn started to pull them back.

"Don't apologize," Eli said quickly.

"Not planning on it." Quinn twisted his fingers. "You know how to take it, don't you?"

"Yes. Fuck yes." Eli relaxed around the motion.

Cock tease or not, Eli was tight, even with his ass no longer crushing Quinn's fingers. Turning his wrist, Quinn moved his knuckles inside, rubbing and searching for the right angle.

"Yeah." Eli's muscles fluttered in time to that satisfied grunt. "Want your dick now, please."

"You're tight." Quinn wrapped an arm around Eli's hips and tried to tease a little space for a third finger.

"Thanks." But the laugh Eli tried to slip into the word stuttered away as Quinn worked a third finger in down to the second knuckle.

Eli's spine rolled, and now there was a little more room for Quinn to move his fingers. "Fuck me. C'mon."

Quinn needed to throw Eli off balance again. "Daddy's busy right now."

Eli groaned and dropped his head to his forearms as Quinn twisted his fingers down to his knuckles.

His slender body rocked with the lightest pump of Quinn's wrist.

Tenderness flooded Quinn's chest with a breath-crushing weight. The desire to cuddle and coax was as strong as the urge to make Eli forget his game and play for real. "Relax. Daddy'll get you there, honey."

Eli's breath sounded caught in a sob. "Do it. Please."

"I've got you." Quinn eased his fingers out. A sudden urgency had him rushing to wrap up and get slick. He took a breath as he lined himself up, praying that first slide into hot muscle wouldn't send him over the edge.

"Come on." Eli groaned it, but his ass was tight as Quinn nudged forward.

Quinn stroked down the sweaty skin of Eli's back, kept a hand on the base of his spine, and pushed down. "Stay right there for me." He nudged forward.

"Shit." It whistled out from clenched teeth. "Your fault. Made me wait. Too long."

Quinn felt that wave again. The one that wanted to wrap Eli up in a hard embrace until Quinn held Eli as tightly as his body gripped Quinn's dick. But that wasn't part of the game he'd signed on for, and based on the way Eli played, that wasn't what he was looking for either.

"Shut up and take my cock, boy."

The words did what the gentle stroking didn't. Eli's ass opened, and Quinn drove inside. They moaned together, and Quinn worked his way down to his balls.

"Fuck, yeah," Eli panted.

Quinn grabbed Eli's hips, put him where he wanted him, and started a good deep rhythm. Eli's body worked him, tight and slick, and for once Quinn didn't miss bare skin. Without the barrier, that tight a grip after all that teasing would have had Quinn coming after a dozen thrusts.

Knowing Eli didn't have that kind of help made Quinn smile, until he saw one of Eli's hands slide down under his chest.

Quinn slapped Eli's ass in time with a thrust. "No."

The effect was electric. Muscles rippled along Quinn's cock, tightening around the base, but Eli didn't stop working his hand underneath them. Quinn spanked him harder, hand landing in the same spot, fingers thudding into the crease under the swell of his cheek. Eli's body milked him with quick pulses. Quinn landed a blow sharper and lower. After a harsh gasp, Eli slid his hand forward, away from his cock.

"Don't make me tie them, boy."

Eli bucked, his body rolling and shaking. Quinn got a foot on the mattress and rode with him, driving in and letting Eli's motion take over for a minute.

"Please, Daddy. I have to come." The voice was raw, nothing Quinn had heard in any of Eli's moods so far.

"When I say. I've got plans for that dick of yours." The shift had left Eli's cheek more exposed, and Quinn landed a slap on some still-pale skin.

"I don't top," Eli managed to huff out.

"I didn't say that's what I wanted. Right now you're my boy, and you don't come until I say you can." Quinn smacked him again.

"I'll get hard fast." A thin, choked whine.

Quinn grabbed Eli's hips and fucked him fast and deep.

"You can still fuck me after I come." Eli's head was grinding into the mattress and he turned it, lips and cheeks stained bright red, lashes dark against his cheeks.

"I'll do what I want."

Eli's desperation only made the need to hold him stronger. The need to watch him break, give in completely, and let Quinn take care of him got twisted up in his determination to make Eli stop thinking he could bargain his way around him.

Eli's hand slipped down once more, and Quinn lunged forward, pinning him on the mattress and grabbing both his hands.

Eli tried to move his hips, grind against the sheet, but Quinn held them under his weight. Eli's ass became impossibly tight as his legs were forced together. All Quinn could manage was to swivel his hips in a counterpoint to Eli's ragged gasps.

"I'm going to fuck you until I come, and you're going to have to wait for it, boy."

Eli bucked and fought to free his hands. "Please. Please, Daddy."

Quinn put enough weight on Eli to keep him from getting a good grind on the mattress and fucked him hard. A roll of fear in his stomach told him he was as close to losing control as Eli, but he couldn't resist pinning both Eli's hands with a left-handed grip so the right could land another electric ripple-inducing swat on Eli's ass.

Eli bucked again and then shook. Quinn landed a few more smacks, and Eli grunted and went limp.

His face was turned up enough to make his words clear. "Come in me. C'mon, Daddy."

Fuck that. "Quinn." He ground the word out between gritted teeth with the last bit of sanity he had left.

"Come in my ass, Quinn."

"Yeah." Quinn arched his back and let everything go, hips working his dick against that incredibly hot grip, Eli's dark lips the last thing he saw before orgasm squeezed Quinn's eyes shut, streaks of silver lightning behind his lids as he plunged into all that pleasure and let it fill him, empty him.

He dropped his head onto Eli's shoulder, panting while the aftershocks tingled along his nerves. Eli's ass clamped around him again, and Quinn's dick jerked in another spurt that hurt as much as it was good.

As soon as he could get some spit in his mouth, he was going to give Eli the sweet blowjob he deserved, fingers rubbing inside his ass until he came apart while Quinn watched.

He lifted himself on his arms. Even the condom felt extra heavy as he stripped it and tried to get it someplace it wouldn't make a mess.

"Roll over and let me suck you, honey."

"Okay." All the desperation was gone from Eli's voice, though he sounded eager enough. "But I'm shifting out of the wet spot first."

Chapter Four

IF ELI hadn't just had the best orgasm of his life—and given the fact that he still sometimes jerked off three times a day, he had to be well into five figures—the look on Quinn's face would have been the high point of the night.

"You little shit." Quinn sat back, staring at the spot where a string of come hung from Eli's slick, softening cock.

"Here's a tip. If you don't want someone whose ass is one big erogenous zone to come, don't spank him when there's anything but air on his dick." Eli tucked his hands behind his neck and leaned back against the pillows, legs spread. "But like I said, I can get hard again pretty fast—sooner if you stick something in my ass—and I'd love a blowjob." He winked. "Daddy."

Eli winced as Quinn used Eli's discarded briefs to wipe at the wet spot. He'd have to go commando to get home, and his black jeans were tight enough to chafe.

"You're something else," Quinn muttered.

"Tell me something I don't know."

As Quinn put his fists into the mattress and loomed over him, Eli's ass slid into a dip, the sheet rough on the skin where Quinn had been leaving his handprint.

Eli knew he did a damned good job of controlling a wince, but Quinn must have seen something else. "Sorry." But a grin made the apology a lie. "Need to roll on your stomach?"

"I like it rough." Eli shrugged, swallowing back an *I've had worse*. He wouldn't know until he checked for marks the next morning. And it wasn't what he'd meant to say. He'd had pain without great sex to make the sting worth it before. That didn't have the same ring, so he kept his mouth shut.

"I noticed." Quinn's tone had that amused dryness Eli had been hearing all night. Screw him and his nonchalance.

"You were fucking awesome, by the way."

"Thank you." There was that same gravity, hiding the fact that he was laughing at Eli. "You were fucking awesome yourself."

Eli could nonchalant it with the biggest I-don't-give-a-shit prick on the planet—which wasn't Nate, though his friend probably made it in the top five. "In that case, if you don't feel like driving me back downtown, do you think you could cough up half my cab fare? I promise I won't feel cheap." He hooked a finger in his shirt and dragged it with him as he slipped off the bed.

Quinn wrapped his fingers around Eli's wrist and pulled him back. "Whoa. Maybe *I'll* feel cheap. You got another date?"

"I didn't seem about to get that blowjob." Eli settled back but gave Quinn a narrow-eyed look.

"Give me a second. You may have noticed that you're a little younger than I am."

Eli tugged at a gray curl that had come out of that tiny ponytail. "And a lot hipper, daddy-o."

Quinn moved fast, pulling Eli onto his side by his hip and slapping the up-till-then-unsore cheek of his ass. Eli wished it pissed him off, but the sting sent arousal zinging from his ass to his dick.

"Hmm." Quinn rubbed where he'd swatted, looking down at Eli's cock. "Are you sure that wasn't only precome?"

It had been quite a load, thank you, but before Eli could defend his balls' honor, Quinn said, "I would have said you're pretty tense for a guy who just got off, but now I'm wondering if it's because your dick is looking pretty happy to see me again." Quinn let his fingers slide down Eli's crack to rub gently over his slick hole.

Eli gasped and rolled to his back. "So suck it."

Quinn leaned forward and kissed him instead, soft and easy.

Eli jerked his head away. "You get off on teasing guys, is that it?"

"Nope. Just you." Quinn held Eli's head between his hands and kissed him, not rough, but so fucking thoroughly that every inch of their mouths was involved, and Eli's dick was definitely more than happy to get back into action. He moved in closer so Quinn would feel it hard and ready against his hip, but Quinn kept kissing him, tongue filling Eli's mouth, gliding and tingling. Lots of times sucking cock made him breathless and dizzy when he couldn't get air, but this was the first time a kiss had done it. And he had plenty of air. He arched against Quinn's body, dick rubbing the soft hair and ridges of Quinn's lower belly. The rim bounced over a muscle, and Eli groaned into the kiss. God, the man must do crunches in his sleep to have abs like that.

The rest of Quinn's muscles were just as strong and capable as they rolled Eli on top, letting him grind against Quinn while that kiss went on. Eli swore his fingertips were tingling from it, hell, even the tips of his hair, and he wanted—needed—something hard and deep inside to balance all that gentle pressure. He tried to move, to get Quinn with an agenda that would involve something fucking Eli's ass, but Quinn didn't do anything but shift his grip to the back of Eli's head and wrap the other arm around his waist.

Eli shoved, and Quinn let him go, a puzzled look in his eyes. Eli braced himself with his hands next to Quinn's ears.

Quinn's gaze softened, and he brought a hand up to rub his thumb across Eli's lips. They still tingled from that kiss. Eli dragged Quinn's thumb into his mouth and sucked.

"Come back down here. I'll get you off." Quinn's deep voice rumbled between them.

Eli didn't have any doubt about that. Quinn knew what Eli liked and wrapped it up with a hot Daddy bow.

It came as a shock to his dick, since Eli's higher brain could usually be counted on to agree with the one between his legs, but that wasn't what Eli wanted. Well, it wasn't only what he wanted. He wanted the whole Quinn package with his active, forceful participation.

After shaking his head, Eli treated Quinn's finger to a reminder of Eli's oral skills before letting the finger rest on his lips as he spoke. "I want to wait for you, Daddy."

Quinn's eyes darkened, and he cupped Eli's face.

"Quinn," Eli corrected himself, remembering what Quinn had said at the end of the last round.

"Are you turning down a blowjob?" Quinn's smile didn't seem to be mocking Eli now.

"It's not that I don't like them." His tone held a lot more wounded dignity than he'd intended, and he tried to erase it with a grin.

Of course Eli liked getting his dick sucked. He hadn't met a guy who didn't. But he liked the way Quinn had fucked him, hadn't ever had someone push as hard as that, had someone really get what Eli wanted. He doubted there was going to be a sudden shortage of blowjobs in Baltimore. But guys who topped like Quinn? Who made Eli feel safe and scared at the same time? If there were a lot of them hiding in town, Eli hadn't been able to track any of them down.

"Because I've got to tell you, when my dick gets hard, I'm probably going to want to shove it up your ass again."

Eli's dick jumped. They both liked that idea a lot. "Okay."

Quinn ran his hand down Eli's ass, rubbing the still-burning skin. "Not too sore, boy?"

Eli shook his head. "You don't have to play that game if you don't like it."

"Who said I didn't like it? Want me to find that rubber?"

"No." Damn. Maybe Eli could make a midnight run for Viagra. He tried to sneak a look over his shoulder.

"Believe me, it's trying. You are one hot piece of ass to have in my bed."

"I bet you say that to all the boys." Eli grinned and stroked his fingers over the tattoos on Quinn's solid shoulders. A Celtic cross decorated his right, a Celtic triad interlocked with leaping fish his left. "Nice ink there, sailor."

"Because I was."

"Oh my God. I fucked a Marine?"

Eli's ass stung from another hard slap before he got dumped onto the mattress, Quinn holding him down. So maybe Eli'd gotten that wrong. If that's the way Quinn reacted, Eli would be sure to keep mixing his uniforms up.

"Sailors are in the Navy." Quinn's mouth moved close to Eli's ear. "If you want a Marine, I could probably fix you up. Fair warning, he's a cop now."

Eli thought for a second. "Your redheaded friend?" He wrinkled his nose. "Nah. Ginger and short." That earned Eli a solid bark of laughter and a quick kiss. Being right had its advantages too.

"I can't wait to tell him you said that."

"So is that what you do? You're in the Navy?" Eli had never understood why gay people were so hot to serve when they still got treated like shit.

"Not anymore. I kept hoping I wouldn't have to keep lying about my life. I did my five and walked away." Something behind Quinn's eyes said it hadn't been as easy as that.

Walking away before you got kicked out. Now that was something Eli could understand. But fuck if he didn't wish he'd gone to one of those protests in DC before that bullshit law finally got repealed. At least he could have felt he'd stood up for guys like Quinn. "And now?"

"I teach high school."

"Isn't that the same don't-ask-don't-tell kind of thing there?" The teachers in elementary school had never made Eli feel he was weird for being different. The teachers in high school hadn't really been dicks, but he'd gotten their message all the same. *Tone it down. Conform. Stop sticking out, and they won't pick on you as much.*

"Not really. I don't keep it a secret from the rest of the faculty, and who I spend time with is never going to come up in my Global History classes."

Eli had always been out. He didn't really know how to make it a question of what he was willing to talk about. People took one look at him and knew he was gay. Not for the first time, he thought it was a lot harder to look like Quinn, stupid little ponytail and all.

"What do you do?" Quinn tucked a hand under his head and propped himself on his elbow. "That is, when you aren't making men want to fuck you on the dance floor."

"I'm a photographer."

Quinn looked like he didn't know what to make of that, but Eli didn't carry proof of his profession in his wallet.

"I'm on staff at the *Charming Rag*." It wasn't a total lie.

"What's that?"

"It's a local arts newspaper. It covers bands and clubs and events." As much as Eli usually liked to talk—especially about himself—he was wondering when the next round had a chance of starting. Quinn's focused interest made this feel like a job interview.

"Do you have plans tomorrow?"

"Huh?"

"Tomorrow. Saturday. Are you working, or are you free from ten until around one?"

"As a photographer or a date?"

"A date. But that might be stretching it. It's more like a family thing I have to do. I'd like company. Your company."

Eli had never considered himself particularly modest, but Quinn asking him out—to a family event—made him feel like he ought to be wearing a lot more than his necklace. Lying on his side, he shifted a leg forward over his junk. "What kind of thing?"

"A baptism."

Eli had a vision of Quinn standing in a kiddie pool while some guy in satin robes poured water over his head to induct him into some kind of religious cult. "Not yours?"

"No." Quinn smiled, letting Eli feel in on the joke. "A baby's."

Eli arched a brow like he was considering. "What's in it for me?"

Quinn squeezed Eli's ass.

"Besides that."

"What do you want?" Quinn's eyes were steady on Eli's face, no teasing now.

Eli had felt naked before. Now he felt like he wasn't even wearing skin. He winked, trying to get things back to the way they'd been. "I think I'll just have you owe me."

"I'm good for it." Quinn's promise made warmth hit a lot higher up than Eli's crotch.

"All right, then. But I'll need to stop at my apartment for something to wear."

"I think you look plenty hot in your fuck-me clothes, but okay."

Eli put his hand on Quinn's chest and traced down, finding a silky path that tingled his fingers, urging him lower. Hell yeah, a happy trail. When he closed his hand around Quinn's dick, he felt the heat and rush of blood. "What were you saying about fucking me?"

Quinn made Eli ride him, and any idea Eli had about being in more control of the fuck disappeared along with Quinn's dick into Eli's ass. Strong hands yanked him down to meet every thrust. For the first few minutes, the sting from being stretched again so soon kept Eli from doing anything but letting Quinn fill him with hard slams and soft praise.

"That's it, honey. Good boy. You're taking my cock so good."

Quinn angled Eli's hips farther back so the thrusts drove right against his gland, a sharp, bright build of pleasure, and Eli was doing more than taking it. He ground down, worked his ass muscles until Quinn grunted.

"Jesus, you're a hot fuck." Quinn held on to Eli's hips and shifted them, tipping Eli onto his side and kneeling between his legs without missing a stroke.

Eli's calf pressed into an inked shoulder as Quinn held him open for long, deep rolls of his hips, touching all the places inside Eli that ached for this, to let someone take it, take him.

"Harder."

"I told you. Daddy's driving." Quinn's lips barely turned up at the corner, the look in his eyes so hard and focused, Eli wrenched his gaze away.

Quinn stopped moving. "Did I hurt you?"

"No."

Quinn took a slow stroke.

"Fuck me. C'mon."

"I've got you, honey." Quinn reached for Eli's cock, fingers gliding slick and sure with lube and sweat and precome.

Eli wanted the Daddy with the hard edges, thick cock, and heavy hands that gave him something to work against, a sting and slap to push him over the edge. Didn't want these perfectly angled strokes to drive him out of his mind, or the big hand that gave his dick the right kind of friction to make his balls draw up tight and good and ready to go. And shit, it felt perfect, because as much as he didn't want it, Quinn was making him take it. Making Eli come sweet and soft and shaking instead of lunging out to grab at the dizzying power before it passed him by.

"That's it, honey. Come for me. Want to watch you come."

Quinn forced it into him with his eyes and his touch and his dick until Eli couldn't take any more and he was so full sensation tore him apart, flooding his dick and ass with pleasure as it let go, hot and wet. He came forever, and it still wasn't enough. His eyes stung, and he thought he'd gotten come in them and realized they were tears.

Quinn must not have seen them. "Beautiful. Jesus, Eli. You're—"

Quinn turned him again, facedown, and it should have been better, because this was the way he liked it, a man driving him hard into the mattress. But Quinn scooped him into his arms and held him as he drove home with his last thrusts.

"Fucking gorgeous coming for me. So goddamned sweet." Quinn's mouth was sloppy and open on Eli's neck, breath louder than the words. With a grunt that sounded like he'd had been punched, Quinn jerked fast and tight against him.

Eli's heart raced long after Quinn settled them both back onto the bed. It throbbed in his ears and his toes, a hot urgent alarm that only pounded louder as Quinn stroked his back and whispered more praise. Eli called himself crazy and he called himself stupid, told himself to calm the fuck down right now, but nothing could convince his body he hadn't downed three energy shots and his heart was going to slam right out of his chest.

In the deep exhalations that cooled the skin under the hair stuck to Eli's neck, he heard the stillness of two in the morning times two orgasms catch up to Quinn.

"Something wrong?" Some force was left in Quinn's sleepy voice, a solid promise to fix whatever was creating the tension in Eli's body.

"No." That was the truth. He'd just had amazing sex—twice— with an apparently nice guy who found his company pleasant enough to drag him along as a buffer against the boredom of some family event, and there was nothing wrong with any of it. "Just wired."

"Hmm. Wake me up if you jerk off. Want to watch."

The laugh came out despite Eli's chest being so full of his stupid racing heart. "I will."

Chapter Five

QUINN WOKE to the smell of coffee and an empty bed. He'd felt Eli get up early in the morning but had fallen back asleep before finding out if Eli came back. As fidgety as his guest had been, Quinn wouldn't be surprised to discover Eli had taken a cab or public transportation back downtown.

But as he hitched up a pair of jeans and followed the coffee smell downstairs to his kitchen, Quinn hoped he was wrong. Not only because he had the baptism to attend, but as good as things had been with Eli last night, Quinn couldn't shake the sensation of unfinished business.

Eli wasn't gone. Dressed only in the black overshirt he'd worn last night, he stretched on his toes to search one of Quinn's cabinets.

The sight sent blood pulsing to his sensitive cock, which tried to reclaim the morning wood he'd fought with as he peed, but Quinn had to curse the fact that he wasn't twenty anymore, couldn't simply slide up, bend Eli over the counter, and give him the pounding that outfit deserved. The shirt skimmed his hips, and Eli's pale legs made the splash of red on his ass stand out more. A few darker spots that might have been bruises spotted the crease where ass met thigh. Spots from Quinn's fingertips.

He should have been ashamed of leaving marks on that fair skin instead of frustrated by his dick's slow response. But he wasn't. The sight made him proud, God help him, proud that Eli would be wearing a piece of last night for a few days. Maybe caffeine would help more than just his brain function.

"Thanks for making coffee." He unhooked his mug from under a cabinet and poured himself a cup.

He'd wondered if Eli had heard him coming and posed like that, hoping Quinn would take advantage of the geography, but when Eli turned around, his face was wary. The eyeliner was gone, and damn if he didn't look younger. What the hell would Claire say when she saw him?

"What time do you have to be at the thing? The baptism?"

"You live downtown?"

Eli nodded.

Quinn checked his watch. "We've got at least an hour."

"I was going to make eggs." Eli gestured at the pan on the stove and the carton on the counter.

"Or you could go back to bed. Seems like you didn't sleep much."

Eli's shoulders were tense under a shrug. "There'll be lots of time to sleep when I'm—"

"Older?" Quinn suggested dryly.

Eli gave him a half smile. "I was going to say dead, but old will do, old man."

Something vulnerable behind Eli's smile reminded Quinn of a wild animal, trapped and ready to bolt. He tried to keep up the teasing. "And what would your mother say if she knew you were cavorting half-naked in the kitchen of a much older man?"

Eli turned back to the cabinet. "Don't you have any tarragon?"

"What?"

"Tarragon. It's really good in scrambled eggs."

Quinn crossed to him and reached into the back of the spices. "Here."

Eli looked up at him. "What kind of man actually uses 'cavorting' in a sentence?"

"The one attached to this." Teasing hadn't worked, so Quinn went for what did. He grabbed Eli's hand and put it on the fly of his jeans.

"Oh. That." Eli's palm opened, rubbed warm and slow.

Quinn's dick got hot and tight, skin stretching again under the steady pump of blood. Sore but good. He moved Eli's hand back to the counter edge, pinned the one on the other side and, ignoring a little morning stiffness, dropped to his knees.

Eli's gasp made him look up. "Umm. The eggs."

Quinn rolled the tip of Eli's cock over his lips, skin pulsing and twitching as he kissed his way down to the base, and then leaned back.

"A guy could get a complex. Is there some reason you don't want me to suck you?"

Eli shook his head, eyes wide.

"Okay, then." Quinn buried his face between the lean hips, sliding his hands around Eli's ass.

Another, sharper gasp, and Eli bucked forward as Quinn's fingers gripped. He knew what Eli wanted.

Christ, what they both wanted.

"Keep those hands on the counter."

Eli's breath stuttered out, and he didn't offer any other resistance as Quinn learned the taste and smell of Eli's skin, the way his cock fit in Quinn's mouth, a nice downward angle to push it toward his throat.

Quinn's mouth and hands and ears drank in Eli's reactions, his expressive body so much easier to read than the constant shift of emotions in his face. He did like it rough. He moaned and fed Quinn some precome for a light scrape of teeth as Quinn laid his finger over the line of bruises under the firm swell of Eli's ass. He loved a hard, fast suck and pressure on the head more than a deep bob, shuddered for a tug and lift on his balls.

"Wait. Quinn. Condom."

Quinn pulled off for a second. Fucking was one thing, but this was his risk to take, and he wanted the raw taste of him. "Shh. It's okay."

Fingers diving back to run down the crease of Eli's ass, Quinn showed off what Eli's body had taught until tension vibrated in the thighs under Quinn's forearms, a warning throb in the vein under his tongue.

"Shit, I'm—"

Even if Eli's warning had been quicker, Quinn wasn't going anywhere. He drank in the spurts from Eli's cock, softening the pressure as the spasms ended, swallowed, and licked him clean.

After climbing to his feet, he put his hands over Eli's where they gripped the edge of old Formica. "Everything about you is sweet, boy."

Before Quinn could kiss him, Eli wrenched a hand free and put it on Quinn's mouth.

"I know from experience that's not quite true, but thanks." Eli slid the hand down Quinn's jaw, his neck, his chest. As Eli's fingers worked the top button of the fly on Quinn's jeans, Eli rubbed his face on Quinn's chest.

His cock had recovered from last night now, but Quinn stepped back. "I need some breakfast if I'm going to keep up with you."

AS QUINN shaved, a dressed Eli came into his shower-steamed bathroom holding the suit Quinn had just gotten back from the cleaners.

"Is this what you're wearing?"

It was a respectable dark gray, and he'd worn it to job interviews—including the one for his job now. "What's wrong with it?"

"Nothing. If it's a funeral."

Quinn studied Eli in his club clothes. There wasn't a whole lot of damage the guy could do with only Quinn's closet to work from, and showing off was kind of the point. "I'm guessing you have a different suggestion?"

Eli grinned and disappeared. When Quinn came back into the bedroom, Eli was all the way inside the closet.

"Your shoes are black, right?" Without waiting for an answer, Eli flung out a pair of black slacks. "Oh my God." Eli tossed a shiny red gift box into Quinn's chest. "Who was that from and how do I get on her gift list?"

Quinn caught the sweater as it fell out of the box. Black with a dark purple and gray argyle pattern.

His yearly sweater from Claire, though he suspected Alyssa might have guided her selection that time. "It's cashmere," Eli pronounced as if announcing it was made of solid gold.

"Yes."

"Put that on. And…." He went back into the closet.

Quinn's lips quirked, since the whole point of this was his own re-coming out. To cover the smile, he said, "You know, I prefer a guy as hot as you undressing me instead."

"Later. If you're lucky." Eli produced a medium-gray sport coat. "There."

"Well?" Eli asked as Quinn stood in front of his mirror a minute later.

Although Quinn was viewing the whole experience as an odd kind of performance, he had to admit Eli had an eye for putting things together.

"It looks nice. Classy." It felt odd to not be wearing a tie, the V-neck of the sweater exposing his throat.

Eli met his gaze in the mirror. "And not too queer, right?" His lips quirked, then his eyes widened. "They do know? Your family?"

"Yes." At least the ones who counted as family.

"Well, they will if you walk in with me." Eli's eyes narrowed. "Is that why you wanted me to come?"

Christ, he was sharp. Did being a photographer give him an ability to see things better? Quinn smoothed a narrow lapel along his chest. "Will you still come if I say that's part of it?"

Eli studied him for a minute, their eyes both on the mirror. "They know, but it's a don't-talk-about-it thing, is that it?"

Quinn nodded.

"Sure." Eli smiled. "I like being the center of attention." He turned away from the mirror and looked directly at Quinn. The assessing stare felt uncomfortably pointed without their reflections as a buffer. After a few seconds, Eli's eyes softened, and he put his hands on Quinn's shoulders. "I wish I could do something about your hair, but I'm afraid that exceeds my ability." He reached around to flick at the tiny curl in the band.

WITH TIME and a lack of parking an issue, Eli left Quinn driving around the block, promising to be out in fifteen minutes. So he almost dropped his towel on his pass through the living room when he found Quinn taking up a huge amount of the tiny space.

"I found a parking spot. Marcy let me in." Quinn nodded at Eli's new roommate.

Eli's friend Casey had gone down to North Carolina to finish her masters in some kind of -ology. Eli was glad she'd figured out what she wanted to do, but her replacement had seriously screwed up the household dynamics. If he had to attend another house meeting that turned into a discussion on the proper disposal of feminine supplies—which, hello, he ought to be excused from—he was going to puke. Eli forced a smile for Marcy and darted into his tiny bedroom.

Now that Quinn had admitted why he was dragging Eli along to the family event, he'd already planned what he'd wear, and it only took him a few minutes to throw it on. Long enough, though, for Marcy to move from the couch to a few inches from Quinn's nose. God, was she that clueless or just pathetic? Eli came out and slipped his hand into Quinn's.

Quinn threaded their fingers together. His eyes sparkled as he brought Eli's knuckles to his mouth to brush a kiss on them. "Ready?"

Eli grinned back. "If you are."

"Did you forget your eyeliner, Eli?" Marcy's smile showed teeth.

It was on the tip of Eli's tongue to ask if Marcy had forgotten the name of a salon to get her eyebrows waxed, but he was trying hard to be nice.

"Thanks for letting me in, Marcy," Quinn offered, and then they were through the door and down the stairs. "Your housemate. I—"

"Go ahead, say it."

"God, she's really a bitch."

"Damn, now I owe you two blowjobs." Eli stopped on the stair above and gave Quinn a quick kiss that turned into something a lot longer and nicer than he'd planned. Quinn let Eli do the work, and it felt strange to be the one hanging on and pushing his tongue into a different texture and taste. Strange, but good enough to make his gut flood with heat and want. He let Quinn go, studying his face as he straightened. His eyes stayed shut for a second, and when they opened, their attention went right to Eli's lips.

The look stayed soft as Quinn put a thumb on Eli's mouth. "I think I'll try for a week's worth." He smoothed the hood of the sweater hanging over the collar of Eli's denim blazer. "I like you better in your fuck-me clothes"—he tucked Eli's bangs behind his ear—"but you still look—"

"If you're serious about a blowjob, do not say *cute*."

"Hot."

Eli shook his hair free until it hung across his face. "Nice save."

THEY WERE late. Since that was pretty much standard in Eli's world, it didn't bother him much. Besides, it wasn't his party. He wasn't about to blame it on Quinn pinning him up against the counter, because, hey, blowjob. But there was the fact that Quinn hadn't stayed in the car like Eli told him to. He couldn't exactly say why that irritated him so much, the sight of Quinn taking up all that space in the living room, knowing that Eli had a SpongeBob towel, or that his room at the front of the apartment was barely larger than the full-sized mattress on the floor. Yeah, that last annoyed him enough to drop all the blame on Quinn.

Of course, Quinn might blame it on the fact that Eli got out of the car and stared up at the big stone edifice, the rosette stained glass, and the label of St. Agnes Roman Catholic Church.

"Catholic?" He'd been expecting Episcopal or one of the other nice denominations that didn't immediately assume he'd burn in hell forever because he had sex with men. Hadn't Quinn said his family knew he was gay?

"Coming?" Quinn looked back.

Not for a while. Just the presence of all that disapproval would be enough to keep his dick soft for hours. Eli caught up to him.

Things hadn't started yet, but there was a hush of expectation as they hurried down the center aisle. Quinn seemed to be headed into a pew about halfway back from the sparkling gold stuff on the altar when an older woman stepped out from the second row and gestured to them. Well, to Quinn. Though she smiled as she let Eli move past her and her matching purse and shoes and husband to the inside of the pew. Quinn's mom—if that's who the lady was—had silvered-blonde hair and fairly decent fashion sense.

As soon as Eli's ass hit the hard wooden bench, the contact reminded him exactly what he'd been doing the night before. He could see the rationale behind church construction, the suffering guy staring out at you while you suffered on really hard wood after a fun weekend. Enough to bring on the guilt.

"Uncle Winn." A sweet-sticky breath hit Eli's cheek, and Quinn turned to the pew behind them.

"Hey, Tommy the Terror." Quinn reached back for the toddler who was no doubt aptly named, as he was standing on his mother's nice skirt.

"No." His mother scooped Tommy the Terror back into her lap. "Don't encourage him. He has to learn to sit still."

A male arm clapped Quinn on the shoulder, and Quinn offered a buddyish handshake across the seat back.

The guy had sandy-brown hair, the woman blonde. It was hard to tell which one might be Quinn's in-law versus sibling. In fact, mother, father, or the next generation, none of them looked like they could be related to Tall, Dark, and Sexy next to him. The men weren't short or soft, but they didn't have Quinn's rangy muscles and lean face.

Eli realized he wasn't the only one staring. The man who'd gripped Quinn's forearm was giving Eli a steady once-over without the slightest trace of cruising approval. Eli had an idea he was being measured for a coffin.

"Dennis Laurent." The man offered his name without a smile. The last name didn't help. He and Quinn hadn't gotten as far as last names.

"This is Eli," Quinn said, smiling enough for both of them.

"Hi, Eli. I'm Paula." The woman kept a firm grip on Tommy the Terror but gave Eli a friendly nod. "You met Tommy, and this is Faith." She tilted her head toward a preteen girl with ribbons in her hair who was ignoring her family in favor of whatever reading material she'd found in the rack in their pew.

Eli was tempted to follow her excellent example—if he didn't think the material might spontaneously combust when he touched it. When Quinn had invited Eli along, he'd completely forgotten how complicated the whole family business could be. It was easy to do, not having one of his own. He'd seen himself offering support for Quinn if things got disapproving with some aren't-straight-people-weird humor, but from the steady look Dennis was giving him, Eli thought he might be the one in need of protection.

There was a general rustling and some warm-up notes on the organ when a side door opened and a woman who looked a little older than Eli snuck into the pew behind them. She earned a stern look from the mother, which she returned with an unrepentant grin. She whapped Quinn on the back of the head before sitting next to the Dennis-Paula family.

Eli wanted to kiss her—on the cheek. Not only was she later than they were, but the tips of her silver-blonde hair were a faded magenta. He hoped she was Quinn's sister. In fact, he hoped if he turned around and suggested a run for it, they could be out of the church before the guys in robes got their act together. But the organ hit a few notes and everyone stood up. The mom passed an open songbook their way.

Eli took advantage of the shared book and the cover of bad singing to whisper in Quinn's ear. "I am not looking forward to putting my butt back on that hard seat, thank you very much."

Quinn's breath stuttered over the word *lamb*. "Not in church." But Eli could hear a trace of amusement in that grumble.

Things dragged on. Eli rummaged through the material on the rack in front of him, barely controlling a whispered *Score* when he found a paper program. Baptism to follow Saturday's 10:30 mass. *Yeah, thanks a lot, Quinn.* He skimmed the families until he found the Laurent baby. Okay. Now he could ID the players. He looked around as he checked off the names.

Unseen baby: Gabriel. Mother: Christine Laurent. If he sat up really straight—ouch—he could see a blonde woman in the first pew. The older people on her left must be her parents, the grandparents with the DeForest last name. Now for the rest. Father, Peter Laurent. Another blond, taller, in the front pew. Laurent grandparents: Claire—the lady with the nice smile and fashion sense—and Roger. Godparents: Alyssa Laurent and—a-ha! Quinn Maloney. Well, that explained a little of what Quinn was doing in the middle of all these blonds.

Quinn didn't go up for communion like the mom and dad did, but as other family members went up, Eli got a look at the parents of the baby Gabriel. The Dennis Laurent behind him and the baby's father were clearly brothers. Maybe Quinn was a cousin? Related to the mother? But it was the Laurents who seemed to know him well.

While her parents went up for refreshments, the magenta-tipped godmother slipped into their pew and right up next to Eli, who was kneeling in serious gratitude that the pressure was off his ass again. He hoped God had a sense of humor about his prayer.

She nudged him. "Alyssa. Ex-sister-in-law. And you are?"

Ex-sister-in-law? Quinn had been married to one of them? Was he—no, in this family it would have to have been a she—dead? Did you become an ex if the spouse died? No. So a divorce. Catholics didn't get divorced, except when they did. Was she here? The family seemed awfully happy to see their ex-in-law who was now gay with a really young male date, the steady glare from Dennis being the exception. Eli felt like he'd been dropped in a telenovela.

Eli realized his mouth had become frozen while he worked through that, and Alyssa was staring at him wide-eyed, waiting for an answer. "Um, Eli," he said like he wasn't sure what his name was. At the moment, he wasn't.

"Nice to meet you, Um Eli."

Somehow when they were supposed to offer their neighbors the kiss of peace, Quinn's lips were otherwise occupied to the point where he shifted around Eli to get at Alyssa.

Eli heard "Not another word or I tell everyone you have Bieber Fever" from Quinn as he embraced his former sister-in-law. As threats went, Eli thought it was fairly effective.

He accepted a kiss from Paula and a handshake from both Dennis and Faith. Tommy was sleeping on his mother's shoulder.

If Quinn thought shutting Alyssa up would save him from questions, he was deluded, but they'd wait until they got in the car. At least that's what Eli told himself as Quinn and Alyssa went up to take their places as the baby's godparents. So far no one had acted like Quinn had done anything odd by bringing Eli to the baptism of his former wife's nephew. If it really were a soap opera, the ex would burst into the church right before the end of the day's show.

She didn't.

Eli wondered if there was another reason he was here, but unless he got Alyssa talking again, he wasn't sure he was going to hear it. Really, what did Quinn owe him on the basis of last night's sex and today's favor? Definitely not the history of his life. If Eli had any hope of having his curiosity sated, he was going to have to hope Alyssa wasn't too afraid of being outed as a fan of the Prince of Tweens.

Eli watched and listened as the assembled parents and godparents made their promises about bringing children up in the Church on behalf of the babies. It was like a Holy Assembly Line. Posing for pictures with the newly minted Catholics followed. He stood off to the side as Peter, the father, put baby Gabriel in Quinn's arms. Maybe Eli was so focused on figuring it out that he was inventing things in his head, but at that moment the cameras and conversations stopped abruptly. A look passed between Peter and Quinn, no more than a second long, but the blond's cheeks pinkened and he stepped back, and everything got sparklingly clear in Eli's head.

A side chapel promised escape, and Eli slipped into it, staring at the candles at the feet of what he assumed was St. Agnes, who had a palm frond and a lamb in her arms. He wondered what kind of gruesome history had earned her sainthood. She looked pretty serene about it now. Eli wished he could get his face that expressionless, especially when Quinn found him a few minutes later.

"Does it bother you?" Eli asked.

"What?"

Eli knew Quinn wasn't playing dumb. There were a couple of different ways to interpret that. He picked his first question of the day, half-hoping for a fight that would get him out of this mess. "Repeating that BS up there. About the Church."

Quinn didn't get angry, just took two dollars from his wallet and fed them into a slot in a brass box next to the candles. "It's not BS to me." He glanced over at Eli. "Give me a minute, okay?"

Quinn lit a candle and knelt at the rail, head bowed over his hands. Eli had only known him for twelve hours, but Quinn was all too easy to read. Of course he'd never be the one to walk away from a marriage. Quinn was the kind of guy who met his commitments. The baby's father had been the one to leave, and based on the family's reaction, Quinn hadn't deserved that. So how did everything end all nice and sweet with Quinn being the baby's godfather? Given that look between them, things weren't ended, especially not on the new dad's side.

Quinn had said he was bringing Eli along partly to make a Big Gay Statement. Now Eli knew what the other part was. Quinn wanted to score one off his ex, maybe make him jealous. Eli didn't know why Quinn couldn't have come out and asked, but okay, this Eli could do. Hell, this he would be good at. By the time he was done, Quinn's old flame would be as green as the palm frond in St. Agnes's hand.

Quinn stood up. "Ready for a party?"

"Born ready, baby." Eli took Quinn's hand.

THE CAR trip to the luncheon was mostly silent as Eli tried to find a decent music station, since Quinn's car had no hookup for his iPod. As Eli hit the Tune button again to escape a commercial, Quinn said, "You're quiet."

"I'm digesting."

Quinn gave him that smile—the one that was both laughing at and with Eli. "What?"

"Information."

Twelve—okay, thirteen—hours of acquaintance didn't give Eli any more rights to Quinn's past or to be pissed about being used to make someone jealous. As for the second, Eli was looking forward to it. Quinn was a nice guy, and it didn't take much to figure Peter, the bastard—apologies to the nice Claire Laurent—had hurt Quinn. There was one thing Eli hadn't been able to work out on his own, and he didn't know if Alyssa would have full intel on it.

As they pulled into the parking lot, he unbuckled his seat belt and popped the door. "Just one question."

"Just one?" That damned smirk again.

"Peter—the ex-boyfriend you brought me here to make jealous—did he get that woman pregnant before or after he dumped you?"

Chapter Six

QUINN DIDN'T know how long he sat in the car. But the car door slam was a distant echo and Eli had already disappeared into the Brickdoor Tavern when Quinn managed to shake off his shock. Why he should keep being surprised at anything Eli did, Quinn didn't know, but he'd better follow Eli before he had a chance to leave the rest of the family gaping like freshly caught fish. He caught his breath in relief when he found Eli in the entranceway, hanging his denim blazer on the coat rack.

Eli cocked his head at Quinn. "It's kind of warm in here." He stripped off the hooded blue sweater too, then unfastened the next button on his sport shirt to reveal the silver chain and began rolling up his sleeves. The shirt was shot through with metallic stitching and narrow shining stripes of bright blue against the black background. Quinn had been wanting to run his finger over the lines to see if they were as satiny as they looked. Actually, he desperately wanted his hands on Eli, and the shirt would be a nice excuse.

But the sound of laughter and conversation reminded Quinn why they were here. "She doesn't know," he whispered.

"Who?"

"Peter's wife. She doesn't know… about me. About us. Me and Peter."

Now Eli looked like he should be the one staring back from behind the glass at the National Aquarium. His mouth opened and closed. "Are you kidding me?"

Quinn shook his head. "That is the—"

"There you guys are." Of course Chrissy would find them.

Everything behind Quinn's rib cage shrank under the familiar combination of anxiety and guilt. Because she should know. Had a right to know what might be waiting for her down the road, but he could never be the one to tell her.

She shifted Gabe to her other shoulder. "Eli. It's so nice to meet you. Alyssa told us your name since Quinn here's been keeping you a secret."

"Yeah, he's a secretive guy, our Quinn." Eli gave her a big smile and put his arm around Quinn's waist. "Gonna have to talk to him about that."

"Well at least he finally brought you around to meet the family. And speaking of, here. I think you're the only one who hasn't held him. Grab the opportunity now. I just changed him."

She stuck the baby into Eli's chest, and he grabbed him. He looked like he'd never handled anything as exotic as a one-month-old baby, but after a bit of juggling, he tucked Gabe onto his shoulder, neither hand losing contact for an instant.

Chrissy laughed. "You should have tried holding him in that satin gown Claire lent us. He was slippery as an eel." She put her hand on Quinn's arm. "I want to thank you for being his godfather. It means a lot to us both."

"He couldn't refuse. Not after you asked him in front of everyone at Dad's birthday." Peter came up behind his wife, crowding the little vestibule.

"Quinn's been telling me how proud he was that you asked him," Eli said, a light sway to his hips that could have been all about the baby, but the motion reminded Quinn of how hot Eli looked dancing. Man, Eli had one hell of an act.

"Really?" The delight in Chrissy's voice made guilt squeeze Quinn hard enough to drive out that memory.

"I didn't catch your name." Peter put his arm around his wife, and Quinn thought if he were going to be trapped in a French farce, there at least ought to be an extra door around to escape through.

"Eli. Wow." He jiggled the baby. "This is one *big* boy you've got here. Must take after his dad."

Only someone who knew Peter well, someone who'd run his hands down that chest, grabbed his waist, and held him as their bodies slammed together, could really tell through his dress shirt, but Peter had packed on about ten extra pounds since his marriage. Right then, picking up a hot piece of ass in black eyeliner ranked as one of Quinn's best plans ever.

"Everyone's waiting." Peter turned and walked into the restaurant.

"He's adorable. Thanks for letting me hold him." Eli handed Gabe back to Chrissy.

She beamed. "You're welcome. We all love Quinn, you know."

"I know. It's so hard to fight it. Why would you try?" Eli flashed Quinn a wink.

Or maybe picking up a way-too-smart piece of ass in black eyeliner was the most dangerous thing Quinn had ever done.

Quinn plastered himself to Eli's side, though he couldn't make himself give in to the way his hand itched to ride possessively, almost proudly, on the lower part of Eli's back. The habit was too well ingrained from all the years spent around the Laurents when he was with Peter. The family knew—Dennis had blurted it out since Peter probably never would have—but terms of endearment or physical contact crossed some unwritten line.

Eli couldn't seem to stay inside a line if his life depended on it. Even Peter's dad, Roger, laughed with Eli about some sly remark on Baltimore politics. Roger, as conservative as only a retired cop could be, slapped Eli lightly on the shoulder and asked him what he was drinking.

Eli charmed Claire with shy smiles—though Quinn was reasonably sure Eli had never felt shy about anything in his life. As he punctuated his imaginary story with light touches to Quinn's arm and *right, baby*'s, telling her how glad he was to meet her since Quinn often spoke of her, Quinn felt like a sounding charge had gone off next to his ear, leaving him shell-shocked.

He tuned back in as Eli said, "I planted iris bulbs in the backyard, but the squirrels keep digging them up."

"Really? Where?"

"You know the space between the forsythia and the shed?"

How in the hell did Eli know what Quinn's backyard looked like? Pretty much all Quinn had done after getting Eli in the house was fuck him. Quinn pictured that cupcake of an ass in his kitchen this morning. Right. Eli had been up early, and the kitchen window looked out into the backyard.

"No," Claire said with a regretful smile in her voice. "Quinn's never had us out to his new house. But maybe now that you're in the picture, we can fix that. Give me your email address, and I'll send you an article about bulbs."

"That would be great, Claire. Thank you."

Their two waiters had started bringing out salads, so Quinn urged Eli toward a seat with something like relief. With years of experience at the Laurent table, Quinn knew Claire, Paula, and Alyssa were quite capable of maintaining conversation without anyone else's input. Eli's little performance would be upstaged.

Because the luck of the Irish held true for this Maloney, he and Eli ended up across the table from Peter and the empty seat Quinn knew Chrissy and the baby would be occupying.

Alyssa hadn't made it into the seat next to Peter before she was shrilling, "Oh my God. Finally. You wore it. It looks great on you."

Quinn glanced down. He'd taken off the sport coat. Purple argyle diamonds. God help him.

"You bought him that sweater? We have totally got to go shopping." Eli's voice had taken on a singsong affectation that was nothing Quinn had heard from him before but all too familiar to anyone who'd seen a stereotypical gay man on television. In a minute Eli would start snapping his fingers. "Quinn's closet comes in two colors: gray and grayish."

"Count me in for shopping," Paula put in.

"Me too." Chrissy slid into her seat, handing off a complicated piece of baby equipment and the baby to Peter.

He dragged an empty table over and put the carrier on it. Standing behind his wife, he shot Quinn a disgusted look.

"Quinn hates shopping," Alyssa said as if that was akin to hating puppies.

"I know, right?" Eli added in that same tone. "Sometimes even I'm not sure he's gay."

Peter's chair made a grinding scrape as he dragged it out and took his seat. Unable to meet Peter's gaze, Quinn looked to Dennis for help. Dennis, who'd had his back since the Academy, only stared like Quinn had lost his mind. All Quinn could hope for was that Roger's selective deafness had kicked in.

"The sweater looks very handsome on you, dear," Claire said gently.

"We'll work on it," Eli fake-whispered to Alyssa.

Quinn put his hand on Eli's thigh as a warning.

There was no salvation coming from the talkative women. Claire failed to offer her usual call to action about the latest health threat she'd discovered online. Alyssa fought off a giggling fit, biting her lips, cheeks rounding like a chipmunk's. Paula was occupied with a whining Faith, who was flinging unwanted items from her salad onto the tablecloth.

Crunching on a crouton, Quinn pushed harder on Eli's thigh, praying it would keep him from leaping into the conversational void.

With a smirk that deserved a punch to the jaw, Dennis said, "So how did you guys meet?"

"Why don't you tell him the story, baby?" Eli turned to face Quinn with a half-lidded expression that Quinn guessed was supposed to be romantic but made Quinn think of the way Eli's dark-rimmed eyes had looked when he came.

Quinn jerked his chin in Faith's direction. It wasn't a complete cover. Their meeting wasn't exactly fit for a nine-year-old's ears.

"Ah." Alyssa winked. "We'll talk later." She gestured between herself and Eli.

"You betcha." Eli returned her wink.

Wishing his hand was leaving dents on the brat's ass instead of resting on his thigh, Quinn tried a pinch right above the inseam. He wasn't sure he'd made an impression through the denim until Eli flinched.

A phone buzzed, and Peter pushed away from the table enough to check his display before tucking the phone back into its case.

"I didn't know you were on call." Chrissy turned toward her husband.

Peter's hand paused in the act of bringing a huge leaf of lettuce to his mouth. "I'm not. Force of habit."

A fireman could always be called in, Quinn knew well enough, but he hoped to God Peter wasn't up to his old tricks with a brand-new baby who'd be the one suffering this time.

"What do you do?" Eli asked.

"City fireman," Peter muttered. "I'll bet you're in school."

Eli shook his head. "I work for a newspaper."

"Paperboy?"

"God, Peter. Anyone would think you were jealous," Chrissy said with a light laugh.

In the deafening silence that followed, Quinn missed his stab at a cherry tomato. It rolled off the plate, ricocheted off the basket of rolls, and left a trail of dressing as it spun down to the far end of the table, where Roger caught and ate it.

"Actually, I'm a photographer." Eli's voice was cheerful.

Claire seized the topic at last. "That's wonderful. You know, now that Gabriel's here, I want to get a new family portrait done."

Eli rested his fork and knife on the edge of the salad plate. "I don't have a studio or anything. We do mostly digital work."

"That's exactly what I want. The family has a webpage now, so it would be perfect."

Claire's web update on the rest of the Laurents and her own family took them through the salad course and what felt like an eternity from the plates being cleared to the waiters bringing out roast beef and vegetables, family style.

"You're not a vegetarian, are you, Eli?" Paula asked.

"Nope." Eli helped himself to two thin red-centered slices before passing the plate to Alyssa. "My friend Nate is, though. He eats so much healthy stuff, it makes me sick."

Faith asked for clarification on vegetarianism, declared a newfound affiliation, and reached for another roll. Her mother dumped a pile of broccoli and carrots on her plate and put the roll back.

"Where's your little boy?" Eli asked.

"With my folks. I thought we might enjoy a meal without him reenacting the Battle of Verdun around our legs." Paula tilted her head to look down the table. "Thanks for that, Dad," she called to Roger.

"Roger's a military history expert." Quinn relaxed as the conversation no longer felt like a minefield. "He volunteers down at the *Torsk* and the *Taney.*"

"In the ship museum at the piers," Alyssa clarified.

"Cool." Eli added some carrots to his plate. "Maybe I could get the paper to do a feature. I'll talk to Nate."

"Your vegetarian friend is your boss?" Alyssa asked. The word *vegetarian* made Faith glare at her mother and poke at the mountain of vegetables she'd been given.

"Among other things." Eli winked at her. "But that was in the past." He patted Quinn's arm, and Quinn began counting down the seconds to the next explosion.

He didn't have to wait long. Eli wasn't giving up the stage now.

"Quinn is so lucky to have you all. Do you remember the thing last year with Kellan Brooks? He was on *Get a Job* with Kimmie Stafford?"

"The one whose dad is head of Brooks Blast? The energy drinks?" If it was pop culture, Alyssa knew it. "Right. He came out. It was all over the internet. I showed you that, Mom."

It wasn't all over Quinn's part of the internet, because he had no idea what they were talking about.

"His dad cut him off after he came out. He walked away from all that money to be with Nate." There was nothing affected about Eli's voice now. Strong and warm with awe, it sounded like hero worship. "I know for a fact Kellan turned down half a million. Just to be honest about who he is."

The sound of silverware on the restaurant plates echoed in the aftermath of that conversational bomb. Quinn didn't know whether everyone not looking at Peter was any better than if they'd all stared. Eli had neatly set that up and detonated it from a safe distance. It might have been aimed at Peter, but the shrapnel raining down on Quinn cut deep.

Maybe Eli had a broader target in mind. Quinn knew he deserved it. He hadn't been honest with Eli.

And the thought of meeting Chrissy's kind gaze made his head ache.

Gabe came to his father's rescue with a brief whimper and then a gut-deep wail. Peter was up before Chrissy could blink. "I'll get him."

"So. What are your plans for the holidays?" Claire said.

Eli stretched his arm along the back of Quinn's chair. "Quinn's talking about taking me to Hawaii."

Quinn choked on his ice water. He should have gotten a beer. "That's—"

"You mean you wouldn't be here for Christmas?" Claire was horrified.

"Well, it's still up in the air," Eli said.

Quinn turned a steady, threatening glare on him. It worked on surly fifteen-year-olds. But Eli was made of sterner stuff. He grinned back and continued. "After all, I am a little young to be getting married."

Under a stream of excitement from Alyssa and Paula, Quinn heard Dennis choke out, "Married?"

Quinn began to weigh the advantages of murder over suicide.

SOMEHOW QUINN managed to endure through dessert without having to decide on either option. He gulped a little coffee, took two bites of the overly sweet cake, and looked with longing at the pastries that had been a source of further contention as Faith decided she was a sugartarian instead. Eli had sucked down a napoleon and an éclair while Quinn stuck to black coffee, cursing his thirty-five-year-old metabolism and trying not to think of how obscene the chocolate and cream looked on Eli's wide mouth.

As Quinn pinned his two fifties to the christening gown displayed on the gift table, the women clustered around Gabe, who was apparently doing something precious. Dennis and Peter had followed their father into the bar, and Eli was about to disappear into the men's room. Quinn caught up to him in the narrow hall.

"What the hell do you think you're doing?"

"What do you think? I swear your ex-father-in-law is trying to get me drunk. That's the third Canadian whiskey he's bought me."

"Don't say—"

"Whiskey?" Eli blinked slowly. "Or father-in-law? If you're going to follow me in, give me a minute, because I really gotta pee."

Quinn was a patient man. He taught teenagers, for Christ's sake. But leaning his head back against the Budweiser sign on the dark paneling didn't do anything to control his need to shake Eli and demand to know what the fuck made it so funny to screw with Quinn's life. Knowing he wanted to follow the tirade by shoving his dick so far up Eli's ass he'd taste him for a month didn't help either.

When he went into the bathroom, Eli met his gaze in the mirror, where he stood washing his hands. Eli licked his lips, and Quinn caught sight of himself. His cheeks were flushed, eyes hard and focused, the sweater clinging to his pecs. One thing he didn't look was old. He folded his arms across his chest.

"Exactly what are you doing? And don't say washing your hands, or just sitting on a pillow will feel like burning coals by the time I'm done blistering your ass."

Eli blinked again, smiled, and ran a cool finger along the V-neck of Quinn's sweater. "Mmm. Hot. But I prefer to save that kind of stuff for bed, Daddy."

Quinn did not shiver, even if the jolt to his body could qualify as one. The chemistry between them had nothing to do with Eli acting that way in front of the family.

He grabbed Eli's hand and squeezed, forcing it down to his side. "Listen, you little shit, you do not get to waltz in here and—"

"I didn't waltz in. You invited me." Eli wrenched his hand free and jabbed his finger into Quinn's chest. "And don't think you didn't invite me to do exactly what I did."

Anger beat hot and strong in Quinn's temples, tightened his spine, forced his hands into fists. He took a step back.

Eli followed, crowding Quinn against the sink. "You wanted Peter to think you'd moved on. You wanted everyone to remember the big gay elephant in the room that none of you could talk about because of Peter. I did all that."

The anger wasn't for Eli now. It was for himself, because there was no arguing with that. Punching himself wouldn't help, though, so he unclenched his fists.

"Now." Eli crowded into him in an entirely different way, spine and hips moving fluidly. "You knew what would happen when you followed me in here, and it wasn't just you bitching." He hooked a finger in Quinn's belt. "Jesus. You looking at me like that is getting me hard. C'mon." He yanked Quinn by the belt into the stall and reached around him to lock the door.

Eli wrapped an arm around Quinn's neck, dragging him down, other hand unlatching his belt, his fly.

"We can't." But Quinn's words were an ineffective moan against Eli's lips. Had he known this was going to happen when he came in here?

"We can and we are. So hurry up."

Eli licked and sucked on Quinn's lower lip, forearm sliding over Quinn's dick as Eli got his own pants open.

"What if someone—?"

Eli leaned back against the stall barrier, one leg sliding up to wrap around Quinn's thigh.

"Oh." Quinn's hands landed on Eli ass, shoving under his clothes to find skin, and lifted him up. "God, yes."

Eli wrapped both legs around Quinn's hips, a hand busy getting their dicks together, working what slick he could get from the tips as they started grinding.

Quinn's fingers dug in, and Eli's mouth opened on an almost silent moan. Quinn dove into his mouth, tasting chocolate, cream, then just heat and Eli's tongue meeting his. Quinn's common sense left his brain, riding the blood flow down to his balls, where Eli's fingers teased and tugged, hard enough for an ache that sweetened as their shafts rubbed together. It was dirty, raw, hot, and stupider than anything Quinn had managed even as a desperately horny teen. His—Peter's—family was out there, and he was humping away in a bathroom stall.

Eli's mouth and tongue mimicked what his hand and fingers were doing, stroking along Quinn's lips in long licks as his fingers found the shapes under the tightening skin of his sac. Wet slow kisses as his palm pressed hard flesh against hard flesh, a flick of tongue to chase his thumb over the head, and then a deep suck as he tugged.

Quinn's hips picked up the pace, driving their cocks together, and Eli clung to his shoulders now, legs squeezing. Dimly Quinn's brain sent up a warning flag about flimsy construction and getting caught when the stall collapsed around them, but Quinn told his brain to get fucked and lifted Eli higher, getting the perfect drag of skin and slick cockheads.

Eli tore his mouth free. "Please."

The word made pleasure wash sweeter through his pipes, everything getting so hot at the tip of his cock, it burned.

Eli wrapped a finger in the curl of long hair at the nape of Quinn's neck and yanked.

"Go ahead, honey. I got you." Quinn breathed it along the sweat on Eli's neck.

"Finger me. C'mon. Need it."

Oh Christ. Eli would fucking kill him. Gripping tighter, he inched his index finger into the warm crease, found the velvety ripples damp from Eli's sweat. Soft, but hard too.

"Relax."

"Fuck that. Now."

Quinn pressed. Eli jerked. "Yeah. Gimme two."

Quinn lined up another and shoved. Eli bucked and rocked into him. Trying to hold him, hold them together, was like trying to hang on to that moment right before he came when everything was bright and perfect as the sparks built to the point of no return. Then everything tipped.

Arching farther back, Eli grabbed two fistfuls of sweater and curled his hands around it, muffling his moans in Quinn's shoulder as he pumped hot and slick between their bodies. The wet warmth sliding over Quinn's cock was all he needed to follow over the edge, hips jerking and teeth digging into his lip to keep from shouting.

Quinn managed to keep his feet, dragging Eli back toward him as a bolt in the wall clanged loose. The stall rocked and settled back, amazingly still upright.

Quinn wanted to sink onto the filthy tiles, but he held on as their breathing slowed and Eli tried to separate himself without leaving come all over their clothes. They were marginally successful. The cloakroom was just across the hall. After they cleaned up, a sprint would get them to the extra protection of another layer—and then maybe a quick disappearance.

Eli tilted his head as he scrubbed with the toilet paper. "I think we saved most of the sweater." He hitched his pants back up over his ass and eyed them both. "The sink will help."

Quinn met Eli's gaze and held it. In less than twenty-four hours, this piece of ass in black eyeliner, Eli—whose last name he didn't even know, who was barely a few years older than the kids in his class—had completely rewritten all the rules Quinn followed to keep his life on a peaceful path.

He should have been furious, he should have been scared, and he was, but those feelings were taking a back seat to an overwhelming sense of gratitude—floating on a fresh wave of joy—like being caught in a gentle summer rain that rinsed away the weight of heat and humidity.

He reacted to it the way he would have standing in that sweet shower—he drank in the source.

Eli's eyes were wary, but they closed as Quinn gave him a slow kiss. Eli pulled back, but Quinn took him under the jaw and kissed away that resistance. Almost as soon as Eli was kissing him back, he was reaching out to unlock the door.

"I think we'd better see if we can salvage our clothes with some water."

"I'll run and get our jackets," Quinn promised.

But he didn't.

Because leaning against the door, blocking it with a full body sneer, was Peter.

Chapter Seven

ELI FOLLOWED Quinn out of the stall and felt his body snap into tension. "What?" Eli looked around Quinn and caught sight of the newly straight ex-boyfriend. "Oh."

"You couldn't keep it in your pants for an hour?" Peter's voice was filled with loathing. "There are children here."

"I doubt we have to worry about Faith in the men's room. She can read. And if Gabe makes it in here on his own, I think there's a lot more we should be talking about." Quinn was calmer than Eli could have managed, though Eli felt the absurd need to slip around him. Not to get between them to break up a potential fight, but to shield Quinn from the look Peter leveled at his ex. One that said *What the hell did I ever see in you?*

"Maybe that piece of bar trash you dragged along to humiliate me doesn't know how decent people behave, but—"

Quinn didn't raise his voice, but the soft tone had an edge that cut through Peter's complaint. "You watch your fucking mouth about him."

Eli'd had enough of hanging in the background. He stepped in front of Quinn. "I got this one, baby."

Peter's face was a splotchy red. It might have been puffed with anger, but Eli saw the flicker of something else in his eyes, had seen it in plenty of men's eyes.

Eli ignored Quinn's maneuvers between the sink and the urinals to get back in front and stood his ground. "This 'piece of bar trash' might not know how decent people behave, but he has a keen sense of smell. Someone besides the two of us got off in here, and don't expect me to think one of the old guys from the bar out front came in to whip it on live gay porn."

Peter's flush deepened. "I've been standing here to make sure you didn't get caught. To protect my family from—"

"We've covered the kids, and your father and brother don't strike me as the kind of people to be scarred for life if they trip over people having sex."

"Normal people do not have sex in a bathroom. What the hell kind of thing are you?" Peter sneered.

Quinn put his hand on Eli's back, and Eli stepped more determinedly between them. "I'm the kind of thing Quinn picked. When you were jerking off in here, what got to you most? The memory of his body? God, he's strong. The way he sounds? Those grunts he makes? They're all mine now. How does that feel, Peter?"

Peter turned toward the urinals. "Get him out of here, Quinn. Right the hell now."

"I'll be sure to say goodbye to your beautiful wife." Eli let Quinn push him through the door, but when it seemed Quinn was going to stay back, Eli grabbed his hand.

"No." Eli tugged. "Leave him. He made his own fucking mess."

"Pull yourself together, Peter" was all Quinn said before he followed Eli into the alcove where their jackets were.

"Here." Eli handed Quinn his sport coat and shrugged into his own blazer. After tucking the stained tails of his dress shirt into his jeans, praying no one saw him looking like a nerd, he handed his hooded sweater to Quinn. "Hold this over your arm in front of the spot. There."

"Eli—"

"I know. I'm something else." Eli spread the sweater out a little bit. "Just one more service I provide. Tell them I have to go take pictures for something."

"A photographic emergency? In the arts community?" Quinn produced a smile without his usual mockery in it.

"It can get pretty wild." Eli nodded solemnly, then focused on buttoning his blazer. That smile was freaking lethal, especially to a guy with two Canadian whiskeys, a recent orgasm, and Peter-needs-his-ass-kicked adrenaline in his system. No wonder it had Eli's stomach doing backflips. But as amazing as the smile was, Eli'd had more than enough of dysfunctional fun for one day.

"I'm so sorry you have to leave," Claire said, and Eli managed to keep her hug confined to an arm pat. He might have been exaggerating about his sense of smell, but he was pretty sure he and Quinn weren't exactly exuding freshness. "I'll call you and we'll set up a time for the family picture, all right?" she continued, maintaining her grip on his arm. "Be sure to bring a camera that has a timer so you can be in the shot too."

"Absolutely."

"And don't forget our shopping date," Alyssa added.

"I'm so glad you were a part of this." Chrissy managed to get her arms around Quinn, though he gamely kept the sweater draped in front. "I know it meant a lot to Peter."

Eli barely managed to avoid swallowing his tongue.

Chrissy let them go with a "We'll be in touch," and then they made it safely into the parking lot. Quinn settled into the driver's seat with a long sigh.

"Thanks. I think." He started the car. "Where to?"

"I was going to suggest your place again. I had the whole Facebook post planned out. My Thirty-Seven-Hour Date."

"But now?"

"My apartment would be good, thanks."

"I guess I owe you some kind of explanation." Quinn stared straight ahead but didn't put the car in drive.

"You don't owe me anything, really. I got fucked. I got fed. I could have skipped the church bit, but other than that, it wasn't a bad date. Believe me. I've had worse."

"That sounds like an interesting story." Quinn backed out of the space and headed east out of the parking lot.

"I don't kiss and tell."

"Except on Facebook?"

"It was going to be very general, I swear. I never give any incriminating details like tattoos or Daddy kinks."

Quinn's hands tightened on the wheel. "I'd never done that before."

Eli hadn't ever found anyone who gave him as much as he could handle before either, but he wasn't admitting that. "Really? You're a natural. I loved it."

Silence followed them downtown. As they waited at the light on Broadway in front of Johns Hopkins, Quinn turned to face him.

"Ten years," he said without any need for clarification.

"Fuck." Eli couldn't picture that length of time. Being with anyone, living anywhere, having the same job. Ten years. To have something that felt that solid and then— "Damn."

Quinn shrugged and took a left on Fayette. "What's funny is that I'm a lot happier now."

Eli wasn't. The weight of it seemed to press him into the seat. He wanted to get out and jog the rest of the way. There wasn't any parking, for which Eli was grateful, but there wasn't any traffic eager to move Quinn along when he double-parked in front of the apartment.

"So I owe you one," Quinn said.

Owed him—oh. Their agreement. But Eli was thinking about ten years of a family where you suddenly didn't belong anymore. How did Quinn stand it, being around them because, what, they felt sorry for him?

"No problem, like I said."

Quinn's half smile looked hesitant this time. "Eli, I want to see you again."

"You're sweet."

Quinn's eyebrows shot up. "Sweet?"

"And hot. And fucking awesome in bed. But that whole thing— it's kind of more complicated than I'm comfortable with."

"Welcome to life, kid."

"And thanks for ending this on a patronizing note, Daddy." Eli shoved open his door.

"Wait." Quinn crooked a finger in Eli's belt loop, but instead of copping a feel, which would have done a lot to fix his last stupid remark, he fished Eli's phone out of his pocket. He fiddled with it for a couple of seconds before handing it back. "Now you've got my number if you change your mind." He unhooked his seat belt.

Eli supposed a kiss wouldn't be a bad ending either, but Quinn didn't kiss him. He twisted Eli's lapel around a fist and dragged Eli close enough to growl in his ear. "Because I always keep my promises."

ELI PEELED off his clothes and crammed them in the top of his laundry bag. Not that he had enough money to do laundry. Or to write the check for his share of the rent that Marcy was going to be in his face about, though it was only the tenth and it technically wouldn't be late until the fifteenth.

"But it's due on the first," she'd whine again, like she had been since she moved in. Which wouldn't be a problem except blah-blah-blah dropping ad revenues and if Nate could keep any photographer on staff he'd keep Eli. But when most of the staff writers got cut, so did Eli, and now he was down to getting paid per assignment.

And none of that would suck nearly as much if the hottest sex of Eli's life hadn't just happened with a completely unavailable, hung-up-on-his-asshole-ex, wrapped-up-in-family-drama, gorgeous, sexy, not-at-all-an-arrogant-dick man.

He flopped onto his mattress. If Casey hadn't moved down to nowhere North Carolina, they'd sit on the couch and analyze Quinn until Eli either erased his number or figured out a way to get the awesome sex without the complications.

Someone came in the front door and down the hall into the kitchen. Marcy. Whenever she came home, she dropped off her stash of stolen creamers and artificial sweeteners, lemon, ketchup and Tabasco packets, and whatever else she'd stuffed in her purse. Then she'd sigh and open the fridge, sigh and close it, reopen it like the contents had changed, and then close it. She was always on a diet. Eli was tempted to eat an entire carton of ice cream in front of her every night since he never gained a pound, but he'd puke before it sank into her thick skull.

He had to get the hell out. Everything else was too complicated to deal with, but since Nate and Kellan had moved into an apartment with a laundry room in the basement, and it was almost Nate's fault Eli didn't have any money, now at least he had a plan.

ELI CAUGHT sight of Nate dragging his scooter through the front door of the building and jogged the last quarter of a block. The weight of his laundry duffel and the two sodas he'd brought as a bribe made the last ten steps a hell of an effort, especially when Nate looked up and glared.

"Now you're stalking me at my house? I told you we don't need you until next weekend."

"I'm only interested in your amenities right now." Eli turned enough so Nate could see the bag.

A window overhead opened. "C'mon up, Eli." Kellan's deep voice floated down.

As Eli stepped into the hall, he said, "There isn't anything, though? No assignments? Something else I can do? Filing? Cleaning?"

Nate's face tightened. Someone who didn't know him would think he was mad, but Eli wasn't fooled. Slinging an arm around Eli's shoulders, Nate muttered, "I'd do anything if I could, you know. I hate this."

A lot of Nate's rougher edges had rubbed off after a year of living with Kellan's smile. But Eli was all sweaty from his run, so he ducked out of the hug. "I know."

Nate took the laundry bag from Eli's shoulder and started for the basement. "At least tell me you brought your own detergent?"

Eli held out his hands. "It was heavy."

"You're lucky Kellan likes you." Nate shoved the bag back at Eli and took the grocery bag.

"Oh, *Kellan* likes me."

"He only likes you because you bring him soda." Nate thudded up the stairs, and Eli lugged his laundry down into the musty-smelling cement basement.

After his clothes were folded and stuffed back into the bag, Eli offered to make dinner as a thank-you.

Nate replaced the large skillet Eli had unearthed from the cabinet. "No thanks. We were planning on"—Nate's gaze flicked over Eli's shoulder in Kellan's direction—"ordering in," he finished with a sigh and an eye roll.

Eli didn't care. He was having a crisis. Kellan and Nate could fuck or whatever else they'd been planning another time.

Kellan had his phone out before Nate could finish exhaling. "Pizza, all veggie, coming up."

"Pizza?" Nate's brows shot up.

"After last night, you know I deserve better than bean scum." Kellan had a sexy voice, deep with a ripple of laughter in it, but it couldn't make Eli shiver like Quinn's did.

Eli leaned against the counter. "Ooo. I want details."

"Not a chance." But Kellan put his arm around Eli's shoulders and leaned next to him. "Instead you can tell us about tall, dark and—"

"Old?" Nate suggested.

With a deliberate stare at Nate, Eli pushed away from the cabinet. "Gimme old any day, because that was absolutely the best sex of my entire existence." He reached into the fridge for a bottled water and rubbed it over his face and neck. "I get hot just thinking about it."

"Ouch. Score." Kellan's laugh rumbled through the kitchen.

Nate folded his arms. "If it was that good, why are you plaguing us with your presence when you could be having 'the best sex of your entire existence.'" His tone didn't need air quotes. He made his sneer do it for him. "Did you give him a heart attack? Make him run out of his little blue pills?"

Eli wiped some condensation off the bottle, then licked it off his thumb. "Nope. I cut him loose. Great in bed. Way too much baggage."

"Besides the stuff under his eyes?"

Eli made a hissing noise that made Nate's cat Quan Yin yowl in answer. "Step back, Kellan. I think we're on the verge of a queen out. Jealous, Nate?"

"Be serious," Nate scoffed.

"Sounds kinda jealous to me." Kellan picked up Yin and cuddled her. She flopped contentedly in the cradle of his arm.

"You'd be happier if you dated guys closer to your age."

"Hey, Gray," Eli said as if he were addressing Nate at the advice column he did for the paper. "Did I ask for your advice?"

"You're not going to find some kind of substitute for—"

"The father who threw my ass out on the street while I was still in high school? God, take a few psych courses in college, and you too can be an annoying know-it-all asshole. Do you think that's what Kellan is doing? Looking for a substitute father?"

Eli wondered how Nate could type out his advice if he always had that judgmental, defensive, arms-folded thing going on.

"Kellan's different. His father—"

"Everyone is different." Eli threw up his hands. "I'm different. Did it ever occur to you that maybe I date older guys because they're hot? And they usually have their shit together?"

Nate blinked, but he didn't answer.

"The guys my age are fucking infants. Either they just came out, or they've had it so easy they have no idea what life is like. They've never had to worry about where they're going to live." Eli swallowed hard. That was one of the things he'd come over here to stop thinking about.

Yin jumped up on the kitchen table and sharpened her claws on the paper before sprawling out. Eli ran a hand through her long hair and then rubbed his face in her fur. It made him feel better for a second. He'd like to have a cat, but he had enough trouble keeping a roof over his own head.

He felt Nate come up behind him but slipped away onto one of the kitchen chairs and kept petting Yin. When he was sure his face was under control, he looked up. "Where's Kellan?"

"Probably went to pick up the pizza. He doesn't like it when things get loud."

"And yet he lives with you."

"We manage." Nate's face twisted in a wry grin.

Eli rubbed Yin behind her ears until she purred and snugged herself against his arm.

Nate was one of the most opinionated dicks on the planet, but living with Kellan had done more than smooth his rough edges. It had actually given him some people skills. He let a few more minutes of silence tick by before saying, "Tell me about this guy. I promise to avoid dispensing know-it-all advice for ninety seconds."

"That would be some kind of record. I think you're just trying to pick up sex pointers."

"Don't need any."

"He really doesn't." Kellan came back in and slid the box onto the table. Yin sniffed it, gave Kellan a disappointed look, jumped down, and walked away, fluffy tail curled in disdain. "I want to hear this too."

"There's nothing to tell." Eli scooped a slice from the box.

"How did you find out about the baggage, then?" Kellan asked.

"He took me to meet his family."

Nate choked.

Kellan whacked his back and said, "Before or after you...." He waved the slice of pizza in his hand.

It was kind of adorable that Kellan could still get a little shy about gay sex. "Fucked?" Eli finished for him. "After." He remembered the bathroom. Oh yeah. "And before."

Nate took a long drink. "So did he also propose?" he managed to rasp out.

"It wasn't like that. Exactly. He had a thing he had to go to. And it wasn't exactly his family."

"That's a lot of *exactly*'s. Stick to photography and swear to me you'll never try writing," Nate suggested.

"Stop editing the entire population of Earth and let him tell the story," Kellan said.

Eli was enjoying this now. He shifted out of direct range and watched Nate take another bite of pizza. "He already had plans to go to a baptism. The family is his ex-boyfriend's, but they're still close."

Nate swallowed the pizza and reached for his soda. "The family or the boyfriend?"

"The family, mostly, but Quinn stood as the baby's godfather." Eli watched Nate drink. "Even though his ex-boyfriend is the baby daddy."

X-treme Cream soda launched in a spray across the kitchen.

There were parts of Nate that would never change. Eli held up a napkin. "God, you're so fucking easy."

ELI DIDN'T know much besides the bare bones of the Quinn and Peter and Chrissy soap opera, so there wasn't much detail to give. He hadn't actually come over here for Nate's Hey Gray advice, which tended to be snarky and cynical enough to sell papers. As much as he loved Nate, it was Kellan Eli wanted to talk to—without Nate's acidic remarks burning holes in the conversation.

As Kellan tossed away the trash and wrapped up the remaining two slices of pizza, Nate pushed away from the table.

"I've got to finish up my column for this week."

The *Hey, Eli, don't let the door hit you on the way out* came through as clear as if Eli were wearing a Nate translator. Putting on as pathetic a face and as plaintive a voice as he could manage, Eli said, "Can I stay over?" Into the silent glance between his friends, he added, "She hates me. I don't know why."

"On the couch," Nate agreed with a sigh.

"But you guys have a king, and I swear my hands will stay on top of the covers."

"The couch," Kellan said firmly.

Nate slung an arm around Eli's shoulders. "Behave."

Eli managed to duck the kiss that followed enough that it landed on his ear. "Yes, former boss." He couldn't avoid the light swat on his ass. It only reminded him of where he wasn't spending the night.

"Want to watch a movie?" Kellan dropped onto the couch, legs stretched onto the coffee table, remote in his hand.

Eli hurried to get his head in Kellan's lap before Yin could steal the spot. "I still can't believe he let you get a TV, let alone one bigger than an iPad. It must be true love." Eli settled on his side, legs stretched out, head on Kellan's thighs.

Kellan stopped flipping through the on-demand listings, resting a hand on Eli's head. "And does that bug you?"

"Huh?"

"Nate with me, I mean."

"No. I told you that when you got together."

"Yeah?" Kellan's fingers stroked through Eli's hair until Eli wanted to purr like Yin. "Then how come you don't let him kiss you or hug you like you do me?"

It didn't have anything to do with being in love with Nate. Not that Eli really had been. He'd only thought he was. Thought that after they'd fucked, Eli might wear Nate down for some more sex and maybe boyfriend status. But then Eli had seen Nate and Kellan look at each other, that one time, that first night Kellan stayed. Eli knew he'd been totally wrong. *That* was love. He wasn't saying he believed in soul mates or whatever, but he'd known right then Nate was completely unavailable. Forever.

Eli waved his hand, wrist flopping. "But, dahling, I've *had* him. You are something mysterious."

"Yeah, right. Is it the job thing? You know, he threw up all night before he went in to tell you."

"It's not the job either." Warning Yin off Kellan's lap territory with a glare, Eli sat up so he could make Kellan understand. "I love him—love you both, but not that way. If he thinks I'm pissed at him, I'll go blow him, okay?"

"No you won't." Kellan yanked Eli's head back down but kept him carefully on his thighs.

Kellan let the subject drop. Good thing, because Eli wasn't sure exactly how to answer him. It was different with Kellan. Not that Eli wouldn't have jumped into bed with him if Kellan had hit on him before he and Nate got together, but since Eli and Kellan hadn't—wouldn't ever—cuddling didn't feel all that different than if Eli were Kellan's cat.

Kellan started sifting his fingers through Eli's hair again and clicked on a movie that started with an explosion and sirens, or maybe Kellan had resumed watching something else. Kellan loved disaster movies. Eli didn't care as long as those fingers kept stroking his hair so he could drift into pleasure.

Maybe he dozed, because the next thing he knew, his phone buzzed with a text.

Smell last night on the sheets. Gonna jerk off. Too bad you're missing it.

Eli smiled. *Think you're the one missing out,* he sent back to Quinn. And then a second one. *How'd you get my number?*

Had it since I met you.

Arrogant, toppy, sexy man. Without thinking too much about it, Eli let his hand slide down his body to his hip and then over his crotch.

"Eli." Kellan's voice yanked him back to the fact that he was on his friends' couch.

"What?" Eli tried for innocence, but his voice was a little husky for that.

"If you're going to sext, gimme ten seconds to get out of the room, okay?"

"No." Eli curled his arms around his chest. "I'll behave."

The volume of explosions decreased, or maybe it was a slow point in the movie. "Tell me about this guy, really," Kellan said.

"He's perfect to fuck, but seriously, I can't handle all that family drama." Kellan should appreciate that. Family was a touchy subject for them both.

"So?" Kellan urged.

"So what?"

"So, it's not as if you gay guys have any trouble just—"

Eli cranked his head to look up. "*You* gay guys?"

"Fine." Kellan rolled his eyes. "It's not like *us* bi or gay guys can't just do the friends-with-benefits-thing easy. You don't have to do the family thing."

"But that's the problem. I think Quinn is the family thing."

"Then I guess you're screwed."

"Thanks a fucking lot." Eli rolled back to face the random destruction on the screen.

Kellan petted his hair again. "At least Nate would be happy you remembered 'a lot' is two words."

"Tell me he edits your texts."

Kellan gently flicked Eli's ear. "Maybe I won't tell you the nice thing he said about you."

"What?" Eli looked up at him again.

"He may act like a total brat most of the time, but I swear he's got more common sense than guys twice his age," Kellan quoted.

"I was hoping for something about my ass."

"What I mean is, you'll figure it out."

"I hope so." Eli started to drift off again as Kellan made that soothing stroke through his hair.

"Good. Because you can't spend your life on our couch."

Chapter Eight

"AND WHO else would be there?" Quinn tucked the phone under his cheek as he washed his coffee mug in the sink.

"Just family." Chrissy was as warm and friendly on the phone as she was in person. Quinn bet she was smiling.

"And why is it at your house?"

"Paula decided she would surprise him. He's being grouchy about birthdays. And Claire's having the downstairs bathroom redone. I know it's short notice, but please say you'll both be there."

Both? Quinn bit back the word before surprise spilled it from his lips. Eli. Right. Christ. Stalling for time, Quinn stared out at the backyard. The space between the shed and forsythia bush was bare. Eli again.

"I'm not sure what his work schedule is like this week."

There was a bit of silence on the other end of the phone. Oh. Quinn was probably supposed to be asking his imaginary boyfriend what his schedule was. "And he's not here right now," he added.

"If he can't do Tuesday, we can make it—" The sound of a baby's screech interrupted whatever she was going to offer as an alternative.

Quinn heard Peter in the background. "Hey, Chris, I think he wants that thing from you I can't give him."

A muffled moment, a hand over the receiver maybe, then Chrissy was back. "Here. Peter wants to talk to you while I take care of Gabe."

"Just a minute." Peter's voice was gruff. A door opened. Apparently they were taking this outside.

"That was kind of a convenient interruption. Did you pinch him?" Quinn asked.

"No, I didn't pinch my son. Jesus." When was the last time Peter hadn't sounded tired and bitter when he spoke to Quinn? More than a year now, maybe longer.

"So what do you want?"

"I want you to not have made a fucking scene at the baptism yesterday. But since it's too late for that, you're going to drag your little piece of ass over here. because Chrissy's convinced that he's about the most perfect thing ever and aren't you two sweet." Peter's teeth were clenched, his voice tight.

Peter probably wasn't even angry. Quinn doubted anything hit Peter deeper than self-preservation. The clenched teeth meant Peter was trying not to throw up. Quinn borrowed a bit of Eli, though his tone was dry. "We are. I know."

"Well, I don't know what kind of game you're playing, but if this is what it takes for my wife to—"

"Be convinced I've never had my dick up your ass? I'm not sure that ship hasn't sailed. But I think what would make everybody happy is knowing you won't pull the same shit on her."

"I told you. I'm—I've always been—"

"Straight except for me. Right."

"I don't give a shit what you think. Just make sure you both show up." Peter clicked off.

He'd always done that when he was losing an argument. Hang up. Take the dog for a walk. Say he'd been called in for overtime.

Quinn had barely put the phone on the counter when he fielded a call from Alyssa, who wanted to know if she could talk to Eli, and then Claire, who had to tell him how much she enjoyed meeting Eli and Quinn should always feel welcome to bring his friends to meet the family. If Roger called to ask Eli to go bowling, Quinn was going to impale himself on a barbeque fork.

He left to go buy some iris bulbs for the backyard.

Over the next six hours, Quinn left Eli a voicemail and a call-me text. The bulbs were long-since entombed with a bonemeal shroud, and Eli still hadn't called back. Eli might not deserve all of Quinn's growing frustration, but Eli had to shoulder some of the blame for this mess. He was the one who decided to put on the boyfriend act for the family, spinning out lies until he had them running off to Hawaii to get married.

Quinn had done enough sitting around and waiting the last few years of his life. He drove downtown, parking a block from Eli's apartment.

The walk only made Quinn more determined to spread around his own frustration. But the frizzy-haired girl, Marcy, wasn't much help. After a girl with multiple piercings on her face joined the conversation at the door, it got a little easier.

"Eli's always forgetting to charge his phone." The spikes in her lips glinted as she spoke. "Nate lives on Washington Hill. Corner of Lafayette and Broadway. I dropped him off there once. Third door in from this side of the corner. Uh, on the left—no, right."

"Thanks."

Chasing Eli to Nate—boss, vegetarian, ex-boyfriend Nate—could really only come down on the side of creepy old man stalking younger guy, but Quinn still drove to Washington Hill. He found a place to park and then tried to tell himself he might run into Eli on the street. If that happened, it wouldn't be like he actually went and knocked on the door. There were a few people enjoying a Sunday afternoon outside, walking dogs, sitting on stoops. None of them were Eli.

The third door in had three buzzers, but two had two last names. Liu/James and Gray/Brooks. There was the third possibility. Schmidt. Damn, he wished he'd paid more attention to the name Alyssa was flinging around about the guy who'd come out and turned down his family's money. Firmly silencing the voice in his head that told him this was far beyond stalking, he looked up the *Charming Rag* on his smartphone and found the masthead. Gray, then.

He pushed the buzzer, getting a masculine "Yeah?" in response. "My name is Quinn Maloney. I'm a friend of Eli's. I—"

"Shit. Did something happen to him?"

"No, but—" Quinn wasn't sure he could be heard over the buzz freeing the doorlock and the speaker calling for Nate.

He climbed to the second-floor apartment, to be met halfway up by a twentysomething blond who had two inches and probably twenty pounds on Quinn. He looked familiar, and Quinn remembered meeting him at the club on Friday, though he couldn't drag a name out of his memory.

"What happened to Eli?"

"Nothing. He's fine. I just—"

A shorter, slighter, dark-haired man with a neat goatee stuck his head out. "Told you. He's fine. Could we move the drama inside and stop giving the neighborhood another free episode of *Queer Theater*?"

Quinn followed them into a kitchen/living area.

"Kellan." The blond introduced himself again. "We met at the Arena."

"Right."

As Quinn found himself the object of two intent stares, Kellan's curious and Nate's openly hostile, a sense of the idiocy, if not downright disturbed nature, of Quinn's search began to take full root.

"Uh, I was trying to get a hold of Eli, and I know he doesn't always charge his phone."

Kellan burst out laughing. "Eli keeps an emergency charge on him. That phone never leaves him. He feeds everyone that line when he doesn't want to talk to them."

"So, Quinn." Nate leaned against a kitchen counter. "Pretty desperate measures for a booty call. You know, I've heard there are clubs, online dating services. Maybe you could meet someone your own age."

"It's not…." He should leave. While he had a shred of dignity. What the hell had he been thinking chasing a one-night piece of tail all over Baltimore? And worse, because Peter fucking told him to? Quinn did need a therapist more than a date. Probably should have started seeing one after the hospital, like they'd wanted him to. "Something came up, and I need to talk to him."

Nate straightened out of his slouch. "Asshole. What did you give him? Herpes? Syphilis?"

"No, nothing like that." *Christ, this is insane. I am insane.* "Forget it."

"He went down to the Inner Harbor to take pictures," Kellan said.

"What the fuck?" Nate snarled.

"Thanks." Quinn turned for the door.

"Maloney." Nate's voice snapped out like a commandant on an inspection drill. "You do not want me pissed at you."

Quinn nodded. Rather than inviting a defensive anger, Nate's protectiveness made Quinn glad Eli had friends who would look out for him.

The Inner Harbor was a pretty general location, so Quinn did a lot of wandering. It was sunset when he found Eli staring hard at the massive brick power station which had been converted to a home for upscale chain restaurants. As the sun disappeared, the wind picked up and the temperature dropped, sending most of the tourists indoors.

Eli's hair whipped in his face, but he didn't stop looking at the building, the outlines of neon glowing as the daylight disappeared. The buildup of frustration from the long search, at Eli stirring up the family with his made-up romance, disappeared on a long breath. The back of Quinn's neck tingled at the release of tension. He wanted to walk up and wrap his arms around Eli, stand with him until Quinn understood what Eli was seeing. How exactly had Eli gone from not-my-type to can't-keep-my-hands-off-him in less than two days?

Eli's gaze didn't shift from the building as Quinn approached, but he said, "I wish I could have seen it before they fixed it up like this. Back when it was industrial."

"I could take you over to Dundalk. That's all warehouses and shipping."

Eli made a face and shook his head. "I guess there's nowhere between ugly and homogenized into a mall."

"Halifax."

"Huh?" Eli looked toward Quinn.

"Nova Scotia. When I was in the Navy, we put in there once. The harbor is fixed up with restaurants and parks, but it probably looks more like what you're thinking. It's more narrow, has an old feeling, ships still use it. Lots of cruises stop there."

"Are you offering to take me there?" Eli turned to him, hands in the pockets of his denim blazer. If he had been taking pictures, his camera must be in his backpack now.

"I thought you wanted to go to Hawaii for our honeymoon."

"Oh, right." Eli looked down. Then he shrugged and grinned. "I think I'll settle for Hawaii. I can be packed in ten minutes."

"That's not on offer either."

Eli shook his hair out of his eyes. "So what do you want?"

Quinn knew the conversation would go better if they were closer, touching. Preferably naked in bed. Eli sitting on Quinn's hips, hands tracing his tattoos. Both of them sweaty and slick but looking for more. *Pliant* wasn't a word Quinn thought anyone could use in connection with Eli, but maybe then he'd be receptive.

"There's another party."

Eli had been holding himself still; now he was rigid. "And? You need to come out again?"

"No. Everyone thinks we're dating."

"So? Tell them I'm out of town, tell them we broke up, tell them anything you want. What's another lie on top of all that mess?"

"You're the one who turned it into a lie."

"Like the lie you're all telling yourselves about that dick you were with? The way you all lie to make his bullshit marriage work?"

Anger surged back, buzzing along his skin. "I didn't ask you to do anything other than to go with me."

"Consider my work a bonus for the awesome sex. You're welcome. Goodbye." Eli walked away to stand at the railing and stare out at the water.

Quinn followed him. "Whatever I did to piss you off—"

Eli laughed, but his hands squeezed the railing. "Nothing. Your conscience is free."

"I don't get it. You certainly seemed to enjoy yourself."

"No, you don't get it. What am I, some fag-in-a-box for you to take out to play with when you need to entertain?"

"No. I told you I wanted to see you again. Before everyone started calling me about you."

"I don't get it either. Who the fuck are these people to you? Why does it even matter what they think or do?"

"They're my family." Quinn wanted to shout it but held it to a whisper.

"No, they're your ex's family. But if you want to tie yourself in knots over it, go ahead. Just don't drag me along." The words had a final ring to them. Words said before hanging up or walking away, but Eli remained at the rail, which meant he hadn't stopped listening.

"I thought you were leaving."

"You leave. I was here first." Eli shoved at him with his hip. Quinn shoved back, fighting a smile.

The wind brought fresh bursts of boat exhaust and oil from the bay, the smell so familiar Quinn could almost feel an engine rumble to life beneath his feet, though he hadn't been on a ship in six years.

It was a story Quinn didn't like to tell, and thank God he didn't have to often. The people who mattered knew. Now he told it to the soft slapping waves in the harbor, and Eli could listen if he wanted to.

"About a year before I left the service, I got sick. I'd had a headache, and my neck hurt. We were a day out of Norfolk after six months at sea. I only remember feeling really sick, the worst I'd ever felt in my life. I remember going to mess, and then I woke up in the Naval Medical Center in Bethesda almost three weeks later, feeling like I'd rather be dead. But Claire was there. She held my hand when I wanted to tear off my own skin from the pain."

"What was it?"

"Bacterial meningitis. They gave us a vaccine when we joined, but I picked up a kind they don't vaccinate for. Four other people on the ship got it. One died, and one of them is deaf. They put me in a coma for treatment, and Claire came down every day. Sometimes with Roger, sometimes with Peter or Dennis. Even when they had to wear full hazmat suits to see me, they came in. I was in a coma for a week, and they sat with me. Claire read to me. Roger read to me." Any light had turned to shards of glass tearing through his eyes into his skull, scraping every nerve until it screamed. He'd wanted to hide away from the pain, but somehow their voices kept dragging him back.

"What about your parents?" The change in Eli's voice meant he was facing Quinn now, but Quinn could only look at the waves, the sharp tips silver and green and pink from reflected neon.

"My mom died of cancer when I was seven. My dad couldn't cope. I went to live with my grandparents when I was twelve, but they moved to Arizona when I went into the Academy. They sent a card."

Eli made a disgusted noise.

"I was barely sitting up when they discharged me, but instead of letting me go to a rehab, the Laurents took me home." Quinn straightened up and let go of the railing. "I was lucky. No amputations, no scars, no brain damage. The headaches come back sometimes." *Headache* was a ridiculous word for splintered glass in every inch of his brain, his hair feeling like needles driving into his skin, but that's what the word was. "I'd cut off my own arm before I'd hurt them. Before I did anything to upset Claire. She saved my life."

Eli spread his hands out along the rail. "A bit of background would have helped before you put me on stage."

"I underestimated your ability to ad-lib."

"Give me a script this time." Eli turned so his back was on the rail. "When's the party?"

"Tuesday at six thirty. It's Dennis's birthday. Chrissy's hosting."

Eli winced.

"I know. No script. Just try not to go overboard. Maybe take it down a few notches."

"That I can do."

"C'mon, I'll give you a ride home, unless…." Quinn let it hang there, hoping.

"No thanks. I want to walk." Eli pushed up and leaned in. Quinn met him for a too-short soft kiss. "Night, Quinn."

This time he did walk away.

Chapter Nine

WITH NO idea in his head but escape, Eli headed west. His feet hit the pavement faster and faster, wind and speed and exertion making his nose run until he had to wipe it on his sleeve. No matter how far he got from the spot where he'd left Quinn, the words followed him. *She saved my life.* Quinn hadn't been exaggerating. Eli could hear that in his voice. The only thing that had kept Quinn alive was the hold of that family.

Eli didn't regret a thing he'd done or said to embarrass that asshole Peter, but when he replayed the way he'd acted, he knew he could have been less obnoxiously manipulative with the rest of them. Quinn should have told him.

He could have died. Quinn could have died. But that was years ago. Why should it matter? The feeling that kept Eli climbing up away from the harbor, driving him toward the bars, made no sense. Why should the idea that Quinn had almost died make Eli's throat tighten around the sharp, quick breaths he was taking?

Eli hadn't known him then, would never have known him.

His steps slowed as he approached Grand Central. That had been his plan. Hit the biggest place to cruise. Maybe find a different bed to sleep in to avoid the confrontation with Marcy. It wouldn't be the first time he'd had sex with an equal interest in a place to stay the night.

He reached into his pocket for his wallet, took out his cell, and reread the last two texts he'd gotten before Quinn tracked him down.

Careful. Kell told the crazy stalker where you were.

He went to lots of trouble to find you. That's hot. I like him.

Eli tucked the phone away and went into the bar.

The Sunday night crowd was big enough to make Eli think he'd have competition from pros—if he meant to go through with it.

What was so bad about home? He'd go back to the apartment, tell Marcy he couldn't make the rent, and promise to be out in two weeks. And in two weeks he'd have—he stopped thinking about that and leaned into the bar, more than aware he couldn't even afford a drink. A hand slid onto his back, followed by the weight and pressure of a taller body beside him. A signal to the bartender, and Eli had a rum and coke in front of him. He was going to thank the guy, get a look at him and decide what he wanted to do, when the hand on his back slid possessively down to the top of his jeans, a light circling pressure.

Eli let himself sink into a fantasy that Quinn had followed him, found him as irresistible as Kellan's text suggested—rather than the truth that Eli was only an accessory to keeping the family happy. Quinn's hand drifted over his ass, and Eli tipped his hips to meet the touch, skin tingling, a light buzz in his balls as he gulped enough of the drink to keep the fantasy alive.

The fingers on his ass dipped between his legs, a light brush forward, and then dug into the still-bruised crease as the hand gripped hard.

The fantasy evaporated. Eli wriggled free. "Thanks for the drink."

Before he could get clear, the guy's hand wrapped hard around Eli's upper arm. "What's your hurry? You were shaking your ass at me just fine."

Eli got a good look at his face. Hard eyes, flat nose. Probably had it broken in a few fights. Grand Central attracted a lot of men who were only gay when they had a dick in their mouths, men who lived a straight life outside of what they managed to sneak off to get here.

"I said thanks for the drink." Eli tried to pull free without turning it into some kind of shoving contest.

"Whore."

"Mmm." Eli sucked down the rest of his drink and leaned into the unsuspecting son of a bitch. "I like dirty talk."

The man released his arm, and Eli's hand shot down, grabbing the guy's nut sac and giving it a twist so he had his attention. "I said thanks. If you're looking for a whore, it's going to take a lot more than a six-dollar drink to get over having to look at your face. I'm going to move on, and you're going to let me. Clear?"

The man grunted, eyes squeezed shut, lips thinned in a grimace of pain.

"Thanks again." Eli moved off to another part of the bar.

He'd inhaled the drink fast enough to get a little buzz but couldn't seem to get into the spirit of things. None of the guys who made eye contact were hot enough, tall enough, or interesting enough for Eli to do anything but flick his glance away in apology.

He was thinking of taking out his phone and playing a game to kill time in case something better turned up later when someone crowded into him from behind as he watched a few guys shoot pool. If it was the same asshole from before, Eli was going to tear off his balls and feed them to him.

"You don't seem like the type to just watch," said a vaguely familiar voice in his ear, while an interesting package pressed into the small of his back.

Eli wasn't making the same mistake twice. He turned.

"Jesus." Round blue eyes under sandy lashes blinked in surprise.

"Fuck me." Eli knew his own eyes had to be bugging out of his head. "Peter."

Peter recovered first. "I was thinking about it." As his wide mouth curved in a smile, Eli was furious with himself for noticing the full lips, the lazy blink of those eyes, the broad solid shoulders, everything that would have made Peter hot enough to fuck if he weren't Quinn's slimy, cheating, closeted ex.

Eli wished for a wall at his back, protection and room to breathe as Peter filled in the space Eli had made by turning around. "Does your wife know where you are?"

"Does Quinn know what a little slut you are?"

"Well, it wouldn't be the first time he's made that mistake." Eli managed to get his back against a post supporting a partition. It felt a little safer. "But Quinn and I have an understanding."

"Liar. He'd never go for that. Tell me really." Peter leaned in so his lips brushed Eli's ear, and maybe getting his back to a wall had been a mistake. "You're one of his students, right? He paid you."

Eli laughed and turned his head, hoping the ends of his hair whipped Peter's face. "I'd have paid him. God, remember his cock? The way he moves it. Mmmm." Eli licked his lips, only half faking the enjoyment of the memory.

Peter's hands landed on the post above Eli's head. "Who do you think taught him that?"

Eli laughed again. "Not you." As much as Peter deserved to have his nuts twisted, Eli would have to settle for just fucking with him. He reached up and put his hand around Peter's neck. "You're aching for a dick in you. Bet you're dying to suck me off."

Peter leaned down, liquor-soaked breath strong on Eli's cheek, leg sliding between Eli's. "Yeah. I'll blow your fucking mind."

Eli moved his hand until his thumb pressed against Peter's lips. As he sucked, Eli ground his dick onto Peter's leg once and then shoved him away. "In your fucking dreams, asshole."

Peter's eyes narrowed.

"Oh. And see you Tuesday. I'll try to remember to bring your wife a strap-on."

WHEN ELI insisted he'd find a ride and meet Quinn at his house on Tuesday, Quinn anticipated a disaster. An over-the-top outfit with sequins. A see-through mesh top with matching pants. A kilt and a bright blue mohawk. But opening the door to Eli's knock, Quinn found something worse.

Eli wore a suit. Navy blue, a blue dress shirt, and a red-and-blue-striped tie. His hair was slicked back from his face, and as he made a nervous adjustment to his tie, Quinn could see his nails were free of polish. One hundred percent conservative by anyone's standards. The problem was Eli looked like a fifteen-year-old in his school uniform. Remembering there was a sexually active man long past the age of consent under those clothes set up a battle between lust and shame in Quinn's body.

"What's wrong?" Eli's brow furrowed, a vulnerable confusion Quinn never would have seen with his hair hanging over his eyes.

Quinn swallowed back the response of *Everything* and tried concentrating on anything but how much better that silken tie would look binding Eli's wrists or teasing his cock.

"The tie's too much. I knew it." Eli fidgeted with it.

"What—why?" Quinn managed.

"You asked me to tone it down."

The sickest feeling wasn't because Eli's suit made Quinn feel like a dirty old man, or that it drew more attention to Eli's age and slender body than if he'd been wearing the kilt and mohawk; it was that Quinn had forced Eli into something so wrong on him.

"I didn't ask you to turn it off. You look—wait. I'm fucking this up." Quinn moved so Eli could step into the house.

Eli nodded.

Quinn shut the door and turned back. Running a finger along the tight collar of Eli's shirt and smoothing his tie, Quinn said, "You did this for me. Because of what I told you."

Eli smiled. It still looked wrong. Quinn missed the self-confidence behind the grin that showed that one slightly crooked tooth.

"Now that's the kind of response that will get you a blowjob, Mr. Maloney."

Quinn controlled the urge to shudder. "Christ. Please don't call me that." There was the grin he'd been looking for. "In the interest of time, I'll settle for a kiss."

Eli leaned in and Quinn hunched down to meet him, but all he got was a light brush of lips. Quinn caught Eli's face in his hands and held him, drawing back enough to see Eli's face. "What's wrong?"

"I don't understand the point of revving the engine if you're not going to drive somewhere."

"You are the opposite of romantic. Did anyone ever tell you that?"

"I am full of romance. I like sunsets and the ocean and beaches and flowers and love songs and Shakespeare in the park and all that kind of shit." Eli's cheeks flushed. It was adorable on him. "I don't get what any of that has to do with sex."

"I'm not talking about sex, Eli. I'm talking about a kiss."

"Fine. I'll kiss the romantic fuck out of you."

Quinn stepped his legs out and bent his knees to get to Eli's eye level and waited.

Peeling Quinn's hand away, Eli licked his lips and wrapped his arms around Quinn's neck. The kiss was a brush of lips and tongue, slow and deliberate. Quinn kept his mouth soft, waiting. Eli took a more determined grip on Quinn's neck and kissed his lower lip, his upper lip, gentle sucking pressure. When Eli's tongue darted out to flick at the corner of Quinn's mouth, he had to reach out for Eli's hips to keep from grabbing for his head and taking control.

Eli's kiss grew more determined, pressure increasing, a hot wet tickle from his tongue teasing sensitive corners. Quinn's hands slid around to Eli's back, holding him, fighting the urge to lift him close and tight. Quinn forgot what he was trying to prove. Calculated or not, Eli could kiss. The fingers on Quinn's neck tightened, and he lost himself in Eli's taste, his breath, the smell of his skin, and the slide of lips. When Quinn opened his mouth, Eli didn't take any more ground than the inside of Quinn's lips, a tingle that echoed down to his ribs, making Quinn's breath catch.

Eli eased back enough to breathe words onto Quinn's mouth. "Well? Romantic enough?"

"My heart's aflutter."

Eli sank away. "All the fluttering is in my balls."

Quinn loosened the knot of Eli's tie and slid it free. "Here. Save this and"—he palmed Eli's crotch lightly—"that for later. I'll be right back."

Upstairs, Quinn exchanged his jeans for slacks, keeping the green sweater with the wooden buttons at the V-neck. As he came back down, he caught Eli with his thumb on his lips and confusion in his eyes.

Eli dropped his hand. "You didn't have to change for me. I've never cared what other people—"

"I care." Quinn tucked his arm around Eli's waist and tasted his mouth again. "God, much as I want to fuck you, I could stand here and kiss you for hours." He coaxed Eli's tongue to follow his, let the kiss get hotter until Eli elbowed him.

"Bastard." Eli pressed his hand into his crotch. "Now I'm going to have to think about your ex fucking his wife so I don't flash a tent pole half the night. Or"—he pressed himself against Quinn—"you could help me out. It would only take a minute or two."

"Later. I'm not showing up smelling like sex."

"If they turn blue and fall off, I'm taking yours," Eli muttered as he slid into the car.

QUINN FOLLOWED directions and parked down the block so Dennis wouldn't see the car. Alyssa met them at the door. "Oh my God, Eli, what happened? Did you let Quinn dress you?"

"No. I had a job interview and there was no time to change," Eli explained. Quinn looked at him with raised eyebrows, but Eli wouldn't give him an answer.

Alyssa led them into the kitchen. "I thought you liked your job at that paper—what was it?"

"The *Charming Rag*. I love it. But you know how the economy is. I'm freelancing now, and I need some regular income."

Another lie to explain the clothes, or was Eli really having problems? Why didn't Eli tell him about it? *Because as soon as you see him, you've got your tongue or your cock in him. Or you're whining about your own problems.* He tried to hold Eli back with a hand on his shoulder, but Eli wriggled free and escaped to the family in the kitchen. Claire stepped away from the stove to kiss them both on the cheek.

"Chrissy's feeding the baby now. Everyone is out back, since fixing a board on the porch is the excuse to get Dennis here. I don't understand why he's being so difficult."

Because thirty-five feels a lot older than thirty-four, Quinn wanted to explain. *And it feels embarrassingly ancient when you can't keep your hands off a not quite twenty-three-year-old.*

Eli went through a brief recap of an explanation for his suit with Claire, the variation being her response of "I'm so sorry. It's a terrible time for young people especially."

Quinn had been straining his ears for the familiar sound since they arrived, trying to tamp down the spread of cold fear in his stomach. No jangle of tags. No click of claws. Hubert was probably out on the porch. He was just too stiff to come in to greet Quinn, smart enough to know Quinn would be there in a minute. Hubert would whine and sit at Quinn's feet and give him the where-have-you-been look with his big brown eyes.

He made his way out onto the screen porch, but Hubert wasn't there. The dread that had been waiting launched itself into his throat, burning into the back of his skull as he searched the living room, checked under the dining room table.

"Quinn." He heard Peter call him back, and then Chrissy put her hand on his arm. "I'm so sorry. We had to put him to sleep. I thought Peter would have told you."

Quinn was out of the house before she finished talking, down the block, leaning against his car and trying to get air in past the icy fingers squeezing his lungs shut.

He knew who was behind him without turning. Eli wrapped himself around Quinn's back. The heat from the palms flattened on his chest loosened Quinn's breath.

"I've only seen him twice since Peter moved out."

There was a minute of silence and then Eli said, "After ten years, you should have been there."

Quinn turned in the circle of Eli's arms, leaning against the car. "Yes." Eli got it. It wasn't that Quinn wanted to, but that he needed to. To lay hands on Hubert and tell him it was okay. To say goodbye. Somehow Peter's cheating, his betrayal, his leaving, nothing felt as deliberately cruel as denying Quinn that goodbye. And what was worse, Quinn knew it was nothing more than Peter's selfishness and his need to hide the past from Chrissy that had made Peter's decision for him.

Eli moved them into a comforting sway, the warmth of his understanding thawing the anger that was all that held Quinn together. He tried to step away, but Eli held on.

"I can't. Not now."

"So we'll leave."

"I can't do that either."

"Don't let him fuck with this too." Eli pulled Quinn in tighter.

Quinn took a deep breath and put his head on Eli's shoulder, let the gentle rocking drag out a few tears, relax a little of the pain radiating through a tightly clenched jaw.

"Thanks," Quinn said as he lifted his head.

Eli shrugged without letting go. "That's what boyfriends are for." He pressed up and kissed a tear from Quinn's cheek.

Quinn shared the taste with a quick brush of lips. For a guy who couldn't see the point of a simple kiss, Eli was acting like… "Mr. Romance," Quinn said aloud.

"Don't let it get out. I have my reputation to think of."

They'd straightened up, but Eli still had his arms locked around Quinn's hips when Dennis appeared over Eli's shoulder.

"What the hell, Quinn. I don't get what's going on with you. You've never acted like this—"

Eli spun around, stepping in front of Quinn like when Peter had confronted them in the bathroom. The idea of Eli taking on someone Dennis's size in Quinn's defense should have been funny, but the thump in Quinn's chest had nothing to do with amusement.

Eli stepped closer to Dennis. "Quinn is dealing with your brother's shit. Again. He came here expecting to see their dog. The one Peter forgot to tell him was dead. And then Peter sent you out to stir up more trouble."

Dennis looked to Quinn for confirmation. Quinn's nod might have satisfied Dennis, but the exchange only made Eli angrier.

"I'm standing right the fuck in front of you, Mr. Laurent. You could at least look at me."

"Look, kid. Whatever the fuck you're doing with Quinn here doesn't give you the right—"

"No, you look. And open your fucking eyes when you do. Your brother is an asshole of epic proportions, and the way you all let him get away with it is only making things worse. If someone doesn't step up, Quinn isn't going to be the only one dealing with the fallout."

Eli stomped off toward the house but then turned back. "And that thing Quinn and I are doing is called sex. Quinn is gay. Gay, gay, gay. Your friend fucks guys. You may have been enjoying some kind of straight-guy denial so far, but get that through your head. Quinn likes cock." With that, he strode up toward the house.

Dennis gave Quinn a helpless, confused look. "He never told you about Hubert."

"No." Quinn swallowed. "Sorry we missed the surprise."

"I wish I did. When will they stop acting like birthdays are some kind of sacred institution?"

"Your mom or your wife?"

"Both." Dennis stared at him, and Quinn pushed away from his car. "So. You're gay, huh?"

"You got that newsflash?"

"Kind of hard to miss. What the fuck is with you and that kid?"

"I know he looks young—"

"I'm not worried about jailbait. I'm worried about you."

Quinn shrugged. Maybe once things with the family settled down, he could figure out how he felt about Eli—besides the sex Eli had been so determined to point out. That was part of it, but not all; he knew that already. "He keeps things interesting."

"I've noticed."

CHRISSY WAS on a mission to make up for Peter's behavior. Operating under the illusion that any cuddling would compensate for the loss of Hubert, she barely waited until Quinn was seated on the couch before dumping a squirming Gabe onto his lap. The baby scowled for a few minutes and then settled. Quinn figured he'd probably just shit. He lifted the bundle to his shoulder and tried a hesitant pat. No way was he pining for fatherhood. After a brief wet hiss, the baby fell silent.

"You're magic," Chrissy said. "I've been trying to settle him down for an hour." Quinn knew a setup when he saw one.

"Do you want me to put him down?"

"Would you? Peter, show him. Thank you. I thought I'd be walking him all night."

Ah. A double setup. Aside from random squawks and gurgles, Gabe had been fairly unnoticeable during dinner. He'd only howled when the birthday serenade had been in full voice, and Quinn could scarcely blame him. His male cousin was particularly shrill. On the way to the stairs, Quinn and Peter stepped over a recreation of the Battle of Anzio formed out of random fast-food toys from Paula's purse.

Peter flipped on the lights in the room at the top of the stairs to reveal a nursery in soft shades of yellow. Peter hated yellow. Quinn had wanted a warm soft gold in the bathroom, but Peter had sworn it would make him puke to match the bile color. Now that Quinn thought of it, the house was full of the shade—in the dining room, the kitchen, the gold-colored carpet on the stairs. Maybe that's why Peter's face in the wedding pictures looked so sour; he was glaring at the carpet.

"Put him on his back," Peter instructed.

Quinn lowered the sleeping infant into the crib.

"I never thought you'd want to be there. Thought I could at least spare you that. I'm sorry, Quinn." Peter's words were soft, so sincere Quinn could almost believe him if he didn't know Peter's wife had put him up to it.

"You could have asked."

"Okay. It's not like it'll come up again, so I can't very well fix it." Before Quinn could back away from the crib, Peter put a hand over his on the rail. "I miss you sometimes. I didn't plan for it to go like this."

Damn him. Quinn slipped his hand free.

Peter's fingers tightened on the crib rail. "Don't think it's always easy for me. You're the only guy I ever—"

Quinn looked away.

"You know," Peter said, voice thick, "forget it. Hate me. I can't fix it."

Quinn wasn't falling for this. He'd seen too much of Peter's selfishness to believe he ever thought of anyone but himself. Then Peter had to do that blink thing, like his eyes were filling as he stared down into the crib, reaching out to pat his son's stomach, drawing a sticky sigh from the baby's lips. "Did you ever think about this? About us doing this?"

It wasn't only sex and familiarity that had kept their lives intertwined all those years. They'd shared a lot at first. But Peter had never mentioned anything about an urge to be a father.

"No matter how many loads I dumped in your ass, I didn't think it would come up." Maybe Quinn was more bitter than he thought, or maybe he didn't like the way the elephants getting into Noah's Ark on the lampshade were leering at him.

Peter shook his head, a disgusted snort barely escaping his throat.

"You could have told me. Why didn't you ever say anything?" Quinn asked.

"I think you answered that pretty well yourself."

Chapter Ten

ELI WATCHED Quinn come downstairs, an expression on his face like he'd been gut punched. Fucking Peter again. Quinn's whole tangle with Peter's family was a fucking shame. For Quinn, and for Eli.

Because a guy like Quinn would be worth waiting for until he came to his senses over how *over* him his ex was. Except Quinn never would. Not with this mess pulling him back all the time. The whole Laurent family was a tourniquet cutting off blood supply to a healthy life away from them. The only way to save him was amputation. But since Quinn credited them with saving his life, that would never happen.

When Roger lit a cigar in the living room—who still did that kind of thing around other people anymore?—Eli slipped out onto the now-empty back porch to breathe some non-1950s air. He should have kept going out into the backyard, because Peter came out after him.

"Get bored listening to the grownups talk?" Peter said.

"Why are you following me? Here to offer another blowjob?"

Peter leaned back against the table, legs spread wide. "Taking me up on it? Gonna let me in on what's so special Quinn had to have it in the bathroom at my son's baptism?"

"Seriously? This is because you're jealous?"

"Of you?" Peter made a disgusted sound in the back of his throat. "Not a chance. I don't fall in love with men. I fuck them sometimes. You queers get that confused."

"Right. *We're* confused." Eli rolled his eyes. "I'm going to tell Quinn, you know."

"Tell him what?" But the smugness in Peter's face said he knew what Eli meant.

"That you hit on me."

"You'd risk losing your sugar daddy when he finds out you were fucking around." Peter folded his arms across his chest.

No one, least of all Quinn, had ever asked Eli to be faithful. If he had a boyfriend like Quinn, it wouldn't be hard. But he didn't have a boyfriend. Or Quinn. "I told you—"

"Right. You have an understanding. Bullshit." Peter straightened up. "Fine. Go ahead and tell him. He'll never believe you anyway."

Damn. Eli wished he'd worn his boots with the heel. Though they wouldn't have put him at eye level with Peter, he'd have a harder time looking down at Eli like that.

Eli stuck his hands in his pockets. "What makes you so sure?"

"Because I know Quinn. I've known him for sixteen years. How's that stack up compared to a piece of boy ass?"

"It's good enough for Quinn." If he were anywhere but here, Eli could cut Peter to pieces. Tease him and then tear him a hole big enough to fist without lube. But Eli was trapped by these stupid clothes, this stupid fake happy family, his stupid promise to behave.

"For a month or two. Then he'll be looking for a real man." Peter stepped toward Eli to whisper, "He loves to get fucked, you know. Goes nuts for a dick in his ass. Comes so fucking hard."

Quinn had told him not to come. *I've got plans for that dick.* Was that why? Eli would never be comfortable topping like that. Not with Quinn.

"I'm still going to tell him," Eli said. *And then I'm washing my hands of all of your family bullshit.*

Peter laughed. "Good luck with that, kid."

The bastard sounded too much like Quinn. Eli tightened his fists in his pockets. "Why are you wasting your time out here while your dad gives the baby lung cancer? Shouldn't you go fake some more affection with your wife?"

The back door opened. "Hey." Quinn headed for Eli, a smile chasing off some of the tired look from Quinn's face. "There you are."

Eli felt a smile slide up to answer, despite Peter, despite everything. Quinn's hand cupped the back of Eli's neck. Maybe Quinn thought he could make Peter jealous. Maybe Quinn had never known what kind of a manipulative piece of shit he'd been involved with all those years.

"Eli wants to tell you something." Peter's dare was open, mocking.

"Then he'll tell me when he wants to." There was an edge to Quinn's voice, but his smile for Eli was the same look of indulgence Paula gave her war-obsessed toddler.

Eli sealed his lips against the desire to take the bait. It wasn't that he believed Peter. But Eli had promised Quinn he would tone things down, not make a scene. And who knew how Peter would spin things.

Eli slid his arm around Quinn's waist. "Later."

"Tell him now," Peter insisted, an unpleasant smile on his wide lips. Quinn's fingers caressed the back of Eli's neck.

Eli turned to look up at him. "I think someone should tell Roger not to smoke indoors when the kids are there."

"It's one cigar," Quinn said.

"Like I said, I can't very well tell my father not to smoke in my house," Peter added smoothly.

They were looking at each other, Quinn and Peter, a moment of shared sympathy over the dramatic concerns of a child. Eli moved away from Quinn, but between the screen, the table and Peter, there wasn't anywhere to go.

"Are you ready to leave?" Quinn rubbed Eli's neck. "I'm getting a headache."

"Probably the smoke." Peter laughed.

Eli should have given him the nut-twist treatment at the bar. It was never too late. He shot Peter a glare, and Peter responded with a slow, challenging smile.

Eli smiled back. *Oh, it's coming, you bastard. Just you fucking wait.*

QUINN TOOK the interstate loop to cut through Towson on his way home.

Eli had been eerily silent since they left the porch, his goodbyes to the family nothing more than flat nods. Now he said, "Where are we going?"

"My house." It hadn't occurred to Quinn that Eli might want to go somewhere else. He'd been interested enough before they went to the party. And there was that tie in his pockets.

"I thought you had a headache." The muscle under Quinn's hand shifted as Eli bounced his foot against the floorboards.

"I did. It's fading." The prickle of warning, the lights at the edges of his vision, all that had gone as he left Peter's house. He loved seeing the rest of the family, but right now he could do with a few months off without having to disappear to work at a summer camp.

"I'm glad. But you can still take me to my apartment."

"What's wrong? Did you really lose your job?"

"I don't want to talk about that." Headlights flashed across the sign for I-95. "South, Quinn."

Quinn put on his blinker and took the ramp, waiting until he'd merged before saying, "All right. What did Peter say to you?"

"It's not what he said. It's what he did." Even over the bump and thud of the tires on pitted asphalt, Eli's shifting and slamming around in the passenger seat was audible.

Maybe Eli had come upstairs and seen Peter's performance in the nursery. The fake contrition, the I-miss-you lie. They were barely past the stage of a hookup, but Quinn could easily imagine a stab of jealousy at the idea of Eli cuddling up to his ex.

Quinn waited. More shifting and then Eli blurted, "He hit on me."

"On *you*?"

"Yes, on *me*. Why the fuck is that so hard to imagine?"

"I meant—" But it was exactly what Quinn meant. "Why would he?"

"Thanks a fucking lot." Eli kicked at the floorboards. "Doesn't this car go any faster?"

"C'mon, Eli. Peter's not going to do that in his house."

"He did."

Eli was probably so used to going to bars that he thought five seconds of eye contact was as good as a *Your place or mine?*

"Maybe you misinterpreted—" A loud sigh cut Quinn off.

"I suppose I misinterpreted him grinding his dick into my ass and offering to suck me off at Grand Central the other night too."

"Grand Central?"

"Yes."

"When were you at Grand Central?"

Eli's voice became a little less certain. "Sunday night."

"Sunday?"

The stab of jealousy Quinn had imagined at the idea of Eli with his librarian-looking ex was nothing compared to the reality. It landed hard and fast in his gut, a hot flood of anger spilling out until his ears throbbed with it. Eli had left Quinn and his offer down at the harbor and gone to trick at the biggest pickup bar in Baltimore.

The tiny rational voice telling him he had no right drowned in seconds as the flood washed over him. He had every right. Some anonymous bastard had seen the fading spots from Quinn's fingers. Maybe left one of his own on that perfect pale curve.

Quinn barely stopped for the light at the bottom of the ramp before yanking the car right.

"Not so sure now?" Eli said, though if he had half a brain, he'd keep his mouth shut. "Peter will fuck anything, Quinn."

"I guess you would know."

"Oh, fuck you. Don't take this out on me because you're pissed at him." Eli reached up to brace himself against the door as Quinn squealed around a corner.

"This has nothing to do with Peter." With two yanks on the wheel, Quinn slammed the car into a spot on Eli's street.

"Right. Whatever. Feel free to lose my number." Eli flung off his seat belt and bolted from the car. Quinn took off after him and barely caught the outside door before Eli could slam it.

"What part of *lose my number* did you miss?"

"The part where you can tell me what to do."

Eli took a deep breath. "Listen, that forceful-Daddy crap only turns my crank in bed, so drop it."

"I'm not playing a game with you, Eli."

Eli looked up at him sharply. In the dim light from the single bulb on the landing, Quinn read his expression. Startled and still pissed enough to make his eyes almost all black, but not frightened. "Really? Because it sure as hell fucking feels like it. You come down here for a little walk on the wild side, and then you want to go back to your perfect suburbia of dysfunctional families and being *tolerated* by the neighbors. So go back to it. Go back to your chemically green lawn and your repressed sexuality and your high blood pressure and swallow it all until you drop dead of boredom before you're fifty."

For a second Quinn thought he was dropping dead. A heart attack at thirty-five, even younger than his mom's dad. His chest was too tight. For blood. For breath. For everything he was trying to hold on to. Then something snapped, and if he was dying, goddamn, it felt good. Almost as good as coming, because everything he'd kept wound so fucking tight was free. Anger and want and pain.

And the one person who might be able to understand it, might be able to take it and give it back just as strong, stood right in front of him. He reached out and grabbed Eli's shoulders. "You little shit. You're right."

Eli latched his hands around Quinn's neck. "Of course I am."

Quinn kissed him, nothing held back, nothing in reserve. He slammed Eli up against the wall in that tiny space between the door and the stairs and let everything go. Eli's fingers caught in Quinn's hair, pulling hard enough to sting before Eli hiked a leg around Quinn's hip and kissed him back, wet and open and almost as desperate.

It was like *The Wizard of Oz*, instant beautiful color, only Quinn had been living in worse than black-and-white Kansas. He'd been trapped in a monochromatic world of beige, of nice, of going with the flow, not making waves. Eli was the whole supersized box of crayons, with no rules about staying in the lines.

Quinn dug into Eli's pocket for the tie he'd shoved there earlier. Eli tried to shift his dick toward Quinn's searching hand, but Quinn laughed and pressed him harder against the wall.

He lifted his mouth. "Give me your hands."

Eli met Quinn's grip somewhere over their heads. "Fuck yeah."

Quinn did a quick half hitch and then lashed Eli's wrists together with a few passes of silk.

Every twist of the silk around Eli's wrists made him buck against Quinn until he'd managed to hitch himself up against the wall with both legs around Quinn's hips.

"Get me off." Eli licked the words into Quinn's ear. "Please."

Blood stretched the skin of Quinn's cock even tighter. Eli had handed over more than his hands. It was a lot to hang on to, when Quinn wasn't sure how he fit back together after the way everything had just shaken apart.

"I got you."

Eli's bound wrists came down around Quinn's neck as he steered them up the stairs, hands under Eli's ass keeping him locked around Quinn's waist. He only put Eli down long enough to find his keys and shove open the door. Scooping him up again, Quinn carried Eli into the small front bedroom and dumped him on his mattress, Eli's grip pulling Quinn down after him.

Eli twisted until their cocks lined up, then started grinding. "C'mon. C'mon."

Quinn's body wasn't functioning much past the need to pump his hips until he came, but he knew it would be a lot better if there weren't so many clothes between them.

"Wait," he murmured.

Eli's legs stayed locked around Quinn as Eli licked his lips and shook his head. "Just a second," Quinn promised. "Got to get naked."

Eli grunted but relaxed his hold, hands flopping over his head. Quinn sat up and stripped in a second, but as he reached for Eli's fly, Quinn's brain caught on to the fact that there was no way to get his shirt or jacket off without untying Eli's hands.

That wasn't happening. The power of knowing Eli couldn't grab his own cock and hurry things along, couldn't get innovative and sneaky, burned through Quinn's blood like a drug. One hit and Quinn was addicted. He couldn't give it up.

He settled for peeling away Eli's pants and briefs, tossing off one shoe to get them off that leg, as Eli spat out, "Fucking hurry up already."

The first touch of Eli's skin on Quinn's dick shorted out what was left of Quinn's brain function. He needed in. Now.

He licked a thumb, shoving Eli's legs apart with his knees. Eli's bound hands came down and grabbed Quinn's wrist. "Go fast and hard as you want, but not bare. Rubbers and lube in the box." Eli jerked his chin at a plastic bin next to the bed.

Quinn found what he needed. Even the shock of shame that burned his ears couldn't slow him down.

He managed a swipe of lube and his thumb pressed inside. Eli's hoarse whispers matched the demand pulsing in Quinn's balls and cock. *Nownownownow.*

Hauling Eli forward, Quinn drove his dick hard against the tight hole. Quinn's turn to beg. God, he needed to bury everything inside this boy—this man. Cock, fingers, tongue, soul.

He ripped open Eli's shirt, sending buttons flying and pinging around them, and bent to lick Eli's neck. "C'mon, honey, let me in."

Eli's spine rippled like a snake's, and the muscle gave around the head of Quinn's dick.

"Go." Eli's eyes were screwed tightly shut, but his body pulsed again, opening, and Quinn shuddered as he drove forward.

Deeper, deeper, his balls screamed, and Quinn got his shoulders under Eli's knees. Eli slung his bound hands around Quinn's neck, asking, pleading, "Harder," and it still wasn't enough. Something big was slipping out of Quinn's control. Something stronger and more terrifying than the anger that had sent him chasing Eli into his apartment. Quinn should be the one with his hands bound. Should find something to hold him back, because he couldn't stop the deep thrusts against the sweet grip of Eli's body. It wasn't only an orgasm clawing out from inside him, fighting for freedom. As desperate as Quinn was to give in and fly with it, fear kept him holding on to that one last piece.

Eli clung to him, opening mouth and body to everything spilling out of Quinn, to the thrust of his tongue and his cock, to the bruising grip Quinn had on his shoulders.

Quinn raised his head to gasp for air, and Eli tightened the muscles riding Quinn's dick. "More. Want it, Quinn. Want you."

It hit his blood like a burst of adrenaline, hot flood burning him clean, spilling into Eli as Quinn's hips snapped hard, everything tearing free until he emptied himself inside Eli's body, sweet shocks chasing along blood and nerves through the last spasms of release.

He was going to pull out when Eli started pleading, "Don't, please, jerk me off first. Please."

"Let me—"

"No, like this. Now."

Quinn managed to get a hand between them, found the hot skin, so tight, so slick. Eli's ass muscles pulsed and fluttered, and Quinn held his hips motionless to keep the condom in place.

"Fuck. So close. Need…. Shit…. Need…." Eli panted, licking his lips.

Quinn kissed him hard and rough and deep enough to feel the whine in the back of Eli's throat. Fingers tight around the head of Eli's dick, Quinn bit the skin under Eli's ear, then growled, "Come for me. Right now, boy. You'd better—"

Eli's ass clamped around Quinn's dick, Eli's body a tight grip on Quinn everywhere as the first warm splatter shot on their bellies. Quinn read the jerks of Eli's body, the gasps from his open mouth, and kept his strokes firm until Eli started to soften. As Quinn brushed his thumb gently across the slick crown, Eli's eyes popped open. They held a wary expression Quinn had to chase away.

He eased out and stripped off the condom before bending to lick the salty puddle on Eli's belly. The only soft spot on his slender wiry body, covered with a downy hair that rasped against Quinn's tongue.

Eli watched him, eyes glittering in the light from the street. His arms, wrists still bound by twisted silk, stretched over his head. The suit jacket and remains of a shirt were rumpled under his armpits. The sight made Quinn groan a gentle bite onto the skin under his tongue. He didn't want to untie him, wanted the blood and the rush of arousal back so he could fuck Eli again, keep them both in this dizzy, bright, colorful world. A warning prickle on Quinn's neck told him that as soon as he left Eli's bed, Quinn would be shoved back into that flat beige world where he couldn't fit anymore.

He gave Eli's dick a light kiss, then licked his way up his chest before resting his head over the thud of Eli's heart.

"I'm all for a postfuck cuddle." Eli shifted. "But this is really uncomfortable."

Quinn lifted his head. "Sorry."

Eli shoved his hands at Quinn. The silk was damp, wrinkled thin, and parts of the skin underneath had been rubbed red. Quinn cradled Eli's wrists in one hand, running a thumb across the slick fabric before freeing the end. When the tie fell away, Quinn kissed one of the red lines.

"That's not bothering me." Eli shook his hands free and then yanked off the suit jacket and shirt. "God, I hated wearing that." He tossed the clothes into a corner and flopped back onto the mattress.

The tension bled out of the back of Quinn's neck when he realized Eli wasn't going to kick him out. The problem was all they'd done so far was sex and the weird shit with the family. Fuck if Quinn would let this slide away from him when he felt that kaleidoscope rush from something as simple as breathing in Eli's skin.

"Did you have a job interview?"

"No." Eli turned on his side, matching Quinn's position, elbow cocked, hand supporting his head.

"You dressed up for me."

Eli huffed a sigh. "I always dress up. But that was because you asked me to."

"What else would you do if I asked?"

"In bed, pretty much anything." Eli's teeth flashed as he grinned in the dark. Even that crooked one.

Quinn wanted to kiss the smile into his own mouth. "Maybe you should give me a list. I wouldn't want to miss anything."

"That's too much work." Eli twisted so his back nestled into Quinn's chest, ass wiggling up against Quinn's cock.

A hopeful pulse of want ached in Quinn's balls, but nothing was happening for a while longer. "Speaking of which, did you actually lose your job?"

Eli moved his hips away. Quinn tucked his bottom arm up and around Eli's chest to keep him close. "Not exactly." Eli shrugged in Quinn's hold. "I'm not getting a regular paycheck anymore. I still work for the paper, only as a freelance photographer. I don't go to the office except when they call me in for a project. Then they pay me."

It was on the tip of Quinn's tongue to offer help, but he knew that would be an instant ticket home. "That sucks."

"It's all right. More free time. What time do you have to leave for work? Another round would be nice."

"I'll wake you up."

"Mmm." Eli tucked his head back onto Quinn's shoulder. "Depending on how much of a list you've got, we're gonna need at least an hour."

ELI DIDN'T know where the fuck his pants—or more importantly his phone—had ended up, and the fact that he'd managed to fall asleep anyway was a sign of how easy it was to feel safe with Quinn around. Something Eli couldn't get used to. Not with the hold Peter had on Quinn. But he could still have fun, make sure that when Quinn got sucked back into all that useless family bullshit, he'd remember what he was missing.

Quinn had shifted onto his stomach, one arm slung over Eli. He slipped out from under Quinn, then peeled the blanket and sheet away. With his eyes adjusted to the dark, Eli could see every inch of the sexy man in his bed. Quinn was hot, no doubt about it, solid lean muscle, dark hair, including a cute patch of it at the top of his ass that stopped where his spine dipped. A lot of territory to explore. Eli wanted to put little markers on him as he mapped him out, little spaces to claim. It wasn't virgin territory, and Eli didn't want it to be. The sexiest thing about Quinn was what he did to Eli. The way Quinn made Eli feel. Like Eli was something magic, like pure sex called into being. The way Quinn had looked at him tonight, like Eli had the map to the oasis and Quinn was dying of thirst.

If it didn't make Eli feel so damned good, it would be scary enough to have him running.

Quinn grunted and turned his head against the pillow. Right now Eli was going to show Quinn he didn't need an asshole like Peter if Quinn wanted to get fucked.

For him, Eli could give it a shot, throw Quinn on his back and fuck the shit out of him. Make him feel as good as he made Eli feel. It wasn't that he hadn't ever. Just that he liked getting fucked so much more. Quinn was worth trying it out again.

Eli settled his body on top of Quinn, earning a satisfied sigh in response. Yeah, Eli could do this. He moved his thumbs down the sides of Quinn's spine, stroke firm enough to keep from tickling. When he hit that patch of hair, he got his tongue involved, running the point down the crack of Quinn's ass. The muscles in the cheeks tensed and relaxed, and Quinn's legs dropped open. Okay, Eli was committed now. He took a deep breath, the sweaty male smell close to what he'd tasted of Quinn so far, then used his thumbs to hold Quinn open for more serious licking. The flat of his tongue produced some sounds that Eli only heard as vibrations, but as he licked and kissed, Quinn started gasping and moving his hips. Eli'd always thought rimming was a lot more fun to get than to give, but wanting to do this to Quinn, prove that Eli could be this for Quinn, was a lot hotter than only offering on the chance he'd get his ass licked in return.

Eli fluttered his tongue on the hole, on the tight skin underneath, and Quinn let out a gasp Eli could hear. He smiled and worked a finger in next to his tongue, slicking and wetting and pushing until Quinn said, "What are you doing?"

Eli moved the tip of his finger inside and licked around it before raising his head. "That doesn't really need an answer."

"Okay. Why are you doing that?" Quinn pushed up onto his knees. "You want to fuck me, Eli?"

Fuck me, he's big. And powerful. And getting fucked was exactly what Eli wanted. Loved taking all that power inside him. But that wasn't the plan. "Don't think I can?"

Quinn's voice was soft. "Never got the impression you wanted to." He reached back and caught Eli's wrist. "What's going on?"

"Do you want me to fuck you?"

"I want to know why you suddenly think you have to." Quinn turned. He smiled, reaching for Eli's balls, stroking them in a way that had Eli pushing his hips out for more.

Quinn gave it to him, a sweet tug. "You don't have to prove anything to me." Abruptly, Quinn sat back on his heels, hands on his thighs. "Christ. Peter. What did he say to you?"

"Why should I tell you? You won't believe me anyway."

"I know he did something."

"But you can't believe a guy like him would hit on a guy like me." Eli rolled off the mattress, wishing there was space in the room to pace. This was why he didn't like bringing guys here. Not out of consideration for his three roommates. Guys were harder to get away from in your own bed. And now he wasn't even going to get off. "God, can we save this for when we're not half hard?"

"No." Quinn pulled Eli back onto the mattress, pinning him under the weight of his body. "That's our problem."

"We don't have a problem, Quinn. You have a problem. You're hung up on Peter." Eli shifted so that his dick rode the cut of Quinn's hip instead of being squashed by his thigh.

"The problem is," Quinn said, like Eli hadn't just explained it to him, "we're always half hard around each other."

"I see that as a good thing." Eli rocked up.

"It is. But it means we're doing this backward."

"So you do want me to fuck you." Eli stopped rocking.

"I mean, we haven't had a chance to get to know each other. Most of what I know about you comes from the stories you were giving the Laurents."

"And that means I have to be lying about Peter."

"I didn't say that. Tell me what happened."

"At the house or at Grand Central?"

Quinn frowned, his muscles rigid. "The house."

"I went out on the porch because the cigar was disgusting. Peter followed me. I asked if he was offering another blowjob like he did at Grand Central—"

"I thought you said he hit on you."

Eli flicked a finger against Quinn's ear. "Are these on? He offered the blowjob."

"But not at the house."

"Get off me, Quinn. I swear you two fucking deserve each other."

"Wait. I'm trying to follow this."

It burst out of Eli, no calculation, no aim. He slammed the heels of his hands on Quinn's shoulders. Breath whooshed out of their chests as Eli twisted and rolled and dumped them onto the floor. He glared down into Quinn's surprised face. How could anyone be this stupid? Eli hated being right all the time. The hottest sex in the world wasn't worth dealing with how blind this guy was. And Eli still opened his mouth to explain it to him.

"What can't you follow? He fucked around on you. He left you. For a woman. He killed your dog. Now he fucks around on his wife and shoves it in your face because the whole damned family's got you by the balls. And I don't know why I give a flying fuck, but I can't watch it anymore. Now get out of my life." Eli rolled off, panting.

Quinn sat up. "Christ, what an arrogant little shit you are." He loomed over him, jaw hard, lips thin. "If you weren't in the middle of a tantrum, maybe you could understand how much crap just came flying at my head."

"Just now? Quinn, that baby didn't spring out of thin air. It's been a year."

"Shut up for a second. If that's possible. Maybe what I was trying to follow was how I could have lived with him for ten years and not seen him. Maybe what I was trying to understand was why a guy who claimed to be straight except for me is chasing dick all of a sudden." Quinn's hands shot out to capture Eli's face. His grip was solid, voice a harsh whisper. "But none of that fucking matters because I can't stop being pissed about you going to Grand Central when I want you for myself."

Chapter Eleven

"LIKE AS your boyfriend?" Eli tried to swallow his shock, but his throat stuck on the adrenaline-hard slam of his heart. Quinn wasn't lying, wasn't trying to charm his way out of the knee Eli had been planning to relocate his sac with. Quinn was by turns adorably vulnerable and a sexy top, but he couldn't quite pull off charm.

"That's flattering." Eli pasted on a smile, then leaned back so that Quinn came with him. "I know I'm awesome in bed, but you met me what? Three days ago?"

"Five. Which is why you should go on a date with me."

"A date. Like straight people."

"You're saying we can't date because straight people do?"

That wasn't what he'd meant. Eli wasn't completely heterophobic, but there were just so many examples of straight assholes to choose from. Like his own egg and sperm donors. His sister. Kellan's dad. Marcy.

Still, Kellan and Nate did stuff together all the time that wasn't fucking. And they had that Date Night thing that Eli usually heard as *leave us alone so we can stare into each other's eyes for a while before we fuck like bunnies.*

"So dinner and a movie?" Eli said.

Quinn shook his head. "We can't talk during a movie." He ran a finger over Eli's lips. "And I think watching you eat might get us back to horizontal too soon."

"I like horizontal."

"I do too." Quinn kissed him, long and deep, but it was the stroke of Quinn's hips that had Eli in a more receptive frame of mind. "But horizontal is not the main point of a date."

"It can be there at the end, though. You're going to put out, right?"

"Is that a yes?"

When I want you for myself. Of course the only guy who'd ever asked had to be unavailable. If Eli ever did get a real boyfriend, it might not be a bad idea to have tried out the dating thing, although it seemed stupid. They clicked in bed; what else was there to know? Obviously it wasn't going to be some big love thing. Even if Quinn wasn't hung up on his ex, he'd never looked at Eli the way Kellan and Nate looked at each other. Most of what Eli got from Quinn was a reluctant amusement, like he couldn't believe he was putting up with Eli's bullshit, but the sex made up for it. That was the same way Eli felt about Quinn and his family crap, so they were even.

"Depends. What are we going to do?" Eli tried to suggest something now by lifting his legs up around Quinn's hips.

"Get to know each other."

"I don't get why that should matter. Even if we lived together, it doesn't mean we have to like the same stuff on our pizza."

Quinn was giving him that smile, the it's-a-good-thing-you're-so-fuckable look. It should have earned him a nipple pinch, but Eli's stomach got the same melting warmth it did after a long, sweet come. Being fuckable was something Eli aspired to every second of the day.

"All right," Eli said. "Where are we going?"

"Can it be a surprise?"

"Like you dragging me to a Catholic church? I need to know what to wear."

Quinn stared down for a minute, like he was running through a dozen dating scenarios in his mind, trying to fit Eli into one.

"Bowling," Quinn said at last.

"Bowling? Rented shoes and hanging with old ladies named Verna and Flo? That should take sex out of the equation, all right."

"Is that a yes?" Quinn asked again, this time with the smile he always used with Eli. There was something mischievous about it now. Like he was up to no good and wanted Eli to join him. Maybe there was a place that did naked bowling. Then Eli thought of someone named Verna naked and shuddered.

"Who pays?"

"Me, since I asked."

Eli slung his arms around Quinn's neck. The spot where the tie had rubbed Eli's wrists tingled as he touched Quinn's skin. "Convince me. Show me how you'll put out."

Quinn did.

A quick pause for the condom and lube, then he put Eli on his side and went into him from behind, short strokes that rubbed in the best possible way. Explosions of hot pleasure inside and the thick shaft delivering all the friction he could take.

It tore away Eli's breath, but he managed to gasp, "Harder. More."

Quinn's hips kept up that stutter while his hands roved over Eli's body, lips and tongue and teeth on his neck. Eli squirmed when Quinn's hand evaded the thrust of Eli's dick toward it. Instead, fingers rolled over and tugged on his balls, nails scraped the inside of his thighs, and then, God, the pressure on the skin between. Pressure to make everything draw up tight and sweet as heat gathered in the tip of Eli's cock and spilled a tingle of warmth over the head.

"Wanna come." But when Eli reached for his dick, Quinn slapped his hand away.

"And I want you to wait." Quinn went back to rubbing under Eli's balls, but then shifted to a grip pulling Eli's ass open wider, a hard deep thrust forcing release closer even while Quinn kept him from getting there.

"Please."

Quinn had to know what that extra stretch was doing to him, the aching pleasure of it. Fuck yeah, he knew, because he sent a flicking finger hard against the tight skin between balls and ass, a spike of pain so sweet Eli jumped and reached back to find anything to hold on to, any way to coax Quinn into letting him go.

"Gonna be better if you wait."

It was so damned good right now, perfect even, and then Quinn eased off and went back to nailing Eli's gland with a rolling thrust of his hips, a build-build-build of pressure and nowhere for it to go.

When Eli reached for his cock again, Quinn captured his hands more securely than the tie. Soft humid kisses on his neck, under his ear, and Eli was frantic. Too full, too much. He slammed his hips back against Quinn, forcing the friction faster, sharper. Quinn kept Eli's hands trapped in one of his and slid the free hand around Eli's thigh to pin him close, slow them down to nothing but that aching, perfect thrust.

Every game Eli had played, tied spread-eagle, a hand or paddle bruising his ass, a flogger stinging into his crack, nothing had ever forced surrender on him like this deep, gentle fuck from Quinn. Eli had thought he liked to give up control, take a break for a while and let a man push sensation onto his body. This was different.

Terrifying.

Because this was what it was like to really lose control. To let Quinn inside, to let him make Eli feel so much more than the amazing sensations of bodies together.

And inside that surrender was safety. Quinn around him, voice in his ear whispering, "I've got you. Let me make you feel good, honey."

Eli stopped trying to pull their hands down to his dick and wiped the sweat off his face on his shoulder. Quinn didn't let him go, though, but used the hand on Eli's thigh to guide them. Deep thrusts that made Eli's belly loose, quick jerks against his gland that made his belly tighten as he tried to hold on to the dizzying pleasure.

His body was under Quinn's control, but his mind spit out one last try. "Please let me come." The release was there, full and hot, flooding his balls, his ass. Still nowhere to go.

Quinn's only answer was a soft kiss under his ear that became a sharp, shivering bite. Eli gave in.

Let Quinn move his body, move through him and in him, like water rushing, wearing down every barrier, washing it all away. Eli couldn't tell where one wave ended and another one started as heat rolled up his cock, but when Quinn finally wrapped a hand around Eli's shaft, hard desperate friction, those little waves of pleasure turned into a waterfall, throwing him over and slamming him under.

Somehow his hands got free, and he clutched on to any part of Quinn his searching fingers could find. Hair, skin, muscle, bone. Because the come bursting out of his balls was going to wash him away if he didn't hang on. Quinn was right there with him, whispering hoarse *yeah, fuck yeah, honey*'s in Eli's ear.

Eli's heart kept on pounding. Eli had had sex before. Lots of sex. Kinky sex. That hadn't just been sex. If he were in someone else's bed, he'd sneak off to try to figure out if that made him happy or scared to death. But that escape wasn't possible.

Quinn made a snorting gasp and collapsed against his back. Eli had never been more appreciative of whatever chemical it was in a guy's brain that made him want to flop over and sleep after coming. Right now the beauty of a Y chromosome saved him from having to look at Quinn or talk to Quinn. And, as Eli's eyelids got too heavy to lift, those chemicals kept him from lying here having to think about what had just happened.

QUINN HAD never been on a date in his life. In the Navy, trying to date would have been asking to get tossed out. He'd fucked guys, but that was as far as it went. Then he'd been with Peter. After that he'd done a repeat—fucking, not dating.

It didn't have to be complicated. He'd pick Eli up, they'd go do something, talk, and see if they liked each other out of bed—and out of range of the family—and hopefully make plans for date number two.

The *hopefully* part was what kept Quinn squeezing the steering wheel as he obediently waited outside Eli's apartment. There had to be another date. Because Quinn couldn't picture going back to his life before Eli had exploded into it. Couldn't go back to everything so peaceful and flat and boring. So this would work. Quinn would make it work.

Even now he'd listened to Eli's insistence that Quinn not come up to the apartment, though he'd been hungry to see him for the first time in over a week.

Eli slammed the door as he came out, then tugged down his black leather motorcycle jacket. A bright flash of magenta showed underneath, and his usual tight black jeans finished off the outfit. Quinn found himself smiling as Eli threw himself into the car in some kind of snit.

"What made me think it would be easier to have girls for roommates?"

"Are they still pissed about last week?" When Quinn had called to set up a time and day, Eli had complained about sitting through a house meeting where they discussed an appropriate noise level for overnight guests and that some warning about finding a man in the bathroom at four in the morning would be appreciated. Like knocking wouldn't have been better. Like they didn't already live with a man. *It's like they don't think I have a dick*, Eli had complained.

"Not they," Eli countered. "She. Sam was probably listening and jacking off, or jilling off, or whatever it is girls do. But Dana goes along with whatever Marcy says."

No time like now to start a conversation. "So you don't bring guys home very often?"

"Try never. There's barely enough space in that room for me."

"I thought we fit."

"Because you had your dick up my ass."

The flood of memories had an instant effect on the fit of Quinn's jeans. Eli's dark hair against his skin, the way his eyes looked black and deep, the smell of his body, the sounds in his throat, and the feel of him around Quinn's body. Suddenly, taking Eli back to Quinn's house in Mount Washington seemed like a better plan. "That was my favorite part of it."

"So we can skip the rented shoes and Verna and go right to fucking?"

If Quinn played this right, there'd be lots and lots of fucking. He was old enough to wait. "And disappoint her? Date first, dick in ass later."

"Killjoy."

Despite the out-of-place Southwestern-style roofing and stucco on Sunset Lanes in Towson, the place was bright and clean and had decent Tex-Mex food—decent enough that people sometimes went there to eat even if they weren't bowling. Best of all, a gay bowling league met tonight, so Eli might not be able to get in as many complaints about closeted suburbia.

"Damn," Eli said as Quinn parked in the strip mall. "I should have brought my laundry." He nodded at the laundromat next door.

"Now who's going for unsexy?" Quinn grabbed his bowling bag from behind the seat.

"Laundry can be very sexy. The vibrating machines, cotton hot and fresh from the dryer, all that time to kill. Seriously?" Eli looked at his bag. "You have your own ball?"

"And shoes. How unsexy did I just get?"

"I may have to reset my plans for later. I don't know if I can do that with a man who has his own bowling ball. Is it pink, at least?"

"Gray."

Eli shook his head, a mournful expression tugging his lips down at the corners. Quinn had been looking forward to seeing Eli again, but somehow had forgotten the effect Eli had on the rest of the world. Once inside, Eli slung his jacket over his shoulder, revealing a vintage-looking bowling shirt in eye-watering magenta, complete with black piping and his name stitched over the left breast pocket. He wiggled his ass over to get shoes while Quinn paid for a lane. By the time Eli was bending over to lace up his rented shoes, all the guys in the league two lanes over were staring their way.

Jamie came over and smacked Quinn's shoulder before stepping around him to offer a hand to Eli. "I'm Jamie. So, are you what Quinn's been doing with himself the past couple of weeks?"

"He wishes." Eli shot Quinn a narrow-eyed glance. "Don't you go anywhere alone?"

"I used to bowl in their league two years ago," Quinn explained.

"He gave it up when Thursday was the only night what's-his-name was home." Jamie tipped his beer to his lips.

Before Quinn could unzip his bag, four other guys had joined them. Terry, who was in his late forties, was offering to show Eli how to keep score, despite the fact that the computerized lanes did it automatically. Quinn squeezed Terry's shoulder as he bent over Eli.

"I'm showing him how to enter the names," Terry said with a wolflike grin.

"Thank you." Eli gave Terry that sexy blink Quinn wanted to keep to himself.

A spark of anger tightened Quinn's fists. "Aren't some of you in the middle of a game?"

"Not me," Terry said.

"Can I get you a beer, Eli?" Jamie offered.

"Ginger ale," Eli said, eyes wide, the angelic look suggesting he wasn't old enough for beer.

"Enough, assholes." Quinn hauled Terry up from the scorer's chair he was sharing with Eli and shoved him in the direction of the other lanes. "Clear out." Quinn turned to Eli. "What was that about?" he demanded.

"They're *your* friends." Eli shot to his feet to face him. "I thought this was supposed to be a date. Which, despite my limited experience, doesn't involve ten people."

"I knew they'd be here, but I thought…." Quinn was no longer certain why he'd thought being here with them was a good idea.

Eli tipped his chin up, a smile starting to curve his lips. "Were you showing me off?"

Quinn hadn't really thought he'd need backup. Maybe he had been. Maybe he'd wanted to see what color Eli could add to another part of Quinn's old life. "And if I was?"

"Your chances of getting blown later just improved dramatically." Eli tapped his arm and waved down the lane. "So give me some pointers."

Quinn wished he'd taken Eli fly-fishing somewhere in the middle of nowhere so when he stood behind him to guide his motions, it wouldn't matter how hard it left him. After a few seconds of attempting to position him, he suggested Eli try to find his own style.

He bowled a strike. And another one. And then picked up a spare.

Quinn loved the look of delight on Eli's face as the last pin wobbled over and Eli looked up at his score.

"I'm winning." Eli should always look like that, as if someone had just handed him a million-dollar check.

He managed two pins in his next four tries. When Jamie showed up with a can of ginger ale, Eli waved him off. "I'm trying to figure this out."

"It's my turn," Quinn said.

"But I need the practice. We won't count this game."

Jamie stood next to him as Quinn watched Eli hook another ball into the gutter. "So what's with this kid?"

"He's twenty-three." Quinn anticipated by a few weeks.

"I wasn't going to arrest you, man. I'm only asking."

Eli's next ball swerved from gutter to gutter like it was dragged by unseen magnets before hitting the pins almost sideways and leaving a five-ten split. Eli pumped a fist in triumph.

"I want him," Quinn said, simply. Because sometimes, it was as easy as that.

"So does Terry. Hell, everyone here would probably fuck him. Billy's drooling enough to change his shirt, and he's a total bottom."

"Not if I have anything to say about it."

Jamie shook his head. "I don't want to see you get fucked over again. Even if he wasn't twenty-three, that kind of thing isn't realistic. Ball your brains out, but leave the whole mess of love and marriage to the hets."

Love. He hadn't said anything about love. Hadn't said anything about love to Peter, though Quinn had assumed that's what it was. It hadn't felt anything like this. Peter hadn't always been easy, but things had been comfortable. Eli was about as comfortable as a rollercoaster with no brakes.

Eli picked up the split and spun around. The elation on his face made Quinn want to kiss the fuck out of him. Lust, love. Quinn just wanted him.

"You deserve a good time, babe." Jamie slapped him on the back. "But keep your upstairs head in the game."

Eli stopped for a drink of ginger ale and made a face, though whether the face was for the drink or Jamie, Quinn wasn't sure. "What's that about?"

Quinn arched his brows. "He thinks you're going to break my heart." He expected Eli to laugh or find a way to twist it into something sexual.

"Even if I could, I wouldn't."

Chapter Twelve

BEFORE QUINN had time to ask Eli what he meant, he'd turned to flash that perfect ass as he picked up his ball.

"I can't believe I've missed this sport. It's all about fingering holes and caressing balls. So how about a bet?"

Quinn was sure that with anything Eli proposed, losing would be just as much fun as winning. "Stakes?"

"If I win, you do what I want for the rest of the night."

"And if I win?"

"What do you want?" Eli purred it at him.

"You do what I want until oh six hundred. Six a.m."

"I got that, soldier boy."

Quinn couldn't swat his ass here. He did it anyway.

"Sailor." Eli's grin said he hadn't forgotten.

Quinn had never tried harder to lose a game in his life. It wasn't easy. Eli would bowl a strike and then three straight gutter balls. Maybe they were both trying to lose.

Eli managed two strikes and a spare in the last frames, then turned in triumph. "Okay. Feed me."

"They've got good tacos—"

Eli made a face and then shook his head. "No Mexican. My favorite burger place is downtown."

They had driven past Loyola when Eli announced, "Ground beef and mushrooms."

Quinn shot him a confused look before fixing his eyes back onto the road. "Pizza toppings," Eli said, as if that explained everything.

It took a second before Quinn realized Eli was continuing the conversation from a week ago. "Not a deal breaker."

"What is?" Eli asked.

At the moment Quinn couldn't think of anything that would make him want Eli out of his life, but there was something he'd prefer not to have slap him in the face again. "Lying."

"Makes sense."

The streets narrowed, the increase of cars and pedestrians pulling more of Quinn's attention to driving. When Eli didn't offer anything else, Quinn asked, "What's yours?"

"Got a pen? It's a long list."

"I find that hard to believe."

"That I'm picky?"

"That you cut people out of your life easily." Quinn looked over as they waited for a light, but Eli was staring out of the window. "If you had to pick one."

Eli looked back at him, held Quinn's gaze. "Being ignored."

"I'll keep that in mind." Quinn spotted a parking spot, though they were more than two blocks away from the address Eli had given him. "Do you mind walking?"

"I'm used to it."

"Right." Quinn could see why a car wouldn't make a lot of sense in the heart of the city. "Do you have your license?"

"No. But I can change a flat tire, jump a battery, and change the oil." Eli had no trouble keeping up with Quinn's long strides either.

"Remind me to call you next time my car makes a funny sound. Why'd you bother to learn that if you don't drive?"

"I took auto shop in high school. I hated the art teacher."

"Did he ignore you?"

"*She*," Eli corrected, "liked to humiliate people. I got in her face about it and got banned from art class."

"Did she humiliate you?"

"I wouldn't give her the chance. She picked on weaker kids. Teachers." Eli rolled his eyes, but before Quinn could defend his profession, Eli added a wink. "So how do you make your students follow orders? Stand there all intimidating and flinty-eyed?"

"I'm not flinty-eyed."

"Not all the time, but you do that narrow-eyed thing when you give me that look that says *or else*. Makes me want to drop to my knees and suck you off on the spot. Guess that wouldn't work in school."

Quinn shuddered in revulsion. "I'm not sure I can eat now."

He changed his mind when the smells from the restaurant hit his nose. Perfect burgers on a grill—in the middle of October—fresh bread, salty grease from fries. After the platinum-blond host exchanged an overlong kiss with Eli, he showed them to a booth.

"Come here often?" Quinn opened his menu. The hair on the nape of his neck prickled. Eli had taken the seat facing the door, leaving Quinn wishing he really had eyes in the back of his head.

"Not often enough. I know the prices are steep, but the food's worth it."

Quinn glanced down. The burgers hovered around ten to twelve dollars, but that wasn't what he'd wanted to say. "I meant—"

"Oh? Silver?" Eli glanced over at the host. "We both like to dance." He grinned. "Are you the jealous type?"

Any chance of a comeback vanished as Eli leaned across the booth. Unlike what he'd given Silver, Eli's kiss for Quinn was deliberate, thorough. No one paid them any attention.

"Just so you know." Eli sank back into his seat. "I am." He tapped his menu. "I'm getting number four. Mushrooms and jack cheese. They put butter on the buns too." Eli's eyes closed in an imitation of ecstasy.

Quinn told his dick to calm down. It had to eventually. He wasn't going to spring wood every time he caught a glimpse of the one crooked tooth when Eli smiled or opened that smart, pretty mouth.

Eli's gaze went to the door. "Fuck me." Eli breathed it like a curse rather than the invitation Quinn was trying to get his dick to stop thinking about long enough to get them fed.

Eli held up his menu as a shield. "Unlike your friends at the bowling alley, this was not part of my plan. Ignore them and they'll go away."

Quinn looked up as the two men stopped at their table—Nate, the dark-haired obnoxious one with glasses, and the more affable one with the wide smile whose name Quinn kept forgetting.

"Going to introduce us?" Nate said with a sneer.

Eli had been nice to Quinn's friends. Quinn could do the same. "Hi. We've met. Quinn."

"Mind if we join you." Nate didn't make it a question.

"Yes," Eli said, but Quinn got up from his side of the booth and slid in next to Eli. "Remember that whole being-ignored thing I hate?" Eli muttered in his ear.

Quinn rubbed a hand along Eli's thigh and whispered back, "Does it feel like I'm ignoring you?"

"It's not fair to take advantage of a guy who's easily led by his dick." Eli shoved up into Quinn's hand.

"Well, it was nice seeing you"—the taller one tugged at Nate's arm—"but I think we're going to—never mind." The blond broke off with a sigh when Nate slammed down into the booth.

"Fuck me, they're still here." Eli kept his lips close to Quinn's throat.

"Later," Quinn promised, backing it up with his hand on Eli's inseam.

Eli moved away. "I think I should have gotten the outside of the booth."

"Just because it's not a life-or-death situation now, doesn't mean it won't be." Quinn turned toward him. "Think of how much better I'd be at blocking any threats from the zombie apocalypse while you get weapons together."

A snort burst from Eli's lips, and Nate's boyfriend echoed the laugh with a chuckle.

"In that case, you can put your carcass to use saving my skin." Nate pulled his boyfriend down into the booth, then yanked the menu from under Eli's folded arms.

"Sorry, you guys." The blond pulled the cardboard out of Nate's hands and handed it back to Eli. "You know how he gets about his toys."

"And Eli is his toy." Quinn straightened up, glaring at Nate's smug expression.

"I didn't mean it exactly like that." The boyfriend blushed.

Eli put a hand on Quinn's arm. "Besides, Nate got tired of playing with me a long time ago. Ignore him. I usually do." Eli's voice had taken on that singsong quality he'd used when he was showing off for the family—for Quinn's friends. Was he like that around everyone but Quinn?

Quinn kept watching Nate until he realized Eli was playing footsie with the blond—Kellan, that was it—under the table. When the waiter took their order, Quinn stuck a leg out to disrupt it.

The wide mouth curved in a sheepish grin. "Sorry, man." Kellan cocked his head at Quinn. "So what's it like dating Mr. Wright?"

Eli glared. "How long have you been saving that one up?"

"A year." Kellan's grin was completely unapologetic.

"Mr. Wright, huh?" It had never occurred to Quinn to wonder what Eli's last name was. When Eli had flashed his license, he'd been more interested in proof of age. "That's pretty good."

"Shut up," Eli snapped.

The waiter came over with a tray holding their drinks, and Eli's face took on a smirk that promised retribution for them all. "Kellan and Nate's dads used to work for KZ," Eli explained as the waiter distributed four cold bottles of the local cola. Quinn had followed Eli's lead and ordered the black cherry, which had provoked a laugh from Kellan. "And now Kellan's dad runs Brooks Blast Energy Drinks."

Alyssa had said something like that at the baptism. Something about Kellan being cut off. "Old news." Kellan waved him off.

Eli persisted, as if he had a point to make. "Yeah, but what everybody doesn't know is that Kellan is my hero. His father gave tons of money to all the antimarriage assholes, and when he tried to pay Kellan off to stay in the closet, Kellan turned down half a million."

Kellan and Nate were in the middle of some kind of private joke that involved a tally, so Quinn was free to concentrate on Eli—on the lesson Eli had carefully laid out for him. The big blinking neon made it kind of obvious. Quinn would never measure up against that kind of hero worship while he was playing nice with the Laurents. And as long as Eli had Kellan as an example, Eli would never see it any other way.

Eli shoved against Quinn. "Let me out."

"I thought we settled the inside-outside thing."

"Your control issues are all good, sailor, but I have to pee. I know you'll all enjoy talking about me while I'm gone."

When Quinn stood to let him out, Eli leaned forward and grabbed Nate's jacket, dragging him close enough to whisper something at him.

With a wave of his hand and shake of his hips, Eli was gone.

"So what is your problem?" Quinn didn't bother sitting back down.

Nate gave it back with equal directness. "I don't like Eli dating someone old enough to be his father."

"Bullshit." Quinn glared down at him. "This is about you and your… toys."

Kellan bit his bottom lip as if fighting a laugh.

"He's not a toy." Nate leaned across the table. "But if you actually knew anything about him, you'd know—"

"You're the one who doesn't know anything about him." It was clear they only knew all-drama, flirt-with-traffic-lights-for-blinking-at-him parts of Eli.

"You didn't even know his last name until five minutes ago," Nate said. "If you knew what I can't tell you on pain of"—he glanced down at his crotch—"pain, you'd see why this is such a bad thing for him. He needs a chance to hang out with people his own age and figure out what he wants."

"If you know him as well as you think you do, you know Eli's perfectly capable of telling me to go to hell if that's what he wants."

"The problem is he doesn't know what he wants."

"Have you ever asked him?" Quinn dropped back into the booth. "As someone *much* older, let me tell you what I see. You love the way he looks up to you—both of you. You treat him like a pet, keep him hanging around for whatever affection you can spare."

"That's—" Nate shut his mouth in a sudden grimace that had Quinn convinced Kellan had stomped on his foot.

"Get a puppy if that's what you need, but stop pretending Eli can't function without you telling him who or what he wants."

Chapter Thirteen

FOR SOMEONE who'd spent his prime dating years trying to make sure he had a reasonably safe place to sleep at night, Eli thought he was getting the hang of this dating thing. Quinn was fun even when he wasn't playing toppy Daddy in bed. And provided Nate kept his mouth shut, Quinn would never know that although most of the time Eli managed to stay with friends during the first two years on his own, there'd been times when getting blown or fucked by someone who'd give him a place to crash and feed him hadn't been a bad exchange. It wasn't like Eli had ever felt desperate enough to take an offer from a guy who was really disgusting.

Nate would keep all that to himself. He might be a self-righteous prick, but he could be counted on to not spill secrets. If this thing with Quinn was worth working at, Eli didn't want Quinn giving him that pity look Nate got most of the time.

Kellan saw Eli coming, and everything at the table got quiet.

"So what did I miss?" Eli figured he'd earned a good-date cookie, since he let Quinn tuck him into the inside of the booth again.

"They whipped out their… measuring sticks," Kellan said.

"I figured that. Who won?"

"Me, like always." Kellan smacked his boyfriend's shoulder, but while Nate was distracted by checking to be sure the kitchen hadn't tried to sneak in a beef patty instead of the veggie burger he'd so sanctimoniously ordered, Kellan tipped his head at Quinn and flashed Eli a wink to let him know Quinn had come out on top.

When it was time to go, Kellan lifted Eli in a big hug. "I really like him. And he's crazy about you."

Nate gave Eli a very deliberate kiss on the mouth and said, "Be careful."

As they walked back to the car, Eli's stomach forgot he'd inhaled all that greasy goodness ten minutes ago, feeling empty of everything but nerves. This was the part of the date he'd been looking forward to.

The part he knew they'd get right. So why the terrified anticipation of a virgin about to get fisted?

"Where to now?" Quinn said as he unlocked the car.

"I thought—" Right. Eli had won the bet. Everything was up to him. It should have made him relax, but instead he babbled, waving his hands for emphasis, "Well, I was going to suggest my place so we could really curl that bitch Marcy's hair, but let's go to your house. You remember you promised to fuck me if I went out with you."

"Something like that. But you won the bet."

"I think you let me win."

"Or maybe I'm a terrible bowler."

"Right. That's why you have your own ball." But he couldn't put much of a sneer in his words.

The pulse of arousal in Eli's groin was still doing battle with the anxious dip and swirl in his stomach when they climbed the stairs in Quinn's house. It wasn't as if Eli didn't want to fuck, but everything felt different with all this lead-up. How was he supposed to make sure there wasn't a letdown? Dating had its drawbacks.

Quinn glanced over as Eli played with the buttons on his shirt. "Something wrong?"

"I'm feeling a lot of pressure to be awesome."

Quinn stepped over and kissed him. "You already are." His lips drifted over Eli's again, a question and an affirmation. When Quinn started on the buttons of Eli's shirt, Eli put his hands up to help. "I promise to be careful with this one. You look hot in it. Where did you find it?"

"The shirt was in a used-clothes store, but I glued on the piping and my name."

Quinn's kiss had a little more urgency as the shirt fell away, lips parted, breath fast. A tongue on the side of Eli's neck made him slip away before he turned into a puddle at Quinn's feet. After fishing supplies from his pockets, Eli kicked away his jeans and briefs.

Quinn yanked off his shirt, but when his hands went to his belt, Eli stopped him, leading him to stand by the bed. "Still on my bet, right?"

"Sure." Quinn ran his hand over Eli's hair as he crouched on the bed. "I think I remember this position."

"Not quite." Eli unhooked Quinn's belt and opened his fly to pull his cock out. The satiny skin pulsed and tightened as he stroked. He ran first his finger, then his tongue down the thickest vein, flicked his tongue under the head. Fucking beautiful cock, stretching and aching for him. He caressed it with his hair, his hands, his cheek. Wanted it down his throat and up his ass just like that, bare skin and the pump of fluid from Quinn's balls. But since they couldn't have that....

Eli snapped open the minipack of warming lube he'd brought and used his thumb to coat the soft, slick flesh on the head of Quinn's dick. He stroked it down the shaft, and Quinn gasped. "I want it to feel hot like my mouth," Eli explained.

"I don't need it to be like your mouth. I've got that right here." Quinn cupped Eli's cheek and put a thumb between his lips.

Eli tore the wrapper on a cherry-flavored condom and slipped it on Quinn. "But I want to suck you off." He made a deliberate bob almost to the base before backing off. "And I want you to go all Daddy on my ass while I jerk myself off."

Quinn grunted, hips shoving his dick against Eli's lips, so Eli figured Quinn was down with the program. The condom made the little licks and flicks less effective, but taking him deep fast made up for it. Eli opened his throat and Quinn fucked into it, a couple of quick thrusts before the first crack of his hand on Eli's ass.

Eli braced himself with one hand on the edge of the bed and grabbed his dick with the other. Quinn pulled back enough to barely be pushing the head past Eli's lips while smacking him three times on the same cheek. It hurt, enough to want to flinch away, but then he stopped and the warm tingling rush started. Eli groaned and sucked, covering his teeth and trying to get all the way down.

"So good. Good little cocksucker." Quinn grunted out the words.

Eli stuck his ass up farther, and Quinn landed a more gentle series of smacks. Eli backed off enough to reach for Quinn's belt, tugged the stiff narrow leather free of the loops, and handed it up to Quinn.

Quinn pulled him off, grabbed his chin, and forced Eli to look up at him. Quinn's eyes were dark with wide pupils, the lamplight catching the silver in his hair. His jaw was tight, but his lips were soft. "Yeah?"

"Make 'em sting," Eli breathed. "Just watch my balls."

"Tuck them forward and keep them covered."

Needing one hand on the bed to brace himself, Eli couldn't work his cock while protecting his balls, but Quinn snapped the tail of the belt down in a slow rhythm, plenty of time for the sting to turn to warmth spilling from his ass to his dick.

"Christ, boy." Quinn flicked the belt, and the tip whipped into the crease, burning onto Eli's hole. Eli jerked, but as the eye-watering pain faded, his whole body throbbed with the rush of sensation.

"Sorry, honey." Quinn cupped Eli's cheek, belt coiled around his palm, the end trailing over Eli's shoulder. Backing away, he lifted Eli up again. Eli grabbed at Quinn's hips.

"No," Quinn whispered. "You want to get off like this, yeah?" He tapped the coiled leather against Eli's ass.

Eli nodded. He did. Wanted the sting and the flush of warmth spiking the urge in his balls, wanted to ride it all the way to an explosion, wanted the soreness and the welts to last for days of jerking off to the memory of it. Quinn giving this to him, Quinn's attention focused into the burn of the leather on Eli's skin.

"So let me do it right, honey." Quinn moved around behind Eli, hauling him back toward the other side of the bed, spreading his legs wide apart, pushing his back down so his ass was high in the air. "Keep your balls covered."

Eli let his shoulders and knees take his weight as he got both hands underneath his hips and waited for the belt to sear into his skin.

Quinn rubbed the belt over Eli's ass, cool leather against the hot sensation on his cheeks, a soothing rub that spread pleasure all around. Eli sank into it, hand busy on his cock, and Quinn stepped back to crack the belt down.

Eli jerked, then relaxed. With his hand on his dick, the lash was nothing but pleasure, sharp and burning but sweet. Quinn picked up a faster rhythm, and Eli rode the razor edge of pain as the thin belt left line after line of heat across Eli's ass. Just when he thought another lick would be too much, Quinn stopped and stepped close again, the fabric of his jeans coarse as sandpaper on Eli's throbbing skin. His hands went to Eli's hips, and Quinn's cock pressed against the top of Eli's ass. Quinn's bare cock. He'd stripped off the rubber.

Right. That's why he'd stopped Eli from sucking him off. Quinn probably had been doing it raw with Peter for years—not suspecting the guy was the biggest slut in Baltimore. It must be hard to get used to a barrier again. Eli hated the taste of latex, but there were flavored condoms. If a guy wanted Eli's bare cock in his mouth, Eli usually wouldn't object, but other than the whole I-wonder-if-I-can-feel-his-come thing, Eli hadn't spent much time thinking about what it would be like to fuck bare.

He wished he could give that to Quinn. It wasn't theoretical now, but a genuine desire to know how it would feel to have Quinn's come inside, to know there was nothing between their skin. Eli could wish all he wanted, but he hadn't been cautious as hell all these years to throw it out the window because Quinn seemed like a nice guy.

Quinn stopped rubbing his cock against Eli and moved back again. This time the belt stung rapid-fire kisses at the bottom of his cheeks, like Quinn was waving the tail end back and forth. Quinn worked the sting inside Eli's thighs, and Eli jacked his cock fast to ride out the burn, but before Eli could jerk away, Quinn cracked the belt hard again, then stepped back. How many times had Quinn done this? He said he'd never done the Daddy stuff before, and Eli couldn't picture Peter wanting his ass blistered, for all he was a butt slut. Quinn was doing this just for him. Knowing that made the sensations sweeter.

Quinn ran his hand over Eli's ass. "So hot and red. I love watching you. Love the way you show me everything you want."

Proof that Quinn was paying such close attention made heat pool in Eli's belly in a way that had nothing to do with the fire in his balls or ass.

Quinn leaned forward and ran his tongue down Eli's spine. "Want more, or you gonna come now?" Quinn's voice rumbled into the spaces inside.

Eli wanted to do what Quinn wanted to do. Fuck the script and the bet and the illusion of control. Eli wanted to give it all to Quinn.

Quinn smacked the belt deep into the crease at the bottom of his ass, and Eli jumped again.

Stroking the belt gently down Eli's spine, Quinn murmured, "Took it good, boy. Jerk yourself off now."

Eli folded deeper into the bed as he got one hand on his dick, ass high in the air, legs as far apart as he could keep them.

Quinn used a hand to pull Eli's cheeks apart and worked the tip of the belt in quick lashes against his hole, a hot stinging little tongue.

"That's it, honey. C'mon."

Eli kept his lips together, but the desperate groan managed to whine through his head. He'd been high on the edge for so long, it only took a few strokes to put him right there again, the warning prickle not only in his balls now, but everywhere on his skin and deeper inside his ass.

The sting increased, or maybe Eli's skin got too sensitive, but the spike of pain sent him over, heat filling him, flooding him, burying him. Quinn switched to lighter taps of his hand on the cheeks until Eli collapsed uncaring into the streaks of his come.

"Christ." The belt hit the floor, and Quinn scooped Eli up with an arm under his hips. "You are so fucking hot."

Quinn's dick was plenty hot as it slid under Eli's balls and between his thighs, along skin scalded from the snap of leather. After a few thrusts, Quinn drove them both forward into the mattress, his cock riding the crack of Eli's ass, the root driving more pressure on the hot swollen skin around Eli's hole, pleasure and pain making the blood try to stir his own dick back to life.

"Christ," Quinn grunted again as his hips jerked faster. But when he spurted warm and slick along Eli's back, it was Eli's name he kept repeating, and Eli fell asleep to soft wet kisses on his back and neck.

UNDER THE insistent pressure of his bladder, Quinn shifted out of sleep. Eli was lean muscle and warm sleepy skin underneath, and Quinn really didn't want to move. He dragged his watch up to his face. Oh three thirty. Carefully separating their sweaty, comey skin, Quinn eased away and stumbled into the bathroom. On his way back, he switched off the lamp and tripped over Eli's jeans. The streetlight showed him a flash of white as a folded note fell out of a back pocket.

If he got busted, Quinn's story was that a teacher's instincts for apprehending note-passers kicked in, but he knew when he unfolded it he had no reasonable excuse. Eli shared a lot of his body in bed and his opinions with his mouth, but very little of his life. Eli knew everything about Quinn but was hoarding his own details like an old lady hoarded cats.

The note wasn't addressed to anyone, but the content was clear. Eli hadn't made his share of the rent payment in two months, and his roommates wanted him out. Because he'd lost his job? Because he spent his money on clothes like his vintage magenta shirt that reminded Quinn of something he'd seen in the eighties?

He refolded the paper and stuffed it back into Eli's black jeans. When Quinn sat back on the bed, Eli's eyes opened so suddenly and so full of a wary alertness, Quinn's heart jumped at the thought that he'd been caught reading the note.

"Fuck." Eli groaned. "Now I've gotta pee." He rolled off the bed.

Quinn was sure Eli wouldn't have wasted any time tearing into him if he'd been caught, so he lifted the covers and climbed underneath while waiting for him to come back.

Eli lost some of that alertness on the trip to the bathroom, like he'd fallen back asleep while pissing. He hit the mattress hard and let Quinn tuck him down into an embrace without complaint. Quinn reached over his head to the alarm, giving him enough time to either drive Eli home or fuck him before he had to go to work. That decision he'd leave to Eli in a few hours.

Quinn might have felt guilty about trying to influence that decision, if when the alarm chirped Eli didn't instantly arch his ass into Quinn's hand.

"Do we have time?" Eli asked.

"Not if you want me to drive you home."

Eli sank back down.

"But if you want to stay here today, you're welcome to hang around. Or you can lock up. The bus stop is about half a mile, though."

"Ooo. You'd leave me here to go through your porn stash and dig through your medicine cabinet?"

"I think my life can withstand your scrutiny. So, shower now or later?"

Eli arched his ass toward Quinn's hand.

"I was hoping you'd say that." Quinn leaned over to switch on the lamp and find lube and a condom. As he rolled back, the sight of the bruises and welts on Eli's ass drove the breath out of Quinn's lungs.

He hadn't thought he'd hit him that hard. At the same time, a possessive pleasure curled around Quinn's spine, the primitive part of his brain whispering *mineminemine*.

"Christ." He reached out to touch and then his hand fell away. "Your ass. I didn't—"

Eli sat up. "I did. I've spent way too much of my life trying to justify myself. I like how getting spanked feels, and no one's going to make me feel bad about it. You can guilt all you want—"

"Whoa." Quinn dragged Eli down on top of him. "Save fighting for when there are enemy combatants around."

"Sometimes those enemies pretend to be friends."

Quinn pulled Eli close against him, wrapping him in arms and legs. "I wouldn't betray you, Eli."

Eli didn't try to get free, but the waiting tension in his muscles said he was still ready for war. "You make a good shield, but I can handle my own battles."

"Don't turn your back on valuable resources. I got top grades in military history and strategy." Quinn winked. "Brief me."

Eli ground his hips against Quinn's. "Briefing later. Fucking now."

"Deal." Quinn knew the advantage of a tactical retreat. He rolled Eli under him and closer to the lube. Eli jerked a little as Quinn slid a finger inside. Quinn raised his head.

Eli grabbed Quinn's arm to keep him there. "Don't worry. Anything I don't like, you'll hear about."

Quinn knew one thing was a guarantee. He took the sweet waiting dick in his mouth and sucked until the hard length stretched his jaw, all the while fucking his finger in and out of the soft, tight heat.

Eli's hands tugged at Quinn's hair. "Fuck me, c'mon, fuck me, fuck me."

Quinn knelt between Eli's legs and rolled down a condom, Eli's eyes tracking his every move. "You miss it," Eli said out of the blue.

"What?"

"Fucking bare. It must feel really good."

"It feels good fucking you."

"That was almost sweet enough to make up for being so patronizing. Do. You. Miss. It?"

"No." Not when it meant trading Eli for it. Eli looked as if he was going to say something else, so Quinn went on. "Fucking bare feels good, fucking feels good. Fucking you, Eli Wright, feels amazing with a rubber on, so Christ, please, can I?"

"Yeah." Eli flashed that crooked tooth and hiked his heels up on Quinn's shoulders.

It was amazing. Not just the heat or the tightness or the way Eli worked his muscles on Quinn's dick. It was this man under him, strong and unbroken, despite the way the world treated guys who were so open about their sexuality. It was the fingers with black nail polish digging into Quinn's arm, the way those gray eyes kept fluttering closed and then opening to stare back as Quinn fucked faster and harder. It was the outrageously sensual mouth that told the world to fuck itself that was groaning and whispering, "Please, jerk me off, *please*."

Maybe that was the key. That Eli needed Quinn to meet him strength against force as much as Quinn needed Eli storming into his life to shake him out of his rut.

Then Quinn forgot everything but the way sparkling pleasure washed through him and into Eli while Eli jerked and splashed warmth high up on Quinn's chest.

As his heart slowed, Quinn remembered that moment of clarity. He rolled out of bed. "I'll be home by four. Be here."

Eli propped his head up on his elbow. "What? No sixteen hundred, Lieutenant?"

Quinn threw a towel from the bathroom at him. "Be here."

Chapter Fourteen

BEING A housewife was awesome. Eli spent the morning online and the afternoon channel-surfing bad TV, making lots of commentary with no one to tell him to shut up so they could hear. At about three, it occurred to him that maybe he should run down for a pile of clothes. Quinn had a washer and dryer in the back hall next to the kitchen. Eli had called Sam, the only roommate he was reasonably sure didn't hate him, and asked her to box up anything of his that wasn't in his room and told her he'd pick his stuff up in a few days.

He'd thought he'd either have to sell lots of his clothes or beg to store them at Nate and Kellan's, but if Quinn wasn't asking Eli to leave, he wasn't going anywhere.

Quinn brought home a chicken dinner already made and slid it into the oven to warm. Eli glanced between the oven and Quinn's crotch and then raised his eyebrows. Quinn made the right decision, dragging Eli onto the couch and making Eli's toes curl, barely shoving their clothes out of the way as Quinn jerked them both off in his hand.

"Thanks for being here," Quinn said into Eli's neck where the T-shirt he'd borrowed was bunched up.

"You are totally welcome." Eli could really get used to having a boyfriend.

As Quinn pulled out some plates and they served themselves from containers on the counter, Eli began wondering when things would go wrong. There was always a catch, and for the most part, Eli could handle that. He didn't expect a free lunch, and he wanted to see where the hook was before he swallowed it.

Between forkfuls of chicken and mashed potatoes, Quinn told Eli some of the dumb excuses students had given him for not turning in their projects. Eli thought it was kind of mean to make stuff due on a Friday when most of the kids were probably already thinking about the weekend, but he supposed it was better than having stuff due on a Monday.

"So how has it been, freelancing instead of working at the paper?" Quinn asked.

There it was. Clunky segue, but Eli got it. He might not have turned in projects on time and earned straight As, but he knew what was going on. Quinn was expanding his Daddy role. Maybe Nate had been a little freer with information than Eli thought.

"It sucks. I'm broke."

Quinn waited for Eli to go on. Something about his patience dragged the words past Eli's lips.

"And I don't know what else to do. It's not like I didn't try a lot of those part-time service jobs before. But I guess…." Eli had told more than one customer to shove their I-asked-for-skim/diet/ dressing-on-the-side picky shit. "I'm not really a people person."

"What did you like about the paper?"

As pep talks went, this beat one of Nate's *Pull your head out of your ass, Eli* speeches. Eli thought about it for a minute, then pointed at the logo on the bag the food had come in. "I like using pictures to make people do stuff, think stuff."

"Like advertising."

"Did you take a course in career counseling? Look, I know. I think I'd be good at that shit. But they want you to have a degree. I can't afford a degree, and I barely got my high school diploma."

"That's surprising. You're a hell of a lot smarter than most of the kids I teach."

Eli sat back in his chair. "You think some compliments and baked chicken entitles you to the history of my life so far?"

Quinn smiled. "No."

Eli pushed his hair out of his face and narrowed his eyes.

Quinn went on, "I thought awesome sex, bringing you dinner, compliments, and streaming your favorite movie on Netflix while I grade some papers entitled me to a tiny bit of that interesting book."

"Really. You want to know what my favorite movie is?"

"You can watch whatever you want, but according to Kellan, whose number I took off your phone, your favorite movie is some confusing chick flick called *Sliding Doors*. You are a closet romantic."

"That's about all I keep in the closet. You stole Kellan's number to find out what my favorite movie was?" Eli couldn't decide if that was over-the-line controlling or sweet.

"No, I called him to find out what you liked to do. I had a feeling if I asked you, your answer would be 'fuck.'"

Eli pretended to consider for a second. "True."

"As much as I enjoy sharing that favorite activity with you, I have to get these grades done. And a man of my advanced years can only get it up so many times in one day."

"You make up for it in endurance."

"I'm pleased you noticed."

"Does it bother you?" Eli pushed the corn around on his plate.

"Not being able to fuck you as often as I want?"

"No. Being—me being so much younger?"

"Nope. I'm thinking in ten years, people will be even more jealous of my hot younger boyfriend."

Ten years? Like Quinn had had with Peter? Eli couldn't imagine much farther ahead than ten days. He liked this. Liked the idea of a boyfriend, especially one that came in a Quinn package, but ten years? He took his plate over to scrape the uneaten corn into the garbage. "I can cook. If you tell me what you like."

"I remember. Tarragon in the eggs. That was good."

Eli started to wash his plate, but Quinn took it out of his hands.

"I have a dishwasher. Let me switch the cable over to Netflix for you, and I'll work out here."

Sliding Doors felt a little too personal this time, with the lying, cheating bastard of a boyfriend and John Hannah being so adorably sweet to a brokenhearted Gwyneth Paltrow. When John Hannah's character said the line about people coming into your life right when you need them, Eli switched it off. Then he decided Quinn had done enough work for a Friday night and dragged him to bed.

On Saturday, Quinn drove Eli down to the apartment for what was ostensibly a change of clothes. Eli packed as much as he could stuff in a backpack. If the movie was right about fate, Quinn was here for him at a perfect time, since as of the moment, Eli had no place to live.

Late Sunday morning, Eli stretched his really happily tired muscles all alone in Quinn's big bed. Quinn might be older, but he was definitely making up for lost time. Eli wasn't sure he could keep up with him.

He sat up suddenly. For the first time in forever, Thursday, Friday, and Saturday nights had come and gone without Eli putting in an appearance at any of the bars. Maybe there'd be a missing-in-action notice in the personals in the *Charming Rag*. He'd spent the whole weekend in suburbia with his boyfriend, and nothing about that felt boring or tame. Maybe Quinn had earned an extra chapter of information. Eli could keep it from turning into a pity party by leaving out the part where his homeless situation was ongoing.

Quinn was still plowing through a giant stack of papers on the kitchen table. Eli found some cereal and was about to eat it dry when it occurred to him that Quinn probably had milk that hadn't expired in his fridge.

Eli was slurping away at the counter when Quinn glanced up at him. "Does this count as the longest date ever for your Facebook page now?"

"The Arena probably filed a missing-persons report."

"If you wanted to go out—"

"I'd have had to get dressed." Eli ran his hand over the super soft T-shirt of Quinn's he'd appropriated to wear over the one pair of flannel pajama pants he owned. He rinsed off his bowl and sat down at the table, not quite sure how he wanted to say it. For a while, he'd considered it a badge of honor and flung it in the face of everyone he met. He was pretty sure the whole poor, abused, queer kid thing was the only reason Nate had hired him at the paper in the first place.

Eli glanced over at the pile of papers. "You know how I said I barely graduated from high school."

"Yeah." Quinn put down his red pen.

"My parents kicked me out of the house when I was seventeen."

Quinn's face was still, like whatever he was thinking was too deep inside to show. "Because you were gay?"

Eli nodded.

"Shit." Quinn glanced down at his papers and then back at Eli. The calm expression remained, but Eli knew Quinn well enough now to read the tension in the back of his jaw, though it never carried through to his lips. "What did you do?"

Eli shrugged. "Spent a lot of time on couches at friends' houses. My best friend, she and her mom let me stay for the first two months, and it wasn't too bad. But when it was obvious my parents weren't going to suddenly give a shit, her mom got worried about legal responsibilities, and I had to move somewhere else. I didn't always make it to school after that. I was too old to have truant officers chasing me down, anyway."

"Did your parents ever try to find you?"

"You know how you said your grandparents sent you a card when you were in the hospital?"

Quinn's mouth curved in a wry twist. "Still get one around my birthday. With a twenty-dollar check. Very polite and appropriate. I send a thank-you card."

"Yeah, well, I don't get that. I haven't seen or spoken to them in five years. I called my sister a few years ago. She'd already gotten married before they tossed me out."

"And?"

"She told me to never call her again because she didn't want people like me around her kids. My gene pool. It has no deep end. Good thing I won't be breeding."

Quinn waited. Didn't offer an opinion like Nate, or *Gee, sorry, man* like Kellan might have.

"There were a couple of times between friends when I walked all night, slept in the library during the day. And...." Eli hadn't said this part out loud before, not even to Nate, though as smart as Nate was, he'd probably guessed it. "Sometimes I tricked, mostly for a place to sleep."

Eli never looked away, but somehow he missed Quinn getting up because the next thing he knew, Quinn's arms were around him, strong and hard, Eli's name a soft whisper in his ear. "Thank God you stayed safe. Thank God you made it this far." It sounded like a real prayer.

Eli remembered his irrational fear of Quinn being sick, of never meeting him because he'd died of bacterial meningitis. It was good to know Eli wasn't the only one who wasted time on pointless *what-ifs*.

Quinn hugged him for a while, then held on tight while he lowered his head and tingled Eli's mouth with a kiss.

This was supposed to be one of those nice moments of having a boyfriend, someone who gave a shit that you might have gotten killed a few years ago. Knowing that didn't stop Eli's dick from responding to Quinn's kiss or the hands wide and warm on Eli's back. In his defense, he was a guy, a not quite twenty-three-year-old guy, and his body knew what the other man could make it feel.

Quinn didn't mind, or if he did, his hands were acting on their own when they slid down to cup Eli's ass and pull him up tight. Quinn leaned back against the counter, and their dicks lined up for a nice dry hump.

"Yeah. I got you." Quinn groaned and kissed Eli's throat, though Eli hadn't asked for anything.

He knew what he wanted, though. Wanted to pull Quinn's strength and power inside so it would be there as a shield any time Eli needed the boost to his own. Wanted to protect Quinn, too, against the stupid families of the world who took his loyalty and decency for granted.

But Eli didn't know how to ask for that.

Instead he held on to Quinn's neck and kissed him, inviting Quinn into his mouth and his body, and when Quinn reached for Eli's fly, pulled back enough to whisper, "Fuck me."

Eli tossed off the T-shirt and pajama pants in the hall upstairs and hit the sheets naked. Quinn followed, landing on top, tongue and lips stroking and whispering across Eli's neck and jaw and chest, while Eli tried to touch back as much as he could. Quinn held Eli's hands against the mattress and continued with a gentle scrape of stubble everywhere, teasing Eli's nipples until he finally wet them, sucked them, rubbed them. Eli arched and stretched, especially when Quinn repeated the whole teasing thing right above Eli's cock. No reward this time, just Quinn gripping Eli's hips and flipping him over onto his belly and starting at the back of his neck.

No need to pin Eli's hands now. Not when he was pretty sure where this was going. For all it happened a lot in porn, Eli hadn't found that many guys who liked to rim, but the way Quinn was sliding his tongue along Eli's spine made him think he'd hit the jackpot now.

Then Quinn moved back up to Eli's neck again, then down more slowly. The crisp curls on Quinn's chest sensitized Eli's skin everywhere, imprinting a memory of Quinn on every cell. It reminded Eli of the way science films about glaciers had always scared him. He knew the ice wasn't like lava, too fast to outrun, but the illustrations showed them going fast. The idea of that inexorable strength carving deep into the earth had always made Eli uncomfortable, like wondering who authorized these changes that were going to affect all those species.

Quinn was relentlessly gentle, tongue dipping into the crack of Eli's ass, a flick at the top before he shoved Eli's legs apart with his shoulders. When he started, Eli wanted to categorize all the feelings, the scrape of his stubble, tongue sharp or flat, and the wet insistent softness of it. Mostly he knew he was whimpering and whining, struggling to climb down onto Quinn's face for more sensation—*more, more, God, please, more*—but Quinn's shoulders kept Eli in place.

Eli started working for a little friction on his dick from the sheets, not in that *you can't control me* rebellion of his first night here, but because Quinn was rubbing his thumb along the smooth, thin skin between Eli's hole and his balls. It was like Quinn had found a way to rub the gland from the outside, and the flick and jab of wet and hot on Eli's hole was almost enough but not quite. There were all these feelings inside, in his body and his heart and his head, and they kept building, and as urgent as Quinn's touch felt, he was still too tender, and Eli was going to explode.

He started shaking with it, and Quinn lifted his head to whisper, "Relax. Let me make you feel good." Eli stopped trying to tear his hands through the sheets, stopped trying to move and let it fill him. He wasn't scared this time. This was a flip side of the Daddy dynamic they'd played with, and it was safe and good to let Quinn push these feelings in him. Eli wanted it to go on forever, but the need to come built again, sharp and inescapable, and he rolled his head on the sheets whispering, "Fuck me, please, Quinn, fuck me."

The lubed finger was cool, so different from the sensation of spit and tongue, but Eli had been waiting so long he relaxed into it, though Quinn kept the strokes short and angled up, away from the kind of pressure that would send Eli over the edge. He lay there waiting, listening to the tear of the condom packet, and he wanted to show Quinn that he knew this was different, that this wasn't any fuck, that he trusted Quinn.

He'd caught his breath while Quinn wasn't touching him. "If you want to skip that—I mean, if you know you're negative—"

"Don't." Quinn's weight pinned him flat against the mattress. "Don't you ever take those kinds of risks, and don't ask me to make those decisions when my cock's an inch from your ass."

His dick slid between Eli's thighs, and Eli knew the condom was on. He might not be able to tell the difference once they got going, but his skin told him that was latex.

"Okay," Eli grunted. Quinn was probably right, but—Quinn pushed inside while Eli's legs were pressed together, when Eli couldn't push up on his knees and control the angle and speed, and it hurt for a second, not the screaming pinch of muscles not relaxed enough, but too big, too much, too tight like this.

He buried his groan in a mouthful of sheet and then bit down as Quinn fucked him like that, inescapable friction and fullness, Quinn dictating the angle, every feeling. It made Eli feel crazy, like he'd really given up control of his body, and that was okay again, because it was Quinn.

He didn't know how long Quinn pounded into him like that, only that Eli couldn't tell where the sensations started—his ass, his balls, his gland, his dick. Everything was so primed to go that when Quinn scooped him up around the waist, whispering "Ready?" Eli could have cried with the idea of release.

Quinn pulled them onto their sides, his lubed hand working Eli's cock a little too slowly, like Quinn needed to catch back up after the shift in position. Quinn's body held him tightly, a hard, sure promise to lean on while his hand sped up on Eli's dick. Quinn was whispering in his ear, as much a kiss and a breath as actual words. "Yeah, honey. Want to watch you come. Do it for me."

When it hit, the contractions went on and on, a burst that never seemed to want to slow down, like he could never empty his balls until he turned inside out. Perfect, kill-me-right-now ecstasy in every nerve of his body.

Quinn must have been coming too, because his hand was tight around Eli's cock and his voice turned into hoarse wordless sounds against Eli's wet skin, his hipbones jerking against Eli's ass.

Quinn rolled away for a second but was back before Eli's skin could start to cool, wrapping him up in a tangle of sweaty arms and legs.

As Eli drifted in a postcome, almost-asleep haze, he decided a glacier would meet its match in Mount Quinn. No matter what kind of storm Eli threw at him, Quinn was solid enough to wait him out.

Chapter Fifteen

LIKE THE mountain Eli sometimes thought of him as, Quinn wasn't particularly subtle. But that was okay, because Eli wasn't either. On Monday, Eli made two trips down to the apartment to rescue clothes in his laundry bag and backpack. He didn't have any furniture apart from the mattress on the floor and a lamp that was enough of a fire hazard that he was glad to leave it behind. The only reason he had so many clothes was that he'd lived in that apartment longer than anyplace else since the breeders had kicked him out. He already had his phone and his camera.

On the second trip on Monday, a cute gym bunny on the bus cruised him all the way up to Park Heights Avenue. Eli pretended not to notice. It wasn't too hard sticking to one flavor of man when that flavor was Quinn.

He put the stuff in the spare room upstairs, but Quinn had to be aware of the appearance of more and more clothes around the bedroom they were sharing. Eli couldn't miss the appearance of local college brochures either, brochures that had really crappy photos on them. He wasn't thinking about going back to school, but maybe they'd give him a little cash if he took some pictures that made the campus look like someplace rational people would be willing to send their kids—and that rational kids born at the start of the century would consider attending.

He was flicking through some digital images on Quinn's very nice laptop when his phone rang with Nate's ringtone.

"If you're not too busy playing naughty nursing home aid with the old man, I've got something for you down at the office."

"A job?" Pointing out that Nate was only six years younger than Quinn wouldn't do anything but encourage him.

"Better. Money. The check from the article on the summer homeless we sold to *Time* finally showed up. Your share is twelve hundred."

Twelve hundred dollars. Eli knew what the contract had said, but it had taken so long for all the accounting to go through, he had stopped waiting for it. He could have made rent after all—last month's too.

"I'll pick it up tomorrow."

A week later, Eli was still staring at the check. The check that had come with a letter from the editor, from the fucking editor of *Time*, saying he'd be interested in considering other pieces of Eli's work. And if that wasn't enough to convince Eli that if nothing else he'd be able to pay his cell phone bills for a year, he got a return email from the PR guy at the local college. The first one Eli had contacted, because based on the brochure, the place had been marketing itself as a teen convent. The email was an offer of thirty dollars each for five of his photos. Where the fuck had all these offers been the last miserable five months of his life?

Over thirteen hundred wasn't really anything to wave around, but it beat his previous checking balance of twenty-eight dollars—and that was only because a careful search of Quinn's couch cushions had turned up enough bus fare to save Eli from having to make a trip to the bank. The ATM wouldn't give him cash anymore.

Quinn had said he'd be home late, so Eli spent the rest of the afternoon window-shopping online. Not that he was able to buy anything—like a scooter that would make it so much easier to get downtown than the long walk and really long bus ride—but independent transportation didn't seem that far away anymore.

QUINN HAD put this off too long. Not that he needed closure. Watching Peter put the ring on Chrissy's finger had been closure enough. Quinn knew Eli had been right about Peter cheating. He'd tried to forget about it, knew he didn't owe either of them anything, but the very real threat of Peter passing something like HIV to his unsuspecting wife—who could pass it to the baby—stirred some obligation to at least tell Peter the game was over.

It wasn't hard to find a time when Peter would be home alone. If it was possible, Claire would have the calendar of everyone she knew merged on her Facebook page so she could keep tabs on her kingdom. Peter wasn't working, and Chrissy and Gabe were at Mommy and Me Yoga.

Quinn found Peter on a ladder in the back, stapling plastic sheeting over the screened-in deck to winterproof it.

"Hold that for me." Peter pointed with the staple gun at the side edge where the plastic was trying to twist. No *Hi*, no *What are you doing here*. Like Quinn was still an everyday part of Peter's life. How had Quinn let this happen?

"No. Get off the ladder."

"What the fuck, Quinn? I'm busy."

He was only up three feet. Quinn kicked a rung. "Get down."

"You're fucking nuts." Peter climbed down. "What's going on?" He threw the staple gun on the roll of plastic and ran a hand through his hair. "This is because of that kid you're fucking. He told you some bullshit about me and you actually believe him."

"Christ, Peter, why would you even think that if it wasn't true? How the fuck do you manage to fool everyone when you're such a moron?"

Peter kicked the plastic down the slope of the yard, then stood facing away for a few minutes. When he spoke, his voice was flat. "Come into the house."

Quinn ignored Peter's effort to move them to the living room and stood in the kitchen while Peter paced around.

"This isn't easy. Don't fucking think I've got it easy," Peter burst out. Quinn folded his arms and leaned back against the counter. "I was jealous, okay? At first I thought it had to be some kind of joke, but then when I saw you with him here—I thought if I pissed him off or put him off you, I wouldn't have to see that anymore."

"You think watching you get married was easy? Lying all this time?" Damn, Peter was too good at twisting things around. This wasn't about what Peter had done to him, it was about what he was doing to risk the health and safety of his wife and baby. "Besides, your bullshit excuse only works if you hadn't been slutting around Grand Central. Christ, you pretended all those years to not even know where the bars were. Swore you'd never set foot in one."

Peter came to a stop in front of him and grabbed on to Quinn's arms so suddenly he didn't try to stop him. "Because I miss you. I didn't think—" Peter swallowed hard. "I thought if I did it right, had a family I wouldn't still—"

"Be gay?"

"I'm not gay." Peter's fingers dug in tighter. Quinn didn't move. "I like sex with guys sometimes. But you—it wasn't—" Peter released his grip and walked away.

Quinn watched in silence. His chest was empty. Even pity felt a long way away.

"I'm not a total bastard. I know I've fucked everything up. There's got to be a way to work this out."

"What? Have your cake and eat it too? Live with your wife and child and come see me when you need a little something extra?"

The sudden look of hope on Peter's face made Quinn laugh. "No. Never. Not the slightest bit interested."

"Because of that piece of ass you picked up? Are you thinking of going straight? God, he's practically a girl, Quinn."

"Not at all. He's all man." Quinn smiled.

"You'd be a bitch for something like that?"

Quinn pushed away from the counter and shoved Peter into the table. "Call him a thing again and I will punch the words out of your mouth along with your teeth. Is that really what you thought of what we did? Being a bitch for each other?"

"No." Peter tried a smile. It made Quinn's skin crawl. "Can't you see how jealous I am? Doesn't that prove how much I miss you?"

"I don't care what you prove, Peter. And I don't care how much of a whore you want to be to prove how not gay you are. But it's not just you. It's Gabe. I made a promise to God and that child, and it wasn't only to see him confirmed."

"What does this have to do with Gabe?"

"Besides the possibility of having divorced parents? Trust me, I see what parents can do to a kid. But if you pick up the wrong guy and pass HIV on to Chrissy, she could pass it to Gabe—or the next kid."

"I'm not stupid enough to take that kind of risk."

"And I'm supposed to believe you?"

"It wouldn't even be an issue if you'd—"

"If I'd go back to fucking you instead? Do you even hear yourself?" This was too much. Quinn started for the door.

"Quinn. Please." Peter's voice held more emotion than at any time Quinn could remember since he'd met him. A raw desperation on the edge of tears. Grabbing Quinn's arm, Peter blurted, "I miss you. I want—"

Before Quinn could shake him off, Peter pulled him in tight and kissed him. Quinn let him. Maybe he was curious, or maybe he was the one with something to prove. It was like kissing a piece of bread. Nothing. Not even an unwanted spark of desire.

"Don't you feel anything?"

Quinn shook his head. He felt something, all right. But it had nothing to do with Peter. "Because of him?"

"Because this is over, Peter. It's been over. You're Dennis's brother, the father of my godson, but that's it. Those are the reasons I'm bothering to tell you to get your head out of your ass before you lose what you do have."

QUINN SHOULD have done that months ago. He stretched his neck, free of a tension he knew he'd been carrying for years. Not only was he done with that bastard, but he'd moved on to someone better. Nothing he'd ever felt when he kissed Peter could compare to what happened when he watched Eli smile. When he wondered what comments Eli would be making about some TV show, or something in the paper. Every time Quinn thought he'd figured Eli out, he'd surprise him. Quinn loved that about him. Loved him.

Quinn was in love with Eli.

Eli, the man who'd just made himself at home in Quinn's life, taking over the bottom drawer and the back of the closet. Quinn wasn't sure he was supposed to notice. It wasn't a problem. Simply one of Eli's survival skills.

Quinn's hands tightened on the steering wheel. So what did that mean for a guy who'd fallen for Eli? Quinn couldn't blame Eli for being good at staying off the streets, but had Quinn put himself in the same situation he'd had with Peter? Peter had used Quinn while planning the new direction in his life. It wasn't that Quinn thought

Eli would lie and cheat like Peter had. But Quinn didn't want to be nothing more than a way station while Eli figured out the next stage of his life.

He couldn't go through that again. He and Peter had never made any kind of formal commitment, never used words to describe what they were to each other. Quinn hadn't thought *I love you*'s were necessary. The fact that they'd decided to make a life together said it all. Except he had been making a life and Peter had been keeping his options open. Hell, Peter had been gone a long time before he'd packed a box.

Ready or not, Eli, you and I are putting words to this right now.

WHEN ELI heard Quinn come in the front door, the laptop clock showed eight forty-five. Halloween was three days away. Eli's favorite holiday. It could get a little wild, but he was looking forward to hitting the bars with Quinn. Quinn could wear one of those T-shirts that said "This is my costume" if he didn't want to get dressed up. Before Eli could mention it, Quinn stuck his head in the living room.

"Hey. Did you eat already?"

"Yeah, sorry. I made spaghetti and meatballs. It's in the fridge."

With both of his genetic donors working until six or seven, Eli had been making his own meals since he could reach the fridge door. But he hadn't had a regular dining companion since he'd left his best friend's house. This was the first time he'd sat alone at Quinn's kitchen table. After a few minutes of feeling weird, he'd gotten up to eat by the sink.

Quinn came in from the hall, rubbing the back of his neck. Eli's stomach tensed. He hadn't done anything to be guilty about, hadn't so much as left a dish in the sink, but some instinct warned him that whatever Quinn had to say, Eli wasn't going to like it. He mentally started packing.

Quinn sat on the couch next to him, and the tension turned to a complicated macramé knot design.

Quinn finally stopped squeezing the back of his neck. "I'll bet you don't miss those house meetings with your roommates." Clunky intro as always. That was Quinn.

"Except I have the feeling this is about to turn into one." Eli closed the computer and slid it between them.

Quinn didn't offer a denial. "I know they told you to move out." He turned enough to watch Eli. "The note you got. It fell out of your pocket, and I read it."

"Okay." It wasn't anything to get upset about, and maybe Quinn knowing that was why he hadn't said anything about the way more of Eli's stuff kept appearing in the house. But Eli felt like a cartoon character with a ten-ton weight dangling on a string over his head; he had to fight the urge to look up.

"So what are you going to do about it?"

There it was. Time for the *Do you expect to live here now?* conversation. Eli tucked a leg under him. "Remember when I said I'd go to the baptism, we agreed you owed me a favor."

Quinn didn't say anything.

"So what about a place to stay for a while?" Eli had thrown out that question dozens of times. Why was it so hard with Quinn on the other end of it?

"How long?"

What the fuck did that mean? Suddenly there was a time limit on being boyfriends? Didn't they get more than two weeks to figure out if this worked? Eli knew lots of guys who'd gone home together one night from a bar and one of them never left. In spite of swallowing down the sticky lump in his throat, there was a hitch in his voice. "Until I find someplace else."

"Some*one* else?"

Eli stood up. "That's just fucking bitchy." Especially when Eli had turned down the gym bunny on the bus. "I was going to say while we're going out, but since there's a limit on it now…." He had to stop and take a breath. Shit. This hurt a lot more than he thought it could. "A month? Fuck, I'll sleep on the couch if you're sick of me already. I picked up a little work."

"Listen. If you don't—I'm not—" Quinn was having trouble getting things out too, not that Eli gave a fuck. "Maybe we went a little fast. Alyssa's been wanting to move out of her parents' house, but she wants a roommate. You guys could find a place. I'm sure she could cover the security deposit and—"

"Alyssa? Your ex-sister-in-law, Alyssa?" Why did it always come back to that fucking family? Like a bunch of weeds popping up everywhere. "Why can't I stay with you?"

"I like having you here, but—"

"So this is where you say we can still be friends? If you didn't want me here, why didn't you say something before?"

"Before you moved all your clothes here and stuffed them in my spare room?"

Before I started thinking we were a couple. But he wasn't giving Quinn a chance to tell Eli how pathetic and immature that dream had been. "Fine. I'm sorry. Gimme a few days and they'll be gone again."

"Where?"

"Why should you care? Not with your ex-sister-in-law, that's for sure. I've got more sense than to get sucked into all that bullshit family drama. Don't you get it? We queers need to make our own families. They'll never really want us."

"You're not listening to me."

"Oh, I'm hearing you really clearly. I wish I wasn't."

"I love you, Eli."

A sharp stick punched the air from his diaphragm, and Eli felt his eyes go wide with shock. "You sure have a funny way of showing it. If you—then what the fuck is this all about?"

"Because I want you to be with me because you want to be. Not because you have to. Because you don't have any other choice."

"Jesus fucking Christ." The screech burst as the pain twisted inside. Eli winced, watched Quinn rub his head like the sound had scraped his skull. Good. Eli kept right on yelling as he walked toward Quinn. "You think because I told you I used to trick for a place to sleep that I'm doing it now? That the whole reason I carted all my shit to your boring box up here in Nowheresville, two fucking buses from a decent cup of coffee, is because I like your mattress? Fuck you." Eli spun around and sprinted up the stairs to pack.

Quinn stomped up right behind him. "Of course I don't think that. But I want this—us—to go right. I don't want—"

Eli looked up from where he was shoving toiletries into his backpack. "You seriously think I'm going to wake up in ten years and decide I'm straight?" He moved to the bedroom and jammed as many clothes as he could on top. Quinn could throw the rest out. Fuck him.

He turned to Quinn again. "I know Peter fucked you over good, but maybe you should try to keep it from ruining the rest of your life."

"I am." Quinn got loud now, a deep rumble that he softened quickly. "I know. Eli, don't leave like this. I called Alyssa."

"You already called Alyssa. Of course you did." Eli snapped the flap closed on the pack. "You wanted to know about deal breakers? This is one on an epic level."

"Wait. How is this ignoring you?"

"It's one hundred fucking percent ignoring me." Eli pushed past him to run back down the stairs. Something inside Eli was scratching, burning at him so that he could barely breathe. He suspected it was tears, and he was not shedding his first in five years in front of Quinn. "You made up your mind about me, made your fucking plan, and I'm just supposed to go with that? Fuck that." He hitched his backpack over his shoulders. "And fuck you."

"Where are you going?"

"Don't worry. I've learned a lot since the breeders threw me out. I've got the hang of homelessness by now."

"I'm not throwing you out."

"Tell yourself whatever you want since you sure as hell aren't listening to me."

Quinn's throat worked. Eli closed his eyes.

"Can I—drive you somewhere?"

"Thanks for twisting the knife." Eli tightened his jaw against the burning trying to escape through his throat. "By the way, just to make things clear, this is us breaking up. So when the next hot guy hits on me on the Seven bus, I'm taking him up on it. And you can fucking ignore that too."

"Please, Eli, let me drive you where you're going."

"No thanks, Daddy. I can handle it all on my own."

Chapter Sixteen

QUINN SANK onto a chair and waited for the familiar numbness to kick in. It would. It always had. Yeah, he'd get mad, he might throw things at times, but after the explosion, everything would reset. And Quinn would find a way to get through it with a smile on his face. It was better finding out now that Eli wasn't ready—didn't feel the same way. Maybe after they'd both cooled down, when Quinn could be rational and not—as Eli had put it—fucking bitchy, then they could see if—

Light and pain splintered Quinn's skull, driving him out of the chair and onto his knees. The warning prickle of pain had been there when Eli started screaming at him. Because Quinn had suggested Eli was using him for a convenient place to stay. Was the accusation off? Wasn't that exactly what Quinn had told himself? That history would repeat itself because he was so easy to overlook, so easy to leave behind?

Eli wasn't going to calm down. Every minute would give him a million more reasons to never trust Quinn again. Quinn was good at ignoring his instincts. He'd ignored the one that told him he wasn't just sick until it was almost too late. Ignored the one that told him Peter was cheating. Damned if he was going to ignore this one too. He swallowed as much codeine as he could handle and still drive, and took off to find Eli.

He wasn't at the bus stop, though, or anywhere along the streets that would take him to it. How fucking long had Quinn been sitting there like an idiot, thinking losing Eli was something he could just tune out, lock away?

After circling the block near the closest bus stop, Quinn started following the bus route downtown, trying to paste on a veneer of calm. Eli had been angry and walked fast. He'd already caught the bus and was downtown, headed for his friends' place. Quinn could catch him there.

Kellan didn't answer the buzz through the speaker, but looked down from the second-floor window. A minute later, Quinn heard his feet pounding down the stairs.

"Yeah?" Kellan's face was blank.

"I'm looking for Eli."

"Did you lose him?"

Kellan's anger stirred hope. Maybe Eli was here. Safe.

Quinn found a smile somewhere deep inside and forced it to his lips. "He—We had a—Look, I just want to make sure he's okay."

"Why? Did you hurt him?" Kellan handled himself loosely, not like a fighter at all, but Quinn could tell the man wouldn't hesitate to come out swinging if he thought his friend was hurt.

And Quinn had hurt him. Stupidly. "Have you seen him?"

"Nope. Guess you should have been more careful, man." Kellan shut the door.

It was just past midnight. Quinn hit every bar he could think of, found the tall, thin, platinum-blond friend who shrugged and said he hadn't seen Eli since they were at the restaurant together. Desperation even had Quinn at Eli's old apartment, and after a few acidic remarks from Marcy, Sam, the girl with the piercings, said, "When you see Eli, ask him what he wants me to do with his mattress. We've got someone taking the room next month."

Christ, and she was the one Eli liked.

Quinn drove through the city. The area near the Arena never looked safe, but an hour after the bars closed, it made all the hair on Quinn's body stand at attention. *I've got the hang of homelessness by now.* Through eyes narrowed by the pain in his head, Quinn saw them. People hunched low in doorways. Standing around under an overpass. *There were a couple of times between friends when I walked all night, slept in the library during the day.*

Was that what Eli was doing now? Because Quinn had let those doubts back in? But Eli walking all night had been before Eli had Nate and Kellan. Maybe he hadn't gotten there yet when Quinn stopped by, or Kellan was under orders to tell Quinn to go fuck himself. Quinn had to believe that, because anything else tore a hole in his gut that hurt far more than the shards of glass under his scalp.

By dawn he was almost out of gas. He parked around the corner from Nate's apartment. At a decent hour, he'd try them again. If that failed, he was going to call up Jamie and beg, grovel, and plead for him to use his cop-shop resources to get an off-the-record GPS search on Eli's phone. Jamie would give him endless *I told you so*'s, but Quinn wouldn't care. He would owe him forever, proclaim Marine superiority over the Navy, anything to know Eli was safe.

SOMETHING WAS tickling Eli's face. He smacked at it and rolled on his side, into the sofa cushions, trying to bury his miserable existence back in sleep.

"Wake up, Goldilocks."

"Shut the fuck up, Nate." Eli reached behind him and threw a pillow in the direction of the voice. Maybe talking about finding the just-right man and bed had figured prominently in his rant when Nate had picked him up in answer to a pathetic late-night phone call. After Eli's walk of rage had taken him way past the bus stop he knew, he'd found himself in some weird little pocket of industrial buildings and called for help.

Of course, Nate couldn't let the Goldilocks thing go now. "So what you're saying is the guy's a bear? He didn't look that chunky to me."

Without turning, Eli felt around for one of his boots on the floor and tossed that too.

"Give him a break." Kellan's voice came from directly over him.

Eli squinted up to find Kellan holding Yin like a baby. It had probably been her tail that had woken him up. "Sorry, Yin." Eli shut his eyes again. "What time is it?"

"Time for you to get off the couch," Nate said.

"Nope, not enough sleep. Wake me in a hundred years."

"You're mixing up your fairy tales, princess. Get off the couch."

"Why? Life sucks."

"Damn it. I forgot to buy hats for the pity party." Nate dragged Eli's legs off the couch and sat down.

Kellan propped him up from the other side, and Yin walked across Eli's lap. He absolutely was not going to cry.

"So what did he do? Should I go kick his ass?" Kellan asked.

"One: I'm not a girl, Kellan, and two: of the three of us, who was the only one who didn't need hospital care after the bashers jumped us?"

Kellan rolled his eyes. "I didn't call you a girl. You ga—you guys are so sensitive about that shit."

"And straight guys aren't?" Nate leaned across Eli to look at Kellan.

"Me, now, thank you," Eli said. "I realize it's hard for you to handle giving up the princess crown, Nate."

"I should have let you sob into the couch cushions all day." But Nate put his arm around Eli, and Eli didn't try to wiggle away. "So?"

"So, he said he loved me and then he told me to move out. Or maybe he told me to move out and then he said he loved me."

"And what did you say?" Kellan asked.

"I left."

"Silently?" Nate gave Eli's shoulder a squeeze. "I find that hard to believe."

"Whose side are you on?" Eli slammed his shoulders back against the couch, but Nate kept the arm around him.

"Yours, always."

Kellan tapped Eli's knee. "What did you say when he said he loved you?"

Eli thought about it for a minute. "That he had a funny way of showing it."

Kellan winced.

"What was I supposed to say?"

"Eli, are you in love with this guy?" Nate's question was gentle. Probably defaulted to his advice-columnist mode.

"What part of moving in with him and turning down other guys and making him dinner and taking his advice about a job doesn't answer that?"

"The part with actual words, babe," Nate said.

"Do you guys? I mean, I've never heard you guys say it."

Nate stood up and pulled Kellan to his feet. "I love you."

Kellan grinned. "Yeah, you do." And they kissed. Long. With tongues. Until Yin took off and Eli was looking for something else to throw at them. All he had left was his phone and that wasn't happening, so he pulled the blanket over his head.

"It doesn't matter if I love him anyway," Eli said under the fuzzy protection from disgustingly happy people. "If he really loved me, he'd have been over here looking for me already." Like that would happen. Quinn was probably happy to slide back into his old routine.

"Uh, yeah. He would." Kellan's voice had that tone in it that usually meant he was blushing.

"What?" Eli pushed the blanket off. Yup. Kellan's cheeks were red.

"He showed up while I was picking you up," Nate said.

Eli dug under the couch for his other boot, remembered he didn't have jeans on, and went looking for them. "And?"

"I wouldn't let him in. Told him you weren't here." Kellan shrugged. "You weren't. Yet."

Eli got his jeans buttoned and sank back onto the couch. "Probably only his sense of responsibility. Like he'd do for one of his students or for someone in that goddamned family."

"If a sense of duty leaves a guy looking like he's just been kicked in the nuts, maybe," Kellan said.

"Really?" Eli jammed his boots on and pulled out his phone to check for messages before tucking it away again.

"Eli." Nate stood in front of the door. "You didn't answer the question. Are you in love with this guy?"

Maybe. How was Eli supposed to know? "Does it feel like you're excited but mostly nauseous? And does the thought of never kissing him again because it's too fucked-up make you think dying is a good plan?"

"Love?" Nate asked.

Eli nodded.

"Yeah, it does," Kellan answered.

"Okay." Eli took a deep breath. "Then I really wasn't ever in love with you, Nate."

"I'm sure he'll get over it." Kellan kissed Eli's cheek.

QUINN DOZED off, jerking awake with a start to find himself in the car—at ten in the morning. On a weekday. He vaguely remembered calling in sick for the first time in five years as he was dry swallowing codeine. Eli. He started the car and drove around the block. He'd just thought of one last place to check before appealing for mercy from Nate or Jamie.

He hoped the fact that he found a spot in a garage close to the Inner Harbor was a sign that his instinct was right. Despite the mob of school kids on their way to the aquarium and the people running for work with their coffees, Quinn saw him. Standing straight in front of the railing, dark hair blowing around in the late fall wind. Beautiful. Sexy. Safe. And pray God, his.

If he didn't think he might startle Eli right over the railing into the bay, Quinn would have run. As it was, he couldn't stop himself from dragging Eli into a tight hug, face buried in his neck to breathe in his smell, force the imprint of his body onto Quinn's.

"I am so sorry," Quinn whispered.

Eli returned the embrace for a second and then shoved him away. "You fucking well ought to be."

Quinn's arms felt useless at his sides. He needed to touch Eli again. Make him understand with their bodies, with what had made everything so right between them, what had gotten so fucked-up when Quinn tried to force words onto it. "I am. I know I was a little overbearing."

"You think?" Eli pushed the hair off his face.

"A lot overbearing."

"An asshole," Eli challenged.

"Yeah. An asshole." Quinn felt the corner of his mouth lift in a smile he couldn't help. Because of Eli. Quinn stared, filling his eyes with proof that maybe it wasn't too late. Eli wore the same clothes, his eyes a little bleary. One arm was rigid. At the end of it, Eli's fingers were wrapped so tightly around his phone his knuckles showed white.

"Expecting an important call?" Quinn asked.

Eli glanced at his hand as if he'd forgotten the phone was there. "No." He held up the phone for a second, staring at it. "I was going to make one. But I couldn't seem to push the right buttons. Because—"

Eli looked away, and Quinn cupped the hand holding the phone, gently loosening the fingers around the plastic before tucking the phone into Eli's jacket pocket.

"Yeah?" Quinn waited, but Eli shook his head.

"Come home with me," Quinn said, hand still gripping Eli's.

"Why?" Eli met Quinn's gaze, and Quinn's body ached from the pain in Eli's eyes.

"I love you."

Eli flung Quinn's hand away. "I let myself be happy. And you hurt me. I let you hurt me."

Quinn knew better than to expect easy. But he didn't want easy. He wanted Eli. "I was afraid you'd hurt me first. I want you in my life. And all that bullshit about taking it too fast and Alyssa was because I love you and I was afraid you didn't love me back."

"I do. I think."

"You think?" Quinn froze.

"When I was too scared to call you—scared that it was too fucked-up and you didn't want me—" Eli reached in his pocket to touch his phone, then kept both his hands tucked away, shoulders hunched. "I always thought love would be different. One day I'd see him and just like that, I'd know."

"I did." Quinn put his hand on Eli's face. His skin was cool from the wind, but beneath that sensation was the tingle of electricity under his palm, the sense of rightness from their skin together. "You winked at me in the bar and that was it. Hooked."

Eli turned his face toward Quinn's hand then pulled away. "Then how could you let me leave?"

"Let you?"

"You were going to drive me. Fucking drive me out of your life."

"You wanted to go."

Eli shook his head and didn't stop. "If you love me—"

Quinn grabbed him and kissed him, cupping his face to stop the shaking. "I do. Eli, you're the most amazing man I've ever met. And even if you end up breaking my heart, I won't mind, if I get to have you in my life for a while."

"No," Eli said, but he was kissing Quinn back, arms tight around him. "If you love someone, you stop them from leaving."

"I didn't know I was supposed to."

Eli held the back of Quinn's head. "Stop me. Every. Single. Time."

Chapter Seventeen

ELI WOKE with his tackle all twisted under him. Which had happened for the best possible reason. The man he loved had worn Eli out on his birthday. Eli shifted and then rolled onto his back. As soon as his still-hot, tingling ass made contact with the sheet, he remembered why he'd been sleeping on his belly. Having a hot toppy boyfriend who knew how much you loved getting spanked was a big plus on a birthday, Eli decided. But it definitely left… a mark.

He cracked an eye open to look at the new leather paddle on the nightstand. Quinn's last birthday present before bed. The double layer of leather not only stung, it left a deeper heat under the skin. Eli loved it.

The computer with the good digital imagery software had been nice too. But as soon as he read the outside of the box, Eli went hunting for the deposit slip showing the check he'd gotten from *Time* and told Quinn to take it back. Quinn cited a restocking fee, his saved-up service pay, and the fact that he occasionally liked to use his own damned laptop when he got home sometimes, so Eli had celebrated his twenty-third birthday with two awesome presents.

His ass rubbing on the sheets as he shifted around was starting to get him hard again. Technically he had thirty minutes of birthday left. It ought to be worth a blowjob.

Quinn's eyes opened. "Can't get comfortable?" He followed it up with an evil grin.

"A little too comfortable." Eli shoved his dick against Quinn's hip.

"God, you're going to kill me, boy."

Eli's stomach dropped at the same time his dick sprang to full hard life. He loved when Quinn used that gruff, growly voice. Loved him. Yeah. How had Quinn put it? Hooked. Eli wouldn't say he hadn't looked at other guys since they met, but he hadn't really wanted to fuck any of them. Even thinking of his favorite celebrity crush tossing him onto the bed didn't do it for him anymore.

Quinn licked his way down Eli's chest, then paused to look up. "You know, I don't think having a hot twenty-three-year-old boyfriend is really going to fly as an excuse when I stumble into work tomorrow with my eyes still closed."

"They're just jealous." Eli tucked a curl of Quinn's hair around a finger.

Although he left Eli dizzy and panting from coming his brains out, Quinn didn't go right to sleep after. He lay on top of Eli, stroking a hand down his side.

Eli wondered if he should offer reciprocation, but Quinn's dick was silky soft against Eli's thigh.

They'd already fucked three times.

"Thanksgiving is next week." Quinn tightened his hold on Eli before Eli realized he was jerking away.

"No. No fucking way."

"You don't have to go," Quinn said mildly.

"And you do?"

"I want to. Aside from some asshole who shall be nameless, I enjoy it."

"You go right ahead and enjoy it. I'm going to hang out with Nate and Kellan."

ELI HADN'T expected him and Quinn to get along perfectly just because they'd worked things out. Eli knew he tended to take an all-or-nothing approach to things, and Quinn liked to look at all the angles. There was no reason for them to be together every minute, but Eli still felt guilty about abandoning Quinn on a holiday. Not that Eli got sentimental about Thanksgiving. If Eli had a job—a steady one—he'd have been perfectly happy to work every Thanksgiving, but they'd done the photo shoot at the food kitchen last week in order to get it in yesterday's paper.

Christmas was different. If Quinn still felt the need to play nice with the Laurents, Eli could handle it for Christmas. After all, if Quinn hadn't needed a date to help him get through the baptism—nope. Eli wasn't going there.

At least Christmas had the potential for presents and naughtiness with Santa hats and candy canes and filling stockings. Thanksgiving really pushed the whole happy-hetero-family shit. Nate got bent about the holiday for other reasons, calling it "The Whitewashing of the Genocide of Native Americans," so Eli figured he could hang there with them and bitch most of the day.

"What?" Nate said when Eli called.

"Why do you think I want something?"

"Because now that you're happily tucked away with your Navy man, you only ever call when you want something."

"That's the first time you haven't made a crack about his age. You're losing your touch, Nathan." Nate had done a piece about gay veterans, and Quinn had steered him to some resources. There appeared to be a truce.

"What do you want, Elijah?"

"What are you doing today?"

"Why?"

"Because it's Thanksgiving." Eli waited for the usual rant.

"And? You've never given a crap before."

It sounded like a brush-off. "Do you guys have plans?"

Nate huffed a sigh. "Kind of. Except my plan is with the First National Bank of Candace."

"Are you always going to call Kellan's mom that?"

"Since she gave him that car, yes." When Nate got all superior like that, Eli was so glad things hadn't worked out for them.

"Aww. He lets you drive it. Wait, why do you have plans with Kellan's mom?" Eli asked.

"We're trying to set up a surprise meeting with Kellan and his dad. Just the three of them at a restaurant. We're hoping no ambulance will be required."

If Nate had been standing there, Eli would have smacked him. "What the fuck for? Kellan hates his dad."

"It's complicated, Eli. He's still his dad. And... he's not a total dick."

Eli sighed. "He gave, like, a hundred thousand dollars to stop marriage equality in Maryland. He still makes public statements about deviance and corrupting children."

"Okay, yes, he's a total dick, but he's Kellan's dad. I gotta go. Kellan's getting out of the shower." Nate's voice dropped to a whisper.

"Okay. Hey. After your rendezvous, do you think you could give me a ride somewhere?"

"That should be good for reaching minimum safe distance from fallout."

"Oh, I see worse things ahead. Better buy yourself a Fleshlight or your wrist will be so bad from jacking off you won't be able to type."

Nate's whispered "Fuck" conjured the image of him pinching the bridge of his nose. Ha. For once Nate hadn't thought something all the way through.

Even though Nate wouldn't see it, Eli grinned. "Better you than me."

ALTHOUGH ELI had slept in, he'd been downstairs in time to see Quinn leave the house wearing one of his less-attractive sweaters and slacks, a dish of yams in brown sugar and butter in one hand. Eli had found a dark plum corduroy blazer in his favorite secondhand shop, so he could at least look dressed up, even if he showed up empty-handed. When he ran outside to meet Nate, Eli knew it was a good thing he hadn't bothered to make something. Nate straddled his greasy scooter.

Nate shrugged. "Kellan took the car to the restaurant. I had to take a cab home."

"How were things when they saw each other?"

"Sullen, but quiet. At least now I know what to write for this week's column: Why You Should Marry an Orphan."

Nate handed him the way-too-big spare helmet, and Eli climbed on behind Nate, hugging his waist. On the freezing ride over to Woodlawn, Eli thought about Nate's future column. He and Quinn were both as good as orphans. Eli might despise the idea of being dependent on the approval of a "normal" family, but if Quinn thought he needed it, Eli would suffer through it with him. Plus, this way he could keep an eye on that bastard Peter.

Nate throttled back in front of the house number Eli had given him. Claire and Roger Laurent's 2182 Meadowview Drive was a red-bricked split-level in a neighborhood of red-bricked bungalows and Cape Cods and split-levels, just like Quinn's, just like Peter's. Eli suspected wherever Dennis and Paula lived, it was more of the same.

"You going to get back okay?" Nate asked as he relocked the helmet on the back.

Eli pointed to Quinn's car at the end of the driveway. "He's still here. I'll be fine."

"Okay. I'm going down to see my folks in Catonsville."

So much for Nate's orphan-loving cynicism. Eli waved as Nate spluttered off.

For once Eli was hoping to make the opposite of a grand entrance, so rather than ring the bell, he knocked.

Alyssa, now with purple streaks in her blonde hair, yanked him inside. "Oh my God, I'm so glad you showed up. It's been really weird."

"About the apartment thing?"

"What, that? No." She waved a dismissive hand. "I figured you guys were working it out. Sometimes Quinn just needs to get over himself, right?"

It occurred to Eli that he had a nice untapped source of information here. She did seem to know Quinn fairly well, and unlike the rest of her family, didn't avoid actually talking about things.

"No," Alyssa went on, dragging Eli up four stairs to what looked like a formal sitting room. It was empty, but she still looked around like she was checking for eavesdroppers. "Peter showed up late, without Chrissy and Gabe. He says the baby's running a fever and that Chrissy didn't want to take him out. Then he said she was taking him over to see her parents for a while."

"Which?"

"Exactly. The story's changed three times. And Quinn was already here when Peter finally showed up, and there was this look. I mean, I know my brother's a dick, but that was the dirtiest look I've ever seen on him. The temperature dropped twenty degrees. Dennis tried to talk to him—"

"Who?"

"Peter. But he keeps slinking away. He's loading up containers now. I swear, he's taking enough food for ten people but says he can't stay for dessert. Something is going on."

The whole thing about desserts and containers had logical leaps Eli couldn't follow, but the rest of Alyssa's whispered drama update was clear. The shit had hit the fan. Eli closed his eyes. "Great."

Despite the plush wall-to-wall carpet, Eli heard footsteps behind them.

"Hey." Quinn came up and gave him a quick side hug. "I didn't expect you. I remember the words *no fucking way*." He murmured the last part in Eli's ear.

"And miss the excitement?" Eli arched his brows. Maybe Quinn could provide some commentary.

"You guys are so cute." Alyssa headed toward the arch that led into a dining room. "I'm going to tell Mom you're here."

Claire appeared around another weird angle. The whole split-level thing was starting to freak Eli out. He'd rather have secret passages in a haunted mansion.

"Oh, Eli. I hope you brought your camera. If only Chrissy and the baby were here." Somewhere a door slammed with enough force to shake the house.

Claire went on as if the sound hadn't happened. "Did you eat, dear? Come into the kitchen. I haven't even put everything away yet. Quinn and Alyssa can set the table for dessert."

Eli wondered if he were being hauled in for another secret meeting, but Paula and Faith were at the sink washing dishes. Running a monologue about the family history and origins of every spoonful, Claire loaded a dish with food and handed it to him.

"The other boys are in the living room watching a game." Claire ushered him out as quickly as she had drawn him in.

Eli had only the two previous encounters to use for judgment, but he had to agree with Alyssa. Things were really weird. And it wasn't just all the stairs he kept getting lost on.

Eli had made a wrong turn and found himself in the sitting room again when Dennis cornered him. "C'mere. I want to show you something."

Dennis took Eli's plate and placed it on a coffee table before leading him up another set of stairs to a bedroom, where he closed the door.

Weird had just taken a detour into *uncomfortable*.

"Um. I think—" Eli started for the door, but Dennis blocked it.

"The last time I saw you. At Peter's house. You said something about Peter."

Eli couldn't figure out what Dennis was talking about.

Dennis folded his arms. "My birthday. You went on your little Quinn-is-gay rant out by his car. You said something about Peter then."

"That he's a selfish prick?"

"You said something about fallout. I remember that."

Eli bit back a *So why the fuck ask me* and shrugged. "I guess. Something like that. I don't remember exactly what."

"Were you just taking Quinn's side?"

"I'm always going to take Quinn's side." Eli straightened up. Screw it. All these muffled footsteps and staircases and secrets. "But I was talking about the fact that no matter what gender he claims to want to be with, your brother is a cheating whore."

Dennis's blue eyes widened.

"A man whore. He hit on me."

Dennis rolled his eyes.

It was Eli's turn to fold his arms. "I'll have you know most gay guys find me hot."

Dennis looked like he was trying to figure out why.

"Fine," Eli snapped. "Don't believe me. Believe this. He was at Grand Central. I don't know if you know what that is—"

"I'm a cop. I know."

"Well, he wasn't there for the drink specials. He keeps it up, your friends in Vice will be finding him sucking guys off in Carroll Park."

Lips pressed in a thin line, Dennis yanked open the bedroom door.

"You asked," Eli pointed out, but Dennis was gone.

Eli went downstairs and offered to handle the second wave of dishes. With enthusiasm, Faith tossed him her dishrag and went to beg her grandmother to let her make the whipped cream. Quinn came in and leaned on the counter.

"What?" Eli muttered self-consciously. That stare was too sexy.

Quinn stretched around him and rubbed something off one of the dishes. "I hate not being able to touch you all the time," he murmured in Eli's ear.

Eli was about to toss the dish back in the sink and jump the man, but he remembered these people were important to Quinn. Eli could behave for another hour.

Shouts sounded from outside, at first indistinguishable, but then, over the whirr of Faith's beaters, he heard the tail end of "...fucking truth for once in your life."

The beaters clattered onto the table, spraying drops of sweetened airy cream.

"I wonder what that's about?" Claire came over to Faith. "Let me help you, sweetie." She picked the hand mixer up, apparently oblivious to the battle sounds. Faith ran to her mother.

No matter how much Claire tried to ignore it, the sounds were very obviously two men fighting in Claire's backyard. Since the last Eli had seen of Roger, he was sound asleep in a recliner, it was Dennis and Peter.

"Mom! That's Daddy." Faith clung to Paula.

"It's okay, Faithy. I need you to keep an eye on your brother for me. Daddy's fine. I'm going to go talk to him."

Quinn had started for the back door the second Faith dropped the beaters. By the time Eli found his way out—through the living room—Quinn was between the brothers, holding Dennis's arm. At the end of it, Dennis's fist had a grip on Peter's dress shirt.

"Well, that explains it." Peter tore himself free, losing a few buttons in the process. He glared at his brother. "You actually believe this little fag—"

Quinn punched him in the mouth. Eli jumped forward to grab Quinn's right arm.

Peter wiped his mouth and smiled with bloody teeth. "Damn. You finally grew a pair."

"What the hell is going on?" Roger came through the back door.

"Don't worry. He can't hit hard," Peter sneered.

"Don't worry. My foot in your nuts will be hard enough," Eli said, still holding on to Quinn.

"Tell them, Peter." Dennis's voice was low, lethal with threat.

"Tell them what? The kid's jealous. I don't know what the fuck he's talking about." Peter glanced up as Claire came out. "Sorry, Mom."

Dennis paced away from his brother, then came back to face him. "Why isn't your wife here, Peter? Tell me what I heard at the station isn't true."

"It isn't. I'd expect this from him." Peter jerked his head in Quinn's direction. "But not my own brother."

"Dennis," Roger barked out. "Explain this."

"I heard from the dispatcher at the station, Chrissy took the baby and left him. Then Eli says—"

"Eli?" Roger turned with a dismissive look.

Eli let go of Quinn and started to step forward, but Quinn's arm pulled him back.

"Yes, Eli," Quinn said. "Who is, when I'm not asking him to lie for the rest of you, completely honest."

"The rest of us? Heavens, Quinn, what do you mean?" Claire asked.

"I don't know about Chrissy leaving, but I'm through covering for your son." Quinn's last word carried a boatload of disgust.

"Quinn." Peter's cry had an equal amount of desperation.

"I don't know what his sexuality is—"

"Really, Quinn," Claire interrupted.

"But he hasn't been faithful to his wife, and if she had any sense, she did leave."

Roger strode across the lawn and delivered a sharp backhand to his son. "What have you done?"

Peter looked down like a guilty child. "She found a receipt for condoms in my jeans. But she wouldn't have thought—I could have convinced her if—he hadn't been around." He pointed at Eli. "He's what made her think anything had happened in the first place."

The silence was heavy. Eli felt the looks coming at him.

"Well, thank God for that." Quinn put his arm around Eli.

"Amen," Dennis added.

Quinn steered Eli to Claire, who was standing with her hand over her mouth as if she had to block whatever she wanted to say. "Thanks for dinner. Claire." He nodded at the other people on the patio. "Roger,

Paula, Happy Thanksgiving." He brought them to a stop in front of Dennis. "Give me a call, and we'll play a little pickup."

"Sure." Dennis slapped Quinn's shoulder and offered a hand to Eli. "Thanks for being strai—uh, thanks, Eli. Sorry about...." He dipped his head in a way that could have referred to any of the family.

"It's okay." Eli stared a second before he shook the man's hand. "You and your wife should come for dinner sometime."

"Honest, you say?" Dennis grinned at Quinn. "What about the kids?" he asked Eli.

"Ummm."

Dennis gave Eli the same shoulder slap he'd given Quinn.

When they were around the corner of the house on their way to the driveway, Quinn yanked Eli close and kissed him.

One ear cocked for the sound of someone coming to pull them apart for queering up this section of suburbia, Eli kissed him back, lifting up on his toes, loving every breath and taste.

"Thanks," Quinn said when he let Eli go.

"I know I'm awesome, but what for this time?"

Quinn dropped another kiss on Eli's lips. "Just for being my boyfriend." Quinn gave him that smile. The same one that Eli used to think meant Quinn was laughing at him. It didn't mean that. It was Quinn's *Dare you* smile. His *Come on and have fun with me* smile. His Eli smile. "C'mon. I'll take you downtown for some pie."

"How heteronormative."

"I can't have pie on Thanksgiving because straight people do?"

"Fine. Have pie. I want crepes." Eli kissed the reddened tops of Quinn's knuckles. "And you have to change out of that sweater."

Quinn laughed and dragged Eli toward the car.

Stay tuned for an exclusive excerpt from

Bad Attitude

Bad in Baltimore: Book Three

By K.A. Mitchell

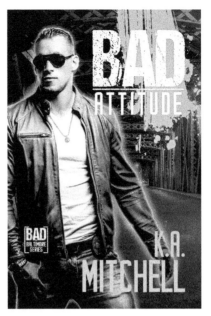

Saving lives never used to be this complicated.

Gavin Montgomery does what's expected of him by his wealthy and powerful family—look good in a tuxedo and don't make waves. When a friend takes a leap off a bridge, Gavin tries to save him, only to fall in with him. At least at the bottom of the river he won't feel like such a disappointment to his family. But he's pulled from the water by a man with an iron grip, a sexy mouth, and a chip on his shoulder the size of the national deficit.

Jamie Donnigan likes his life the way it is—though he could have done without losing his father and giving up smoking. But at least he's managed to avoid his own ball and chain as he's watched all his friends pair off. When Montgomery fame turns a simple rescue into a media circus, Jamie decides that if he's being punished for his good deed, he might as well treat himself to a hot and sweaty good time. It's not like the elegant and charming Gavin is going to lure Jamie away from his bachelor lifestyle. Nobody's that charming. Not even a Montgomery….

Coming Soon to
www.dreamspinnerpress.com

Chapter One

GAVIN WAS far too hot for his own skin. He didn't care if it was barely March. He needed the cold, the distance looking at the sky could give him.

He reached over and tugged at the latch for the roof release, and the Bentley's soft convertible top tucked itself away quietly.

Unlike the driver. "I'm freezing."

"It's my car," Gavin pointed out, tipping his head back and watching the stars spin through the black sky.

"Which I am driving at your request."

"Are you sure you're all right to drive?" The stars' weird leaping patterns and the streaks they left on his eyelids made Gavin dizzy. He clutched the silky leather armrests and looked over at Beach in the driver's seat.

"I'm fine. I only had two drinks, and that was more than an hour ago," Beach scoffed.

Gavin had seen Beach slam down a hell of a lot more than two drinks and function. While studying Beach for signs of impairment, Gavin was struck by the way Beach's straight hair blew around his head until he looked like that teen idol Gavin had caught his youngest sister staring at on her tablet.

An utterly unfamiliar giggle threatened to escape Gavin's lips, and he knew there had to be more than Jäger in the shots he'd been handed. He should have known better than to trust any of Beach's good-old-boy friends. Did that mean Beach had drunk the same thing?

It was hard to tell for certain. Beach high wasn't that different from Beach with a plan, or Beach looking for something to do. Gavin had known Beach for more than half their lives, and there was always a barely contained mania in him.

None of that meant Gavin wanted to risk taking a swim in the Chesapeake, considering they were speeding toward the Francis Scott Key Bridge. The water was a long way down from there.

"Can I put the top back up now?" Beach asked.

"I like the stars." Keeping the fresh air flowing would clear both their heads. "There's a special heating vent in the seat." Gavin leaned forward, and Beach pressed him back.

"Stay on your own side there, son, and don't get handsy." Beach's South Carolina accent rolled that into a drawl. "Hate to break it to you, but there are no stars, Gavin. It's the city and it's cloudy."

Maybe it was the bridge lights, or a plane, or another car. Damn. He shouldn't be this fucked-up. Beach had been wrong. Gavin didn't need to have a good time. He needed new friends.

The lights behind Gavin's eyes swung violently, then shook as the car lurched to a stop. Why were they stopping? On the Key Bridge?

Beach shut off the ignition. "It looks close here."

"What does? What the hell, Beach?" The Bentley was black. They were likely to get rear-ended in a second.

"Fort Carroll. Bet I could swim it." Beach got out of the car.

Gavin looked over the barricade at the vague shape of the man-made island fort. No boats cut the black water. The interstate was deserted. Even at two on a Wednesday morning, shouldn't there be more cars? Other people? He pushed open his door and climbed out. "Beach, get back in the car. I'll get us off the bridge and call Dad's service."

Beach leaned over the divider as casually as if it were a balcony rail in Venice. "I could definitely swim it," Beach said, more to himself than Gavin.

Gavin turned to scan the road in both directions. Headlights. Finally. "Beach, get in the damned car." Gavin took a step toward the crazy bastard, easing his phone out of his pocket.

"I'm not high." But since Beach made that announcement while leaping on top of the concrete divider that was all that separated the asphalt from a drop of seventy feet into the Chesapeake, Gavin was inclined to disagree.

Adrenaline cleared away the weird sensations from the buzz, providing a crystalline moment of focus. "Beach." Gavin pressed nine and held it as he approached the spot where Beach was now shaking one foot out, then the other, like a sprinter preparing for a race. "C'mon. It's freezing. You'll kill yourself, man."

"Nah. Citadel hazing was worse. Call someone to pick me up."

As Beach turned toward the water, Gavin lunged for his legs. But the adrenaline-fueled mental clarity did not extend to his coordination in that instant.

The leather of Beach's shoe burned across Gavin's freezing fingers as he made contact.

And missed.

His thighs hit the edge of the concrete divider, slamming his torso forward in a nauseating blur of black and gray and lights flashing on the water.

Beach was gone, and Gavin was flying after him. In the nonpharmaceutical sense.

His stomach lurched in free fall, and he called on the muscle memory of a thousand goofy diving games he'd played with his brother and cousins, taking belly flop after belly flop to not be called a wuss.

He managed to get his feet aimed down as the winter air rushed up past him. For all that speed, it took a long time to hit the water.

Plenty of time to wonder if anyone would notice if he ever came back up. Plenty of time to wonder how relieved his father might be if Gavin simply disappeared.

The cold shock of the surface slammed up into his bones with such force he wasn't sure he hadn't actually hit a chunk of ice, but then the water closed over his head with a blast of thunder.

JAMIE SHIFTED the mixing straw he'd been chewing on to the other side of his mouth and pictured his dad wasting away with lung cancer. It didn't matter. He still wanted a fucking cigarette.

The Arena was nonsmoking—every place in Maryland was. But slipping out for a smoke would give him a reason to escape all this bullshit Mardi Gras stuff everyone was pretending to enjoy in order to get laid tonight. At a signal from the DJ, the center of the club erupted in a shower of green, purple, and gold confetti. Even over at the bar, Jamie had to duck out of the way of the shiny crap the dancers were flinging around by handfuls.

A club rat wearing eyeliner and flecks of the confetti bounced up to him, one hand suspiciously and conspicuously behind his back.

Jamie's hand shot out to grab the kid's wrist before the glitter bomb struck. "Don't try it, Eli. I'm not in the mood."

There was a brief pout on Eli's pretty mouth. "You're never in the mood."

"Not for that." Jamie chomped on his straw. "Where's your boyfriend?"

"Dancing." Eli flung the handful of color toward the dance floor.

Quinn's height made him easy to pick out. He was dancing—if that halting sway could be called dancing—with a vaguely familiar, tall, slender blond. "Thought you two went off to…." Jamie jerked his head as he let it trail off.

Despite the fact that Eli's mouth had been especially shaped to make a guy think of getting his cock sucked, Jamie preferred not to picture what his friend and this kid half his age were getting up to.

"Nah. He actually did have to piss. I offered to hold it for him, though." Eli shook his hair out of his face. The goth black bangs and pale skin showing through the mesh shirt made him look perfectly at home under the glitter and spiraling club lights.

"Worried someone will steal him away?"

"Not at all." Eli's tongue flicked over his lips.

Jamie glanced away. No wonder Quinn was so fucked.

"You know," Eli began.

Dread snaked its warning through Jamie's guts until his balls pulled up nice and tight. In the year since Eli had moved in with Quinn, Jamie had been subjected to all kinds of statements from his friend's far-too-perceptive-for-a-brat-Quinn-had-taken-in-off-the-street boyfriend. And they always started with those two words.

"If you're looking for something else to suck on to take your mind off cigarettes, my friend thinks you're hot." Eli nodded at the tall blond with Quinn.

Jamie realized why the blond looked familiar and straightened from his slouch. He didn't often get to win a round with Quinn's boy toy. Drawing the straw from his mouth, he said, "Don't get me wrong, your friend was enthusiastic, but… sloppiest blowjob of my life. Don't think a repeat's happening."

Eli cocked his head as he stared at the dancers through the bursts of confetti. "Huh." In a flash, his grin was back. "Maybe you were a little much for him." Eli turned back, staring at Jamie's crotch. "I've always wondered if you're packing enough to back up that attitude."

The kid was sex on legs, past jailbait, and almost as good at the game as Jamie was. Almost.

Jamie grabbed Eli's wrist again. "Don't be shy, then." Dragging him forward, Jamie placed the hand right on his crotch. "Satisfy your curiosity."

He knew he'd won when Eli froze. Jamie slid the straw back between his lips.

Then Eli's fingers wiggled as he cupped Jamie's dick through the denim of his jeans. "Not bad." His hand slipped free. "If you're more of a grower than a shower."

Jamie's chuckle got lost in his throat as Quinn came up to them with the blond in tow.

Quinn acted entertained when Jamie sparred with Eli. Since the kid also made a hell of a housewife with hot dinners waiting, Jamie spent more time at Quinn's now than any time in the seven years he'd known him. Jamie wasn't afraid of any fight, but he'd rather not have it out with his best friend over shoving said friend's boyfriend's hand onto his dick. Even if it had just been a joke.

Quinn quirked his brows in Jamie's direction as Eli shimmered over to drape himself on his boyfriend. Jamie smirked back, but he could see there wasn't any tension in Quinn's posture. There was in Eli's, though, when Quinn's hand squeezed that tight little ass. But their cuddly couple shit left Jamie square in the blond's target scope. Jamie would have been upfront with the guy about a lack of interest, but he wouldn't put it past Eli to slip something nasty into his spaghetti sauce as payback for Jamie making Blondie cry.

"Jamie, I think you've met Silver," Eli chirped.

Jamie knew he wasn't in line for too many favors from heaven. Still, he'd kept the deathbed promise to his dad to quit smoking, and he was planning on giving up cream in his coffee for Lent and not having meat on Fridays. He wasn't sure he'd asked until he got an answer to his prayer in the buzz against his palm. Keeping a hand on his phone was habit. He could almost always be called in, and he'd never hear it in the club.

"Gotta check this." He turned away and read the text. He'd expected to have to get wet when the phone buzzed, but even the confirmation that he'd be spending the rest of the night freezing his ass off diving in forty-degree water couldn't keep him from thinking he was better off than trapped here with Slobber Jaws. Come to think of it, Blondie hadn't been all that careful with his teeth either.

"What?" Quinn said when he turned back.

"Gotta go in. Jumper off the Key Bridge," Jamie said. Though from the APB, he'd say it had to be a pretty important corpsicle they were going to be dragging out of the Patapsco River.

Eli's phone was in his hand. "Probably another poor gay kid killing himself."

"If it is, it's one of the governor's kids."

"Why?" Eli looked up from his phone.

"They're pulling in everyone."

AS THE outboard motor sent the Zodiac Hurricane bouncing up the chop on the Patapsco River toward the Key Bridge, Jamie spotted the lights first. High up on the bridge, flashing blue-and-white from at least ten patrol cars, the red-and-white of the meat trucks waiting on either side of the river, and one from the blinding beam of the city police's search boat as it swept the waves, which were whitecapped from all the action. Behind Jamie's Baltimore County squad, a State Police hard-sided skiff was fighting to catch up.

The sarge's briefing had covered the water temp and estimated chance of survival before the rescue would be only a recovery, but not whose corpse they'd be diving for.

"Christ. Who took a dive? The governor?" Jamie looked up from where he was running a final check on his gear.

"Worse," Sarge called over the chop of the water and the roar of the outboard. "A Montgomery."

Jamie whistled. That would be a fucking media shitstorm. As if to confirm it, a chopper thrummed overhead. He hoped it was one of their teams keeping the vultures off. The police had the bridge sealed now, he could see.

"Which one?" Jamie was betting on the one they called Chip. A pediatric cancer surgeon, he had stress enough to send anyone flying off the Key Bridge. Probably not the hippie chick who was always getting picked up at protests, or the other girl, the governor's daughter-in-law.

"The queer one," Pendarsky sneered from the opposite boat collar. "Probably know him, yeah, Donnigan?"

Jamie spared him a split-second glare. He could practically hear the gears turning in Pendarsky's head as he tried to think of something to say, like Jamie being gay was some big secret he'd just been let in on. Pendarsky was new. Anyone else would have known better.

"Listen, rook, don't go confusing me with your mother. She's the one knows every dick in town."

Pendarsky almost took the bait, but the second he pushed up, the boat rocked and dropped him back on the collar, forcing him to clutch the line to keep from flying in. Their search grid was the south side and downstream. Yancy cut back on the throttle and swung the Hurricane into position.

"Gear up," Sarge ordered.

All that was left was to slide his mask and regulator on, strap the light onto his wrist. Pendarsky struggled now that his wrist was tangled under the line.

"Need some help there, Pendarsky, you fuckwad?" Sarge barked. "Maybe I should just tether you to the boat."

"No, Sarge. I got it."

"Donnigan, you and Geist go in here. Move east till you overlap the troopers. Remember, supposing the bastard was lucky enough not to drown, he's got sixteen minutes left at this temp. Tops. And remember what a Charlie Foxtrot this is going to be even with the best possible outcome."

Jamie flashed the okay sign; then he and Geist went over the side.

The dry dive suit insulated his body with a layer of air, but the icy water still found ways to sting and burn in the tiny spaces around Jamie's mask. The cold seeped through the neoprene on his head, on his hands.

Except for the all-hands-on-deck call because it was a Montgomery, it was a typical search—though they wouldn't be doing this at night if the boats hadn't picked something up—but again, it was a Montgomery.

The lights swept the water downstream of the bridge, though the current was sluggish. They'd find Montgomery in a few days, caught up on something underwater. Chances were if he took the big swan dive, he hadn't tried to save himself once he hit the water.

Jamie didn't get giving up. No matter if it felt like hitting a concrete wall at fifty miles an hour, he'd be swinging, swimming for the nearest land he could find, trying to get his core out of the water, and—Jamie's mind flashed on something he'd seen in the papers a few years back. A big splash with the gay Montgomery son doing some fundraising swim up in one of those long, cold, skinny lakes in New York.

What if Montgomery had changed his mind? What if the cold was enough to make him want to fight, not let the current drag him down? The closest land wasn't necessarily the riverbanks. Who knew when the searchlights had last swept the bridge? They were looking for a drowning victim. Not someone who was swimming for survival.

Jamie veered off the search grid, signaling Geist with a flash of his hand light. Hell, if it didn't pan out, Jamie'd say he thought he saw something.

Geist followed him toward the nearest bridge pylon, moving his hand light across the water. The shoring around the base was made up of head-sized rocks. Not easy to crawl up on, but if Jamie's life was on the line, he'd have managed to haul ass up onto them.

There was nothing on the east side, south, or west. Their hand lights fell short of the next pylon and shoring. Holding his light just below the surface, Geist stared at Jamie in question. Between the thrum of the boats and the chopper sending waves smacking against the shoring, they couldn't have made themselves heard even without their regulators in the way. Jamie lifted his hands in a shrug and put his head back in the water, intending to sweep around the north side before following Geist back to their search pattern.

The waters around Baltimore were always full of sound. Stone and metal shifting and grinding, bass-deep or treble-whining motors, those were all familiar background to the bubbles moving past his ears. But there was something… rhythmic that didn't sound like it came from a motor, a tapping that took on a pattern recognizable anywhere in the world. A pattern only a person could make. Three quick, three slow, three quick. SOS.

Jamie let a little air out of his vest, sinking under the surface to get a better listen. Water carried sound, but it made direction hard to pick up.

Geist swung his light over Jamie as he surfaced. Jamie flashed his own light, then tapped his ears and indicated the pylons on either side of them. Geist pointed, and they separated to search.

Jamie put his head down and swam at speed, panning his light over the north side before making for the next pillar of cement supporting the bridge.

The rocks of the shoring were a dark, uneven lump against the black of sky and the shining black of the water. But as Jamie drew within twenty yards, he was sure that among the rocks, something was moving. Something not a cormorant or a heron, unless they had decided to wear a watch, because one was reflecting his light from a hand and wrist that clung to a rock.

He'd found him. Not just Montgomery, but as Jamie drew closer, he saw that the owner of the arm clinging to the rock was supporting another man.

As Jamie reached for his air horn to signal a boat, the man coughed and gasped in a hoarse voice, "What kept you?"

K.A. MITCHELL discovered the magic of writing at an early age when she learned that a carefully crayoned note of apology sent to the kitchen in a toy truck would earn her a reprieve from banishment to her room. Her career as a spin-control artist was cut short when her family moved to a two-story house and her trucks would not roll safely down the stairs. Around the same time, she decided that Ken and G.I. Joe made a much cuter couple than Ken and Barbie and was perplexed when invitations to play Barbie dropped off. She never stopped making stuff up, though, and was thrilled to find out that people would pay her to do it. Although the men in her stories usually carry more emotional baggage than even LAX can lose in a year, she guarantees they always find their sexy way to a happy ending.

K.A. loves to hear from her readers. You can email her at ka@kamitchell.com. She is often found talking about her imaginary friends on Twitter @ka_mitchell.

Email: ka@kamitchell.com
Twitter: @ka_mitchell
Website: www.kamitchell.com
Blog: authorkamitchell.wordpress.com
Tumblr: kamitchellplotbunnyfarm.tumblr.com

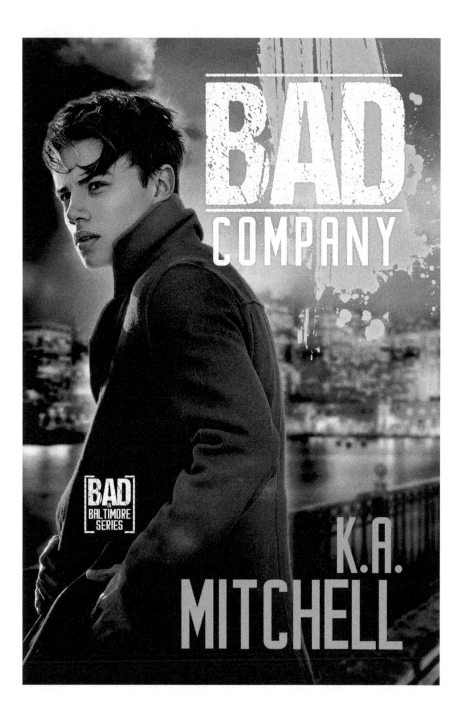

BAD
COMPANY

BAD IN
BALTIMORE
SERIES

K.A.
MITCHELL

Bad in Baltimore: Book One

Some things are sweeter than revenge.

"I need a boyfriend."

Hearing those words from his very straight, very ex-best friend doesn't put Nate in a helpful mood. Not only did Kellan Brooks's father destroy Nate's family in his quest for power, but Kellan broke Nate's heart back in high school. Nate thought he could trust his best friend with the revelation that he might be gay, only to find out he was horribly wrong and become the laughingstock of the whole school. Kellan must be truly desperate if he's turning to Nate now.

Kellan's through letting his father run his life, and he wants to make the man pay for cutting him off. What better way to stick it to the bigot than to come out as gay himself—especially with the son of the very man his father crushed on his quest for money and power. Kellan can't blame Nate for wanting nothing to do with him, though. Kellan will have to convince him to play along, but it's even harder to convince himself that the heat between them is only an act....

www.dreamspinnerpress.com

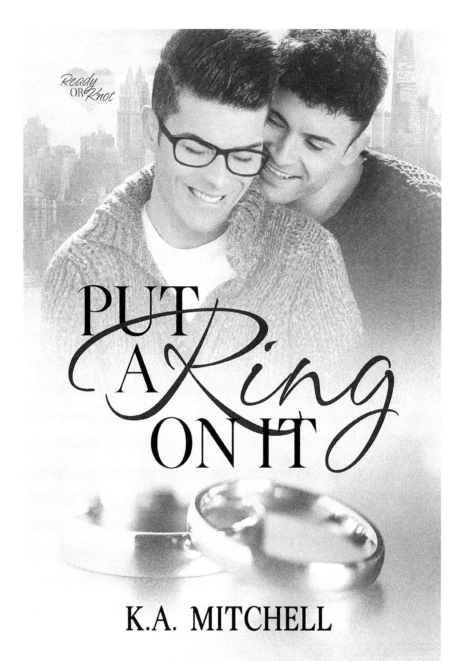

Ready
OR Knot

PUT
A Ring
ON IT

K.A. MITCHELL

Ready or Knot: Book One

Kieran Delaney-Schwartz—adoptee, underachiever, and self-professed-slacker IT guy—lives his under-the-radar life by the motto: Don't try, don't fail. His adopted siblings are all overachievers thanks to his driven, liberal parents, but Kieran has elected to avoid disappointing anyone by not getting their hopes up. He's coasting through his early twenties when he's hit head-on by Theo. The successful decade-older Broadway producer sweeps him off his feet for a whirlwind thirteen months that are pretty sweet, until it all comes screeching to a halt on Valentine's Day, with an unexpected proposal via an NYC Times Square flash mob.

Now everyone wants in on the wedding, except the grooms….

www.dreamspinnerpress.com

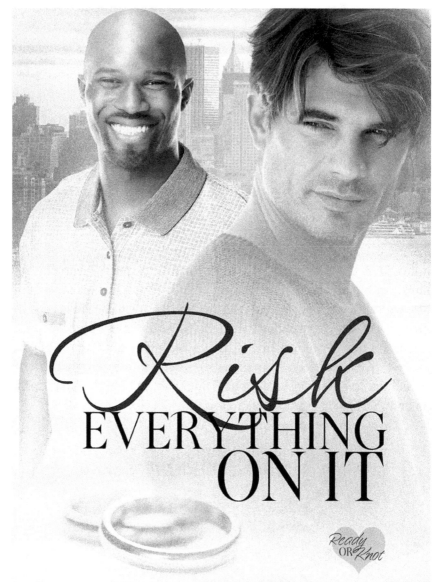

Risk
EVERYTHING
ON IT

Ready or Knot

K.A. MITCHELL

Sequel to *Put a Ring on It*
Ready or Knot: Book Two

Former child star and deeply closeted adult actor Jax Conlon needs a boost to his flagging career. He promised his mom, just before she died. He hopes he's found it in a guest spot with the latest directorial prodigy, but his research for the role gets derailed by an encounter with a handsome stranger with more… hands-on experience.

Oz Parsons is a devoted dad to two amazing little girls. Maybe a little too devoted—he hasn't had anything resembling a personal life since his ex left, leaving Oz and the girls with broken hearts and abandonment issues. So a hookup with a hot guy is just what he needs to let off some pent-up steam without any complications. There's something about Jax, though, that's got him finding reasons to draw things out.

With their goals and families pulling them in two different directions, Oz and Jax have to figure if white-hot chemistry and desire that won't quit is enough to roll the dice and risk now on forever.

www.dreamspinnerpress.com

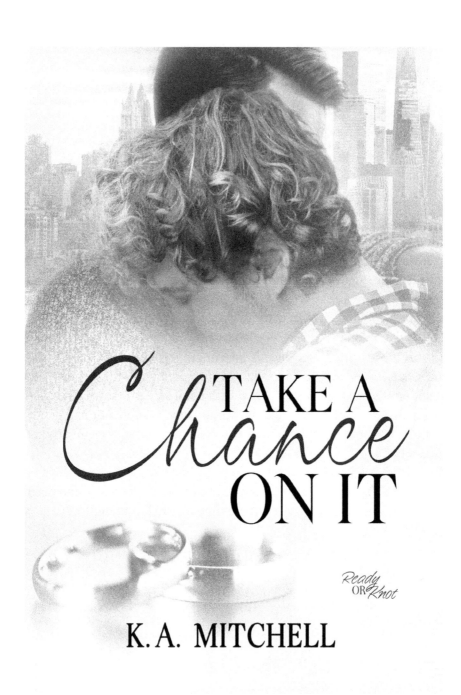

TAKE A *Chance* ON IT

Ready OR *Knot*

K. A. MITCHELL

Sequel to *Risk Everything on It*
Ready or Knot: Book Three

Left at the altar by his long-time lover, Spencer, and in desperate need of quality health insurance, Dane Archer can't say no when his best man and best friend, Gideon DeLuca, steps in. But Dane and Gideon have history, tangled and passionate and complicated.

After seventeen years of cat and mouse, Gideon has realized Dane isn't the kind of man who ever wants to be caught, and he's stopped playing Dane's game.

For Dane, it's never been a game, but sexual fidelity isn't his strong suit. Love is too beautiful for limits, something he's never been able to get Gideon the control freak to understand. Now Dane has nothing but limits, including the timeline on his paper-only marriage to Gideon.

Gideon's the only person Dane trusts enough to lean on, and Gideon will do anything to get Dane through this crisis. Anything but fall for Dane again.

Living together forces Dane and Gideon to stop circling and face what's been between them all these years. They just don't know if they have the power or the time to make things right.

What they do know is that they're not ready for it to be over.

www.dreamspinnerpress.com

Daddy
Needs a Date

SEAN MICHAEL

Also from Dreamspinner Press

AN UNLOCKED MIND

SECRETS

K.C. WELLS & PARKER WILLIAMS

www.dreamspinnerpress.com

CPSIA information can be obtained
at www.ICGtesting.com
Printed in the USA
LVHW081658220219
608478LV00018B/349/P

9 781640 804173